A PALM BEACH SCANDAL

A PALM BEACH SCANDAL

SUSANNAH MARREN

ST. MARTIN'S GRIFFIN ❧ NEW YORK

First published in the United States by St. Martin's Griffin, an imprint of St. Martin's Publishing Group

A PALM BEACH SCANDAL. Copyright © 2020 by Susan Shapiro Barash. All rights reserved. Printed in the United States of America. For information, address St. Martin's Publishing Group, 120 Broadway, New York, NY 10271.

www.stmartins.com

Library of Congress Cataloging-in-Publication Data

Names: Marren, Susannah, author.
Title: A Palm Beach scandal / Susannah Marren.
Description: First Edition. | New York : St. Martin's Griffin, 2020. | Series: Palm Beach novels ; 2 | First published in the United States by St. Martin's Griffin, an imprint of St. Martin's Publishing Group in 2019.
Identifiers: LCCN 2020019359 | ISBN 9781250228086 (trade paperback) | ISBN 9781250772756 (hardcover) | ISBN 9781250228093 (ebook)
Subjects: LCSH: Domestic fiction.
Classification: LCC PS3613.A76874 P35 2020 | DDC 813/.6—dc23
LC record available at https://lccn.loc.gov/2020019359

Our books may be purchased in bulk for promotional, educational, or business use. Please contact your local bookseller or the Macmillan Corporate and Premium Sales Department at 1-800-221-7945, extension 5442, or by email at MacmillanSpecialMarkets@macmillan.com.

First Edition: 2020

10 9 8 7 6 5 4 3 2 1

For my family

Silence may be as variously shaded as speech.
—EDITH WHARTON, *THE HOUSE OF MIRTH*

Tell me all, and be sure that I will never let you go, though the whole world should turn from you.
—LOUISA MAY ALCOTT, *JO'S BOYS*

PART ONE

CHAPTER 1

ELODIE

Aren't the women always rushed? Even if they appear to be graceful, ambling along the limestone path to the courtyard, it's actually a quiet frenzy. More members of the Palm Beach Literary Society file in, the usual glossy and cultured forties to sixties crowd heading toward their tables, chattering among themselves. They are followed by the septuagenarians and octogenarians at a more measured pace. What is fresh are the twenty- to thirtysomethings—daughters and granddaughters of members. Each fixates on her iPhone as if there is no slightly bumpy ground to navigate. Every woman is dressed for her decade. Favored colors—sage green, buttermilk yellow, auburn, deep blues, and purple, left over from last season—show off the preferred designers: Oscar, St. John, Dolce, Kors, McQueen, Etro. Whatever their age, the sunlight flits across their faces as they search for their assigned tables. Women fan themselves with their programs, seeming eager to begin. As they assemble I pray no one trips or is displeased with her assigned location.

At the entrance of the main building, I stand in my peplum dress in blues and greens, and illusion pumps, welcoming the women. I watch how they half wave at one another. I wave back at everyone in a wide sweep. *Too earnest, Elodie,* my mother would warn me. Among the guests for today are loyal members, new members, probable members. For the latter two, I've scheduled this as an eight-thirty breakfast. "Awfully early. I mean, who in Palm Beach will be finished with their holistic Pilates, a Zumba water class . . . an early tennis match by then? It's unheard of!" Nan Payton, the head of the board, said when the invitations were mailed. Snail-mailed.

Except for women who work, I had explained. And this morning Demi Dexter, the most in-demand cosmetic dermatologist this side of the bridge, Halley Hennes, a social worker for the VA Medical Center in West Palm, Tanya Lessinger, a public defender, and Maritza Abrams, the matrimonial lawyer chosen by wives, not husbands, are the first to sit down. Their wrought-iron chairs tip imperceptibly into the sodded earth; each straightens her shoulders and turns to beckon women she hasn't seen before. Five—no, six unknown guests walk toward this table. Colleagues perhaps, out-of-towners from farther north than Jupiter, as far south as Lauderdale. Their nods and greetings are quiet—it is an early hour, no matter what my intention.

As their bodies wobble in their seats, I miss New York City, where I once worked at the St. Agnes branch of the public library on the Upper West Side. It was a diverse group in every way—men came, too, to hear novelists, essayists, screenwriters. This morning's event is pegged the "Literary Ladies Breakfast." Men *could* come, in theory, but they seem to prefer golf, tennis, or going straight to the office. I double-check, without spotting one male among us. From across the courtyard, the doyennes at Rita Damon's table observe the newcomers warily.

The next tier of professionals is more predictable—a specific Palm Beach career crowd. Margot Damon, Rita's daughter-in-law, and Peggy Ann Letts, both real estate agents at the Bailey Group. Kimberly Shawn, interior designer. Allison Rochester, who recently began working at High Dune, her husband's hedge fund, selecting worthy causes to support. Betty McCarter, whose shop sells bone china and sterling-silver trays for the finest homes in the estate section. Coiffed and polished, they huddle as platters of mini croissants and mini pastries are passed. Although they have lived here for years, their accents become interfaced. Miami natives remain heavy on *l*'s and vowels, Southern drawls never dissolve, and a Bostonian cadence rises above the rest.

Last to be seated are those whom I know best. Ardent readers and lecturegoers who come to the library several days a week. There they pluck from the shelves and make requests from the waiting list. These include my mother and mother-in-law, who come together to anything and everything that is offered. As director of events at the Palm Beach Literary Society, I've fought for classes for children, adults, and seniors. There are six librarians whom I supervise, and we share this point of view. Instead of the old template of a private club, we have pushed for free programming. Still, this is an institution founded in 1925 by several Palm Beach matrons and designed by Maurice Fatio during his Italian Renaissance period. Change comes slowly. Long-standing members remain a steadfast clan, champions of this morning's fund-raiser. To avoid stirring things up, we have selected a guest today who is respected and veritable.

And it's a sold-out event. If I add this to our Best-Selling Authors Series, we have a compelling list. Lately I've been braver about following my instincts, wanting to mix it up. I'm proud of my endeavors, my choices for the Literary Society. I've brought in more poets, songwriters, an expert on Shakespeare and women, incendiary playwrights, and political writers. Yet I haven't forgotten how I was watched when I first began. *Let Elodie prove herself to the board, heighten an intellectual curiosity, attract admired authors, a calendar of events.*

"Elodie?" Laurie, my assistant, tucks her wispy hair behind her ears. "I think it's time."

The chitchat is waning. I look around. The literary critic and feminist Julianne Leigh, this morning's speaker, floats toward me in her boho chic persimmon maxiskirt and tan fringed suede booties.

"Oh, sure. Am I holding things up?" I ask.

When Julianne reaches me, Laurie and my mother both take their iPhones out for a photo op. Julianne and I oblige, arms around each other's waists, our smiles radiating toward the tables. "Quite a crowd," she whispers although her microphone isn't on.

"I'm thrilled," I whisper back. "Thank you."

I go over my introductory notes in my head, although I know exactly what my words will be, since I'm a longtime fan of Julianne's.

"Please, ladies, take your seats." My voice is clear. I notice that although we are outdoors, there isn't much air circulating. It could be the humidity—uncommonly high for November in Palm Beach. We should have held the event inside, where the air-conditioning is endless. Except for the setting—twelve tables among the allamanda bushes, birds-of-paradise, and Dombaya. Julianne Leigh hovers at the edge of the front row, waiting for my introduction to begin.

"It is meaningful that everyone is here today for our annual kickoff 2018/19 Distinguished Lecturer Series." I lift the glass of water left on the inside ledge of the podium for the guest speaker. I take a sip and go on.

"I have long admired Julianne Leigh, ever since I first read her work when I was in college. Today she will discuss how the writings of Stevie Smith and Elizabeth Bishop have influenced her. She'll talk about Smith's humor, whimsy, and seriousness, and offer her insights into Bishop's evocative language that describes atmosphere and place. I cannot imagine a better critic than Julianne to interpret these works. And I know that she'll set us straight on that famous line of Smith's, 'I was much too far out, all my life. And not waving but drowning.'"

Applause as Julianne approaches, a whiff of her Guerlain La Petite Robe Noire preceding her hug. I gag, as if I've never been overwhelmed by a scent before. Swiftly I recover and meet her embrace. We swap eye contact, our resident intern snaps a photo, more applause.

As I step down, onto the lawn, I'm light-headed. I move away from the podium toward my mother's table as if it is a goal line, suddenly nauseous. The sun shines too brightly and the clank of coffee cups and silver trays being placed on the tables sounds too harsh. I put my hand against my waist, flat although I'm fifteen weeks pregnant—after three miscarriages, nothing matters as much as my baby's beating heart. My nausea turns to a kind of cramping across my entire middle to my back. I look out at the crowd, whose focus is entirely on Julianne. She begins by describing her ascension in the writing world as if it might be as easy as learning to ride a bike. She is captivating, melodic. I move myself along, daring to stare in one direction. My mother, in front to my left, gets up from her chair so quickly it falls onto the grass. She is staring at me with pity in her eyes.

A sharp pain begins to radiate, this time from my back, sharp enough that it sweeps over me. Whatever air there is dissipates and stylish women on the terrace and in the lavish gardens seem far off, almost photoshopped into a vagueness.

"Are you all right?" Laurie comes to steer me beyond the rosebushes where I'm standing, immobilized. I'm sure I'm answering, yet I can't hear a sound.

"Elodie!" Another person appears. Reassuring, steely. My mother. "Someone, help Elodie. We need help," she says.

Next I hear a woman, perhaps from the last row, shout, "Call an ambulance." Someone puts her hand up, says, "I did." Another woman says, "I'm a doctor." Her words are promising—aren't they? She's suddenly there, taking my pulse, guiding me onto the grass. I couldn't be losing this baby, my baby girl. Not this time, not again. Then the bleeding begins—unlike anything I've ever known.

CHAPTER 2

ELODIE

I look at James and remember what Aubrey, my younger sister, always says: *James is a ten. You married a ten.* Aubrey's imprimatur has no positive effect—things feel imbalanced. I stare at the tiny gold triangle pattern on my hospital gown and then up at the ceiling cracks. Although this is a different room than my last time at South Palm Hospital, the paint, an off-gray dull finish, is identical and splinters in the same places. The single window is sealed and the panes are filmy, while the air-conditioning drones on.

James's face seems dry and tight and he is pacing. His own level of ambition and investigation won't allow defeat in any portion of life. He has an MBA from Harvard. He's the CEO of ANVO, a biotech start-up. He is accustomed to solutions—he is a negotiator, and this isn't easily negotiable.

Instead, he is merely a husband who will pace in his wife's hospital room after her fourth miscarriage in a row. A pregnancy that was convincing enough that we dared dream of our baby, due in May—in time for summer. He is another man completely from the one who kissed me this morning, when I was wrapped in a towel and he was almost out the door to his office.

"Our baby will be very clever," he'd declared last night. We were in bed. I was rereading *War and Peace* and James was reading a book about quantum physics.

"Our baby girl," I said. News we learned last week and have yet to tell anyone except for my mother and my sister, who so get it. Next week, at the sixteenth-week point, we planned to tell Mimi, James's mother. He wanted her to know at the same time as my mother, but I had to keep it sacred for as long as possible.

"Every mother deserves to have a daughter," my mother said when we learned the sex of our baby. James saw how pleased I was when I repeated this to him. Although he might feel that every father deserves a son, especially since he has been fatherless these last twenty years. Who knows what the odds are of having a son? How about just having a child?

"It's been a long haul," he said when we were seated at Bice, waiting for our friends the Shieldses and the Harwoods to meet us. "You're forty, I'm forty-three. I worry about you, your body. Is it fair to have children—for them to have old parents?"

I might have argued that this seemed calculating and that once our new house was finished, many children could live there. That there are plenty of couples having babies at our ages. As if I didn't know James's strategic plan from the night that he'd tapped me on the shoulder and introduced himself. It was thirteen years ago at the Campbell Apartment in Grand Central, during a massive train delay. While we waited for hours, we sat at the bar, trading dreams of success and children. We were so young, it was a theorem. Two years later we were married and I thought perhaps we should take care of it at once—have two children in two years. If there was no model time to have a baby, this seemed like a solution. James didn't like the idea; he said we deserved time as a couple first and we were both trudging ahead with work. Somehow together we let it go. At first I almost kept quiet on purpose. Then when James honed in, there were issues. If only we had done this at the right time in our lives.

Carly Shields and her husband, Wally, were being brought to our table. To the left and to the right, tables were being filled with people we know. Besides, I've always gone along with my husband's logic; I've always appreciated it. We share the canvas, paint in the same palette—that's what James and I do. Later when dinner was over, I decided not to go deeper, knowing this would be my mother's tact.

"Can we go home? Now? I'm so wiped out. I want to be in my bed."

"I'm sorry, sweetie, they said you might need to be transfused—they're monitoring you."

"A transfusion? But I thought . . ."

"Let's not worry about that yet. Can I get you something? Soup, applesauce?"

For the first time since we began the process of starting

a family, of trying to do the most natural thing in the world, James seems desolate.

"No, thanks. I'm fine. Nothing. Please, don't worry," I say.

I wonder if it is afternoon yet. How the time moves in this hospital reminds me of a long delay at an airport. Hours eked out until your flight takes off.

"Is my mom on her way?"

"She should be." James frowns at his iPhone. "I got her text."

Earlier today my mother gave a half smile of approval (she never completely smiles anymore because she says her face has "dropped"). What has happened since then isn't for her. I ought to do something—fix my braid, which has come undone, find a lipstick. I am terrified of how disappointed my husband is; I dread my family's view of me.

"A sip of water?" James holds up the Styrofoam cup with a straw in it.

I shake my head. He moves to the window and pauses as a distinctive patter is heard from down the hallway. A clicking of heels against the tile that could produce one of three women—my mother, my mother-in-law, or Dr. Noel. I am hoping it is not Mimi, James's mother. He must sense this, because his face relaxes when Dr. Samantha Noel appears. For a moment I believe she'll save me, turn the day around, pledge a full-term pregnancy for me. Her pearls and the neckline of her dress show beneath her crisp white lab coat with her name embroidered across the left breast pocket.

"This almost took, Dr. Noel," I say. "I was almost in the clear."

"I know. I know." Dr. Noel clasps her hands together;

her bangle bracelets clink before she lifts the scratchy sheets. "May I take a peek?"

I keep talking. "Well, when this is over, when I'm better, I can try one more time."

Dr. Noel blanches, pauses. "I'm sorry, Elodie, I don't think it's prudent. I'm advising against any more in vitros. I don't think you should become pregnant again."

I know that she is speaking to me—her mouth moves in this fixed, tapered way. What she says makes little sense. This has happened before but I have recovered. I tried again, the in vitro took, and I was having a girl.

Dr. Noel is poking around while I'm panicking.

"James? That's not right. That's not what we'll do. It's not our idea, because . . ."

He stands at the head of the bed and rests his hands on my shoulders. I keep repeating the word *no*.

"*No, no,*" I say again.

There is the weight of his hands for what seems over a minute. He quiets me without a gesture.

Dr. Noel sighs. "We've talked about the statistics. How a woman over forty has a five percent chance of becoming pregnant each cycle. IVFs help, of course, yet they aren't miracle workers—we're dealing with the age of the egg. Elodie, please listen. I am advising you against any more procedures—I'm not confident that you can carry a baby to term." Her voice is terse, final. But isn't she like that? There isn't much compassion coming from Dr. Noel.

James keeps rubbing my shoulders. Dr. Noel stands near him, as if they're team players consoling a fallen teammate. Had I tried earlier in my marriage for a child, I might never have walked into Dr. Noel's ultra-pacifying office filled with melancholy. Dr. Noel, who stands behind her desk to shake hands at every office visit. Like an ad for Shutterfly, a framed picture of her three children, twin girls and an older boy, sits on the corner of her desk.

Light that streams in from the window facing west bounces near me. I attempt to hold my arm up, the one that isn't strapped to an IV, to stop the noise, the wrong answers.

Dr. Noel's lips are thinner than usual when she pulls herself up straight and discreetly finishes the exam. "I will have you monitored for the afternoon."

"Meaning what?" I look at James, who takes my hands in his and kisses my forehead.

"Then we'll see," she says. "That's what I can convey at this moment."

The clatter of her heels begins as she heads toward the hallway. I resist apologizing once more. Have I ruined everything? I should not have put off having a family in my early thirties. Or is it more specific—was I drinking too much caffeine, should I not have gone on Katie's boat only a week ago? I watch James pace the way he does before he closes a deal, when he is concentrating ceaselessly, waiting for the outcome.

Someone is behind him. A nurse? My mother? I can't be certain until I hear James.

"Hi, Mom," James says, his voice low and deflated. Has Mimi, James's poised yet not always to be trusted mother, been waiting in the cafeteria, outside in the visitors' lounge? I would feel better had she fit in another round of cards at Longreens and skipped her visit with me.

"You poor girl." Mimi comes close to the bed. "How are you?"

I know she means well, as my mother would say. I turn away.

"Elodie, dear, James is *distraught*."

"Mom?" James says. "Listen, maybe you could give us a minute. Dr. Noel just left."

"Darling," Mimi says, "James, you look spent. Depleted, really."

At least Mimi has a son to inappropriately fawn over. My lost baby flashes before my eyes. Her deep-pink-and-fuchsia crib sheets are from Carousel Designs—she smells the way other babies smell, only better, more familiar, because she is mine. Next I envision myself strapping her into a stroller for a mother-daughter walk along Worth Avenue. In this trance, I'm such a happy mother that when Mimi appears, I'm magnanimous, handing my nameless baby over. I'm about to announce a name—*What name would that be? Why haven't we narrowed it down?*—when I feel another ripple through my abdomen. My reverie halts.

"I wanted to offer moral support, to check on you." Mimi gives me a small, square smile.

A wave of cramps, more blood. I am afraid; I don't want to be transfused.

"Well, thank you," I say.

My mother-in-law seems to be considering the latitude. Her instinct to safeguard James is always there. James, a good son, attempts to handle us both. My mother, who besides being wise and cautious *likes* Mimi, bought me a book when James and I were first married on the mother-in-law, daughter-in-law, son/husband triangle. I read that mothers-in-law should never criticize their daughters-in-law, that they should avoid driving a wedge into what is already a complex situation. According to that book, it's James's turn to say something.

"James is worried about me." I sound snippy, I can't help it.

Mimi rummages through her handbag and opens a tortoise compact mirror, as if she's meeting friends at the Brazilian Court for lunch and is the first to arrive, with a few moments to primp.

James straightens up. "*We* are worried about you. Everyone is."

Mimi shuts the compact, sighs. She is dressed in the clothes she wore this morning, a floral-print dress and medium heels—both now seem wilted.

"Right, Mom?" James says. "Mother?"

She isn't listening; she arches her neck. "Will you excuse me a moment? I think I see the Carrolls, my neighbors. You know their daughter has had a few problems."

Mimi dares to step toward the door frame and pokes her head out.

"Sure, that's fine." James follows her, escorting his mother to her escape. He is polished. I mouth *Thank you* without speaking a word.

A few minutes after she has gone, I decide I only want to speak with my own family. Probably this is similar to the need someone has after she's given birth—to be with her family over her in-laws.

"Have you heard from my parents?"

"They're here, Elodie. See?" James points to the hallway, where it is true that my parents have materialized.

First my father, in his tennis whites, glances into the room; presumably he's displeased. He probably got the text in the middle of a set at Longreens. My mother is behind him. Like Mimi, she is dressed as she was this morning, when she was proud of me, lapping up the praise for my programming, lavished by a board member, Kira Stengler. Even in my present state, I concede how both my mother and father assiduously sidestep problems. Their motto is "Avoid anything unpleasant"; their caveat is "unless it is for the family." They're visiting because I'm their daughter. Together they are one operative, "the Veronica and Simon Show," as my sister and I call them. Under any circumstance, including my miscarriage. Within seconds my mother is at my bedside stroking my hand while my father walks around the room.

"Dearest, what an ordeal." Veronica, as I call her, angles her head in my direction. "When that ambulance arrived, we were so frightened. Laurie is a fine assistant, so levelheaded. Your librarians—why, two of them came to the podium and urged us all to stay. Julianne Leigh kept going."

"Veronica," my father says. "There isn't any reason to describe—"

"No, there is. Elodie should know the lecture went on. Afterward a few women, members you know well, asked if you had passed out. If you were well."

I don't know what to say. I'm mortified.

"It was a very successful event, in any case," Veronica says.

Simon is at the window. "There are a few black skimmers outside. You can see them clearly *and* the windowpanes need cleaning. They're beyond the main building," he says. "Can you see, Elodie?"

"No," I tell him.

"Simon?" My mother angles her head again.

"A room with a view, isn't it?" Simon says.

Her nude patent Manolos don't click with the same tempo as Dr. Noel's or Mimi's, but near enough, as she hastens toward my father. "What an awful situation it is for Elodie and James." She lifts my father's wrist, code for *Not here, not now.*

"I'm sorry," my mother says. "And so is Dad."

"James knows what to do," my father says.

In the corner, James is on his iPhone. He is so facile, he reminds me of the teenage girls at the Academy who come into the library—ostensibly for literary purposes, but mainly to text or sext with the boys.

"James?" Veronica says.

"I'm trying to find Dr. Noel. She said to reach out directly. I want to find out when Elodie can be discharged."

"I thought you might need to get back to the office. If you do, Simon and I, we can be with Elodie." Veronica is speaking about me like I'm not there.

"I'd like James to stay." Another gush of blood. I'm imagining I *should* be transfused. "James?"

"Of course I'll stay."

A young nurse wearing navy scrubs comes into the room, dragging a cart. "Hello." She looks at everyone and no one. "I'm checking your vital signs. Could everyone step outside, only for a few minutes."

She lifts a digital thermometer from the cart. That's when my father takes my mother by the elbow. My mother stares back at me woefully. If she could stay without him, I'd feel better; the room would feel less leaden.

"We'll be down the hall, sweetie. I'll find a mystery, a thriller, to distract you," she says. "I should have stopped at Classic Books and picked up something."

"We're going. Now." My father leads her away. It isn't that I've not witnessed his brusque delivery—I'm used to it—but that I wish he wouldn't.

More footsteps, female, not snappy, not stiletto. They stop outside the doorway.

"It's me." Aubrey, my younger sister, appears in the very same patch that our parents have escaped. The molecules of air have crossed and the room is reconfigured in a brighter hue. I pull myself up a few inches to greet her.

She has driven straight up from Miami. Although she is eight years younger, we could be twins. Our low hairlines, our overbites, which admirers find becoming, our narrow faces, how we squint the same way. Mostly we are pale, with streaky blond over brown hair. From where I am half-propped up on a hospital bed, she looks awfully tall, beyond her five feet seven, then I notice her platform suede sandals. She moves quickly to my bedside, smelling of organic body lotion and lavender, frowning. "Why the IV?"

"In case she needs any medication," James says.

"Well, I'm with you, Elodie. When this episode is over, we'll go on the Avenue—Ta-boo for lunch, Vintage Tales, Eau Spa. The stuff you like, and it will be *relaxing*. I'll stay with you and James—till you are back to yoga, back to work."

Aubrey bends a bit, drapes her arms around me as best she can. I let her. I let her be closer than anyone, including James.

I face the wall while my sister goes on about it—the

Lake Trail, Balanchine at the Miami City Ballet, a mani-pedi, Swedish massages, the new Alice and Olivia, salty caramel gelato.

Then her sentences evaporate and the walls turn from hospital green to sepia.

CHAPTER 3

ELODIE

Y ou deserve credit for choosing a place that's near the Avenue and we won't be seen by anyone we know," I say to James.

We're at the pool area at the Colony Hotel at noon. We've been ushered to a table with an umbrella and my husband of eleven years and I sit facing each other. My second time out since my miscarriage, and the world feels precarious, precious.

"Being here is a little like playing hooky. I bet we're the only ones who have to get back to their desks," James says.

"We seem older; we're the only ones not in the sun." I point to women in string bikinis on the lounge chairs and a few toned men languidly reading texts on their iPhones. They seem to be trying to get rays, to be tanned if not sun-burned. Suddenly I feel like we might not be as fetching and quintessential a Palm Beach "young couple" anymore. My friends are out and about right now. Some at work, a few at Longreens or Mar-a-Lago, playing tennis, golf, or cards. There are the "girl lunches" at the Breakers beach club or purse shopping, an occasional parent-teacher conference at the Academy.

"We came to talk, Elodie."

At least we are invisible—no friends or family, no members of the Literary Society are circling. Besides, the southeast breeze will blow our words away from us, toward the Intracoastal.

A young woman about Aubrey's age, blond, with a pretty face, hands us two menus, which flap in the wind. Are James and I about to decide on more change orders, discuss delays in deliveries for our new house? A list lights up in my head: custom floors—La Roche di Rex from Italy—closets with windows, an ill-conceived, then restructured terrace off the master bedroom. All this after we've settled the architecture debacle over Mediterranean or Bermuda style. The past year, James and I have been looped together, a team for the house. James usually wins—because he cares so much, because I speak more softly. He holds up his forefinger and middle finger. "We'll have two iced teas."

As our server disappears, I'm tempted to switch my order to a latte. Instead, I watch her go, wondering if she has children, what their names are. Does her husband work nearby? Do they live on the other side of the Intracoastal? Perhaps in West Palm or Lantana, or right in Lake Worth.

"Is living across the bridge more family-oriented?" I ask.

"More family-oriented?" James says. "I don't know. Less tony, that's for sure. There are plenty of families on the island—right in Palm Beach."

If our server has children, they would be very young and very blond.

"Listen, Elodie," James says. "Dr. Noel has said—"

"What? When did you speak with Dr. Noel?"

"When you were at South Palm. She was with you first and you heard what she said and then she and I had a brief—"

"Without me? Don't we speak to Dr. Noel together?"

James raises his arms; his muscles show more than most husbands' do. He's in a kelly green polo shirt and khakis, meaning he might only stop at ANVO for an hour this afternoon, that he has golf plans with clients.

"There were two minutes, she and I were by the door to your room. I wanted to feel her out," James says. "Calmly."

Although I should have been included, I don't say this smacks of betrayal. Instead, I admit to myself that I've been touchy. I give him credit for searching for answers. I wait.

"What she suggested is that we hire a gestational carrier, using a donor egg, a surrogate."

"That's what she said?" I look at his face.

He nods.

"James, stop, please. I don't know what you're thinking," I say.

"I'm offering the options."

"Options? *Options?*"

"Hear me out, please." My husband drums his hand on the arm of his chair.

I move my body about, repositioning myself. My uterus is cramping in the aftermath of the miscarriage.

"It would be my sperm and someone else's egg . . . artificial insemination. Then that woman would give birth to our baby."

"Why not *my* egg?"

"You can *get* pregnant—but fertility declines with age. Your eggs are older, they're less viable."

Less viable. Less potent. In another life I wore La Costa el Algodón mini-slips to bed to entice my husband; his very touch sent shivers through me. I ached for him and for our lovemaking long past the expiration date for romance in a marriage.

For the last two years, our sex life has been a means to an end and we've willingly traded in our shared need in the night for baby making. Between pregnancies that failed, an ovulation thermometer surfaced on my bed stand. That became our measure of seduction and tenderness. The cycles, the injections, subcutaneous and intramuscular. Before that, I used to make him laugh.

"So we're one of those hapless couples without a baby, despite every measure we took. Only luckier because at least we haven't plowed through our savings before we give up," I say.

"The pregnancies that ended, they're a loss for me, too." James's voice is low. "I don't want to give up, Elodie. You know I don't."

"I've researched how some couples adopt a baby in Russia or mainland China. One or two infertile couples miraculously became pregnant once they got back to the United States. We've talked about adoption and traveling to a country where the babies and little children are in need of a home." I put this idea out partly as a magic potion and partly because adoption would be fine with me. "And we would share that experience, if we adopted."

"Not my first choice." James's tone is firm. While the circumstances have changed, his attitude about adopting has not.

"Somehow it could still happen for us. We could have *our* baby," I say. If only it were for sure.

Another round of in vitro isn't happening, I know by the way he shakes his head, and I realize that I've taken hormones for nothing. I swallow hard. How could this be my life? I've watched mothers stroll along the Avenue with their small children, fulfilled, content. Some secretly doling out M&M's, others handing out Polly-O string cheese. Mothers with their children, traveling together from playgroup to painting classes at the Four Arts, on to gymnastics at Gymboree. Over Christmas vacation they add a few days at the Breakers holiday camp, visits to the aquarium and children's zoo. The best is when mothers come into the Literary Society with their small children for the Children's Hour on the fourth floor. We showcase children's book authors, Nancy Tillman, Nick Bruel, and P. G. Bell, while never forgetting *Goodnight Moon* or *Chicken Soup with Rice*. We order new titles as well as classics—the key is that they're imaginative, adventurous, and bold. Books I would select for my own child.

Two days ago I read *The Tiger Who Came to Tea* to the three- to five-year-olds. There is a sister and brother who come each week. The mother sets one child on each knee as they listen. The little girl fusses with her pigtails and wears funky-print leggings and the little boy claps when I turn the pages. That is when I most want to hold my own child close as the world unfolds.

"I want a baby, too, James. With you. I don't want a stranger's eggs. Someone we don't know carrying our baby, being the donor."

"I agree it brings up another level of potential problems," James sighs. "It's too . . ."

"Unnatural?" I say. "I'm uneasy with the idea. Having your sperm shot into her body while I'd be on the sidelines."

"Something like that. I know how you must feel." James leans in, beseeches me. "I've really thought about it, scrupulously."

I want to remind him that I have never failed at anything in my life. James knows, doesn't he? I was a straight-A student who earned academic scholarships for both undergraduate and graduate school. I was summa at Princeton; I have a master's degree in library science from the University of North Carolina at Chapel Hill. I have finished every novel I've ever started reading, including *The Brothers Karamazov*. I've never cheated on a boyfriend, including in high school; I've never stood anyone up. I'm a dutiful daughter and genuinely adore my sister. I worked hard to become director of events—scheduling exhibitions, book discussions, and author talks. I'm upping diversity, explaining to the board why it matters to include grade schools, to offer outreach for children and adults alike. I fought the board for our Writers and Critics schedule, then chased down the talent. Wasn't I taught by my parents that perseverance pays off? Yet not with this, not with carrying a baby to term.

Our server, still young, still potentially nosy, appears with our drinks. I measure the sugar into a spoon, only half full. Then I stir gently. I might skid off the seat; I might disappear.

"Okay, I think I get it," I say. "We have a life. We have our love, our work. Maybe it isn't only about having a baby. We care about each other."

I half believe it—if only I can dispel the baby. My husband leans closer, kisses me lightly on the lips. I can taste the tannic acid from his iced tea. There is something about James today that unsettles me. Like the person I married has gone missing, replaced by this nervous version, a woe-begone man.

"I married you because I love you." James drags his chair to mine. It thumps, making a screeching sound on the patio. "I want children—at least a child. Life would feel incomplete without one. I know I'd be a great father, you'd be a great mother."

I cough, take a sip of Voss water from my glass.

"I was just out of college when my father died. He was very dedicated to me and to my mom. I want that chance, that experience," James says. "Look at you and your mother and Aubrey. Don't you want to raise a child based on what you've had with your family, what you do for kids at the Society?"

"What happened with your father is terribly sad. I know he was outstanding. You *should* be a father, James."

The umbrella over our table almost topples in a mini wind squall that's come out of nowhere. I notice one of the bikini-clad women—a tourist—spreading her towel out on her lounge chair while the sun dips and resurfaces. Carefree, unencumbered. Why didn't I at least harvest my eggs?

What was I thinking—what were we thinking as a couple? I don't dare acknowledge our miscalculation, that when we were first married I was pregnant. It was too soon, so James and I made a decision together to abort. Is he remembering, lamenting that my being fertile is no longer possible? Again the anguish of knowing I'm late in the game.

"This is how I feel, Elodie. I want you that much, *with* children. *I* want to be a father."

When he puts his hands on my forearms, they are like bricks. I try to shrug away from him. He is supposed to talk about the value of us, a "running for office" duo. James is the husband who keeps trim and hasn't lost his hair. I do my best between hot yoga and the elliptical, the Lake Trail with my mother and mother-in-law. My hair is so glimmery lately, it's as if I stole it from Aubrey. Both James and I exude a calm. He should make a pledge about our life together working with or without children.

"Elodie?"

He straightens up, inches away, suddenly confused. Is he mistaking the lunch with me, his wife for better or worse, with a meeting at ANVO? There at *his* company, he gets to push for progress without opposition, without glitches. He brought ANVO to South Florida, where it keeps growing, focusing on the commercialization of drugs in certain areas of the country or why the research on inflammatory disorders matters. I profit from his style, his conviction at ANVO. His promises, from front-row seats to Bruce Springsteen on Broadway to a surprise long weekend in Nassau to flying Mario Vargas Llosa to the Literary Society after I mentioned my hope, happen pronto. Yet he can be humble, and when we are at dinner with friends, he boasts about my lineup of writers, not his latest projects. While James views most of life as a negotiation, I don't forget his private side. That's what I'm after, what I need. Which James is the one sitting with me at lunch?

"I want us to have a child however we can." He looks to the east, although the ocean isn't visible from where we are. We hear the waves crashing.

"So this is what we could do." He stops and holds up his hand, reminding me of the crossing guard in junior high. "Dr. Noel said she's performed thousands of in vitros with donor eggs and she's arranged gestational carriers for couples. She recommends ART—artificial reproductive technology."

Our server comes back with the tray in one arm and does an overly dramatic swirl as she places it on the stand behind James. She begins to unload it, putting a small bowl of salad dressing and an undressed plate of kale in front of me. Swiftly she puts James's already-dressed kale Caesar at his place setting.

The outdoor restaurant is filling up. More women in Eres bikinis with matching sarongs tied around their waists are fanning themselves with their menus. Mostly they use their aviator sunglasses—in pink or rose color— as hair bands, pushing their long, spirally hair off their foreheads. Three women have small children and husbands who hold the younger ones in their arms. Maybe they planned their families together—a toddler and a kindergartner per unit. Did they have tummy tucks after their pregnancies? Or did they do sit-ups for months to drop their post-partum fat? I've overheard women whispering about both at the Literary Society. Fat that is earned. A grandmother—truly, she's a "glamma"—looms to the right of the second husband. Her manner indicates that she's been at a few outdoor resort lunches with her young grandchildren and their clueless parents. My mother and Mimi start zigging through my head. *Everybody's got something that doesn't fit*—Mimi's warning against the illusion that most women are privileged *and* satisfied.

"Jesus, what would our mothers say?" I ask.

"I'm not thinking of our mothers, I'm thinking of us."

"Now that it's on my mind, I can't stop. I'm sorry. It's that my mother's Palm Beach side would try to hide the whole thing. You know how she can be and your mother is sort of the same. I imagine she won't like this plan either. One day we show up with a baby and everyone says, 'Wow, you weren't pregnant. What happened?'"

"Your mom is such a cheerleader for you, she'd make up some tall tale," James says.

As he points this out, I realize how deeply James wants a baby. How important a conversation we are having, how he is searching for a solution.

He is staring at the young families about to order fries and hot dogs for their children. "Maybe we should go." He starts eating quickly, while I can't swallow.

"Are you okay?" I ask.

James is the closest to tears since the days when he first spoke about his father. His jaw is set, but he needs to be held. I get up from my chair and go to him. I kneel beside him and whisper, "James, listen . . ."

"No, not really okay," he says.

I rise and put my hands on the back of his neck, where his skin is warm and strong. He lifts his right arm and motions for a check. The manager catches this and races over, his blue-and-melon-striped tie billowing in the wind.

A table over, two little girls begin their orders.

"Chicken fingers and fries!" the first, who is about five, shouts out. She is chewing on her braid and her bathing suit looks sopping wet.

"One burger! Two milk shakes!" The second little girl, who is possibly seven, also shouts, "Extra ketchup!"

She holds up an iPhone and the younger one squints to see the screen.

"Girls, say please." The mother comes along in her sarong and bikini top with a towel in her hand. "Who is too wet to be eating lunch without changing first?"

Our server looks into the distance, sighs. It occurs to me that she might not have any children after all.

CHAPTER 4

ELODIE

"It is only a shell—a facade so far," I say to Aubrey as we face both the ocean and the Intracoastal. We stand outside the scaffolds that lace together our house-to-be.

"Yeah, but look at the view, Elodie!" Aubrey points to the west, where the sun is setting. Streaks of orange and gold mix with a dusky sky. "And a private beach!" She pivots her head to the east.

I know she's trying her best to cheer me up, remind me of what I have and not what I've lost. Along the shoreline, low waves roll in, scant and steady.

"I know it's dazzling," I say. "Especially this time of year."

"Plus, the season is starting," Aubrey says. "Mom and Mimi are making plans and talking wardrobes."

"You and Tyler should come to the Rose Ball at the Shelteere. As our guests."

Aubrey laughs. "Can you honestly imagine Tyler there? Besides, we've got eight bands to hear before Christmas and three festivals, including Rakaskella and EDC Orlando."

I convinced my sister to come with Tyler tonight. The allure being that the walls are in, so we can do a walkaround. As if she cares or covets any part of this five-bedroom Palm Beach house. How we choose to live has to be far-fetched to her, although familiar.

"I know. But please remember you're invited, if you change your mind. I'm glad you're around more these days," I say.

Whenever she comes to Palm Beach, lithe and lean, with her flowing skirts and flip-flops, the chic younger Cutler sister is welcomed. *I'm back, up from South Beach,* she posts on Instagram.

"Maybe you and Tyler want to come to a black-tie or two, sit at our table."

"I'd like that, Elodie, but most nights, like I said, we're with bands or singers—for the gigs. Tyler really can't get away and I should be there, too."

"Sure, I get that." I mustn't push her too far. Except my mother and I want her in Palm Beach and she resists. This has been going on ever since Aubrey graduated from college; she never bought into coming back to this narrow island with its linear view of life.

Aubrey tilts her neck forward, part sea horse, part dancer, to look at James and Tyler, standing at the dock. James and I only met Tyler at my parents' house an hour ago. When he walked in with his frayed jeans and wrist tattoos, I watched my mother's intake at lightning speed. I wish I had been able to tell her what Aubrey has confided in me, that she has found refuge. Tyler is kind to her and attentive to his work.

"You are sworn to say nothing about him," Aubrey insisted beforehand. "I want everyone to meet him and decide."

What remains in the ether is Aubrey's known pattern. After three months she tosses a man out like rotted fruit, only to drag in another version of the same guy. "Fungible," that's what James calls Aubrey's men. Until now. Tyler and Aubrey have been together eleven months. When he hired her to scout out bands in Miami for his company, Lambent Music, he was working in Los Angeles. There was no office and she was the sole employee. Veronica and I were astonished by how seriously Aubrey took her job, how determined she was to hear the singers, especially women vocalists. The night that he got to South Beach, they met at the Dance Room. Aubrey claims Tyler was splendid. At first they flew back and forth on weekends to be together. Then Tyler decided he could bring performers to Florida as well as find talent in the area. A few months later they hired four full-time people and took office space on Lincoln Road.

Still, she held back from introducing him to us, tough graders that we are. I see where Aubrey is going with this, that our approval matters less than he does. That she doesn't care if Tyler isn't more sophisticated or that our family will judge his every move. That's why I catch my sister's eye and wink. I do the smallest thumbs-up ever, the kind I taught her when she was in eighth grade at the Academy and searching for subtlety.

Aubrey does the same, smiling. The guys come close to where we stand.

"What do you think?" I open my arms wide, convey the space of our house-to-be.

"Wow. It will be something." Aubrey pauses. "I read somewhere that houses are a big deal in a relationship. One of those monumental changes. A stressor."

"Totally," I say. "Katie Kutin sent me these anxiety texts, because after she started building her house on the ocean, she thought she'd lose it. I take what happened to her as a warning."

"I'm not so sure that putting these ideas out there was friendly." James sounds annoyed.

"She's my best friend. If she can't express what happened with her house—the truth about it—who can?" I ask. "She was trying to help me."

"Right, but her work as a physician is grueling, Elodie, that's a big part of it. Plus three children," James says.

"Not that Katie's saving lives can be compared to cultural programming, yet I believe her experience was separate from her kids and her career. She said that building a house is a black hole."

James checks his iPhone. The sun streaks across the horizon as it sinks. Quickly we're at nightfall.

"How's her little boy—what's his name?" Aubrey asks.

"Zachary. Adorable. Really, I try to spend time with him, since he's my godchild. He comes with Katie to the Literary Society. When Katie's on call—every other weekend in the ER—I sometimes take Zachary and Matt keeps the younger ones—with the nanny. Zachary's five and easy—a book lover, too."

"Isn't their new house like right around the corner?"

I feel my sister's question is skewed. Is she asking if we live on the same molehill?

"Yes, two streets over; she's on Kings Road. She says that once she moved in, she was enticed. Then chained to the house and finally it's an albatross. With some strange seduction that keeps going."

"That's grim," Aubrey says.

We can't help laughing. The men look at us. James of the clean-cut, chestnut-hair, broad-shoulder brigade, Tyler of the shaved-head, ripped-torso, dissenter squad.

"Hey, it's going to be quite a house. Just like our digs," Tyler says.

Digs. There is a slight freeze; then James says, "Elodie, you've been to Aubrey and Tyler's place, haven't you?"

"Yes, in October. When I had Columbus Day off. Mom had me bring duvets from Lucille's on South County."

"Duvets?" Tyler asks.

"They're in the guest room closet," Aubrey tells him. "I didn't put them out yet. I haven't even opened them."

"Although it was an emergency delivery from Veronica," I say.

Aubrey and I know what Veronica perceives as critical, including when one of her daughters is moving into a new place. James, too, gets her style. Tyler stands outside our invisible circle—he's only just arrived. But how *would* he fit in? Will he ever fit in? He has walked into a period of our lives when James and I are filled with talk of kitchen cabinets, silent-flush toilets, or social aspirations and the ambushed subject: parenthood. When we lived on Riverside Drive and 101st Street with our dog Cupcake, an Airedale terrier, who could have predicted we would move back to Palm Beach within a year? I want to set my little sister free of any expectations—let her see where her life takes her. I'd like to whisper in her ear, *Come and go. Be a visitor. Do not get caught in the web.*

Although I haven't asked him, plausibly Palm Beach meant little to Tyler before he met Aubrey. Tonight he must be saturated. Before he had time to recover from cocktails at our parents', a true Veronica and Simon Show, James practically dragged us to our house, which is not much beyond skeletal. Except for the square footage, coming in at eleven thousand, large enough that one needn't boast about it, the size is obvious. The copious closets and vast bathrooms seem obscene. Somehow the contrast of our home in the estate section with Aubrey's rental apartment in South Beach, decorated in Ikea, feels like we're braggarts, show-offs.

"C'mon, we'll walk you guys around," James says. "Before it gets too late." James holds up a bottle of Chianti and hands me four plastic cups. With his free hand he dips into the metal storage chest. The workmen have stationed it near what will be our front door. He produces a battery-operated lantern and two ancient-looking Eveready flashlights.

"Are those from Green's Pharmacy?" Aubrey asks. "Dad had them in the garage when we were growing up, didn't he, Elodie?"

I nod. "For hurricanes."

James hands Tyler a lantern and shines his own over the scaffolding and property.

"I don't know," I say. "We don't have to do a tour. Does anybody need a tour?"

"We're here, might as well." James does a circle of light over the Intracoastal. A jagged shadow falls over our faces. Aubrey, my little sister, is exquisite.

"Right, right. Sometimes when we're here, we can't quite believe it. That we're doing this. Building this," I say.

"What a house. Great for a brood of young kids." Tyler points to where the grand staircase will be. "Sliding down the banister!"

No one speaks for a beat. I imagine that my sister hasn't filled Tyler in, given him the gory lowdown. I hold my empty wine cup out to James for a refill. He pours one for each of us. Then Aubrey clears her throat, takes Tyler's hand. "Tyler's right. It's amazing."

Again no one speaks. I try to read Aubrey's face in the darkness. Who could blame her for wanting to head to South Beach now, skip the dinner, escape.

James holds up the bottle of Chianti. "Who wants more wine?"

Aubrey and I shake our heads, like we've rehearsed it, while Tyler thrusts his cup toward James. James pours as if he is a dashing host and we aren't using plastic at a construction site. A future where he'll stand on our stone veranda, pouring Patrón into our Tiffany Diamond Point highball glasses.

"Hey, good with me." Tyler polishes off the wine.

For extra light he opens the flashlight app on his iPhone. He and James are ahead, male warriors on a mission. I stare at the two men as they stand together, both over six feet tall.

"We should be careful," I say, avoiding the periphery, where one could fall two floors. I place my right hand below my belly button, as if I'm still pregnant. I tiptoe around, pointing to the scaffolding. "It's rickety."

James places his hand on my elbow. Tyler motions toward

what will be the sunroom and a guest suite. He asks in a boom-box voice, "Up there, are those the bedrooms?"

The bedrooms. Including the nursery. Aubrey is watching in the dimness. Maybe it's the first time in my life that she doesn't seem in awe of me for anything. She comes close and slips her hand in mine.

"We should go—skip dinner. I'm the designated driver. . . . Tomorrow morning we have an early—"

"Wait, wait," James says. "I've got one question for Tyler. About the audio system?"

"Sure, I can recommend a few. Bose is great. People say you hear every nuance, every drumbeat."

"Excellent." James is pleased.

Aubrey and I are quiet. Then she asks, "What's the architecture going to be?"

"Well, it's a new house, we plan to create it in the style of Howard Major—an early-twentieth-century Palm Beach architect," James says.

"What Mom calls 'tropical classic,'" I say.

I view us from Aubrey and Tyler's stance. Are we nothing but a younger version of the Veronica and Simon Show? Why else build this place? Four blocks to the north our parents have similar views and their own double-vaulted entryway. James and I have been a team for this—geared to match the essentials, which include a library, sunroom, patio with an infinity pool, access beneath the A1A to our own beach and cabana. When I began planning the garden, the shrubs mattered. So did purple cornflowers. After reading four books on indigenous plants, I knew I'd stick with bougainvillea, yarrows, and beautyberries. Only a few months ago I had more zeal for floor plans and decor than I do today. Before the miscarriage.

Out of nowhere the wind picks up. Although I've been in Palm Beach my entire life, I've never adjusted to the sound of the ocean that carries onto land. Or that it happens no matter which side of the island you're on, Intracoastal or by the sea. The shoreline has gone dark and is hardly discernible in the moonlight. I shiver.

"So what about dinner—a quick bite in town? We can take one car and drop you back." I wait for Aubrey to decide.

"That's fine," Aubrey says. "Perfect."

Again the moonless night as we wind down the A1A to Buccan. James's BMW 5 sedan purrs with Aubrey at the wheel.

"You two are quite a pair of sisters." Tyler, in the passenger seat, turns to me.

"Just the two of them," James adds.

"I have two sisters—both back in Portland—and I'm in the middle. They're like Aubrey and Elodie, thick as thieves," Tyler says.

"Did you read about that study on siblings a few years ago? In *The Atlantic*?" I ask.

"I read it!" Aubrey says. "I knew you'd have seen it, too!"

"I kept thinking that for sisters it's a more profound connection. Here's the question: If you're in a sinking boat and there's only one life vest, do you give it to your husband or your sister?"

"Exactly the right question!" Aubrey says.

"Evolutionary psychology provides the answer," James offers.

"What?" Aubrey says.

"It does," James insists. "Because we're adaptive. If you think about it, your DNA is more important than a marriage. The sister will save her sister to preserve their genes." James is doing that brainy, nerdy bit to which he occasionally succumbs.

"Hey, could be the sister *likes* her sister and not her husband," Tyler says.

"Or you could argue that your spouse matters more, since when you got married, you left the family of origin," I say. "There is the idea that loyalty shifts from the family that raised you to the new family or marriage, the family of procreation."

"Oh, Elodie, it's fine." Aubrey laughs. "You would save *James*. *James* would get the life vest."

"Eh, who gives a damn, really. I mean, maybe all three are strong swimmers—no need for the one life vest," Tyler says.

"Right, in a perfect world the strong swimming would save the day," Aubrey says. "You wouldn't have to choose."

CHAPTER 5

ELODIE

Rain clouds darken the A1A as I drive home from the Literary Society. Although it's only six o'clock, floodlights from private homes shine over an opaque ocean. I pass El Brillo, where my parents live, and to the south the pink towers of Mar-a-Lago are the only illumination in a murky sky.

James is waiting on the flagstone steps, as if he has time to spare. The scenario is unfamiliar and my first instinct is to panic. Until I see how happily he holds a food basket with gold and green ribbons.

"Wow, who arranged this?" I ask when I pull up to our house—the home we have lived in for almost seven years.

"Justine's prepares and delivers. I thought we'd try it out. Your sister reminded me last night that you love prepared food."

"True," I say. "But Christina could have cooked tonight. You didn't have to order dinner."

Christina, my parents' housekeeper, who comes to clean twice a week for us, has been especially disheartened by my miscarriage. She had promised that her second cousin, who is a trained nanny, would take care of our baby. To this end, Christina has been among those I've avoided these past few weeks.

James unlocks our front door. "Only the two of us. No interference—an empty kitchen."

I wrap my arms around his neck and we kiss.

"Is there some gift box after this?" I ask.

"No, there isn't," James replies.

"How unlike husbands in the area," I say.

"Right, no assistant from my office has gone on the Avenue to get you a link bracelet from Seaman Schepps."

We kiss again.

After he unpacks the basket, he begins arranging dinner in a purposeful way. He transfers the zucchini and yellow squash into a large bowl. I walk past him toward the double sink, where he has placed a bouquet of deep-violet pansies, marigolds, and primroses, late-autumn/early-winter colors. Suddenly the granite island in our kitchen, the honey-colored hardwood floors, the double doors that lead to the terrace and pool—our entire home—feel dear to me. Why do we need another house—why did I sign up for building a grander, finer version? Not only Katie, but my friend Nina has already completed her upgraded house. She and her husband were enmeshed during the construction—more so than on their wedding day or when their children were born, she says.

"Not that it lasts," Nina said when she heard about the property we bought. "It was our joint venture; then there's an emptiness. I don't even go to the Literary Society for lectures on the architecture, because the house is built. And get this: My girls miss the old house, where they shared a bathroom. Chaz and I tell them this is bigger, better for our family. I'm not sure they believe it."

Our endeavor loops us in a singular pattern, too. The house has a life of its own, and while I was undergoing in vitro, James and I had begun to speak in shorthand about change orders, vintage Belgian door handles, and crown moldings. Less about the family part, the *nesting* part.

"Higher Love," by Steve Winwood, plays on our Sphaeron Excalibur system. James raises the volume a notch and leads me in a dance. We dance around the kitchen and I remember what a fine dancer he is, how strong his arms are, how straight his back is. He knows the steps for real; I fudge well.

"I don't know when we last did that alone and not at a party," I say.

"We are now." He puts his mouth close to my ear.

I want to cling to this, the two of us. Without ANVO, in vitro, the board at the Literary Society, little children lurking about.

James glides back to the counter, places radicchio and endive on two salad plates, sprinkling walnuts from a small glass jar that Justine's has included. I remember our baby's face in the sonogram, her mouth shaped like an O, her tiny chin.

"The couscous was delicious," I say an hour later. "It's sweet of you to have arranged it."

He smiles politely. The dance segment of the evening has waned. James stops eating and stands up, tugging on his shirt collar with his left hand.

"Elodie, I've thought it through."

"Thought what through?" I hope we're about to focus on the house, an incident at ANVO, or my plan to bring the Ukrainian-born mother and daughter poets to the Literary Society. I'm prepared to describe how this afternoon Mrs. A. insisted on "tried-and-true fiction" from the eighties and selected two Danielle Steele books, when I was recommending *The Unbearable Lightness of Being*. I dread any other discussion. That includes our calendar for the season, since I'm not ready to breeze into every party yet. Being back at work is both a panacea and a staggering feat.

Snatching our dinner plates, James clears and piles them in the sink. I'd make a light remark about how few times he has cleared a table or loaded a dishwasher, except I sense the weight of his next lines. I know he is going to talk again about a baby.

I jump up to help out—something my mother would do and my married friends might do, depending on the circumstance. Because tonight most of them, like our parents, are en route to the Norrics' on Island Drive for their party, which we have politely nixed.

James scrapes the food into the garbage, then faces me, leaning against the counter.

"I have an idea, Elodie," he says. "I realized there's a solution. We can ask Aubrey. Let's see if she'll do it for us."

"Ask Aubrey what?"

"It should be Aubrey's egg," James says calmly.

"Aubrey's egg?" My mouth almost glues shut. I'm speaking through a stifling layer, a residue. I repeat, "Aubrey's egg?"

"Aubrey as the traditional surrogate. That's how I see it. Her egg, my sperm through artificial insemination." James's voice is lucid. He keeps going. "I wish we had figured it out earlier, but this is where we are. Your sister carries the closest DNA to your own. She looks like you and has your IQ. You're so close, you're simpatico."

I walk to the window of our sliding glass door; the exterior lights illuminate the patio. I cough twice.

"*Aubrey?* I mean really? Aubrey's egg and another woman carrying the baby?"

"No, not that. Aubrey would be the *surrogate*. It's not done as much anymore, yet easier. Like I said, there'd be in vitro and that would be it. She'd be pregnant with our child. There'd be no hiring a gestational carrier, a random woman."

What he is recommending is unthinkable. Yet my husband has put great thought into the idea. I know to measure my response, not to blurt out, *This is absurd, desperate.*

"And we'd have some kind of control over Aubrey? Isn't she a bit unreliable, a little too hip to be asked? Aubrey does what she wants. How can we ask her?"

Wasn't I the one who brought my little sister to where she is today? From push-up bras to Edith Wharton, Gloria Steinem, Bobbi Brown eyeliner, mean girls at the Academy, birth control in high school, I've been her guide and protector. I taught her *how to be,* such specific lessons that she is the quintessential cool girl.

"You know you'd see her almost every day." James comes to the window, stands beside me. "I bet she'd be in Palm Beach more. She'd rise to the occasion, I know it. She'd quit clubbing to protect our child. It's not work for hire; she's your sister and she'd have a genetic stake in it."

"A genetic stake would matter to her less than the sacrifice. How could it not be that? Look at what the ask is," I say.

"You love each other, Elodie. I haven't seen sisters more connected. She would do anything for you."

"Would she? How do you know? Until now there's never been talk of a test."

There is an image of Aubrey walking with her friends in their miniskirts and Converse sneakers on Clematis Street when she was only thirteen. It was Christmas break. I was secretly following her, a half block behind, my eyes glued to her head. Just in case she needed me to fend off lecherous males or for some extra cash.

I shake my head. "Beyond the idea of asking Aubrey, which seems selfish and unfair and complicated, she has a boyfriend, she cares about him. She finally has this job, this career. Besides that, what you call a connection will change what she and I have. Our *essence.*"

"I don't believe that," James says.

How convincing James is when he pushes for what he wants most.

"James, it seems plain *weird.*"

"Weird?"

"Say that I thought it was a good idea, that it worked for us, James, how can I ask my sister to give up everything that's hers for your sperm and her egg?"

"Our baby," James sighs. Now again, he must be thinking how I've failed, put us in such a position. I wait for him to dispel this, flip it out of his consciousness so I feel less awful.

"Except . . ." I begin.

"Sure, she'll be giving up some superficial things, but look at what she would be doing."

"What she would be doing *for us,* James. I mean, Aubrey's feet don't touch the ground. The collective lie, the one my parents tell, is that Aubrey will be back to live a mile from us. Some bullshit about her studying for a degree in musicology in Miami, that it's the only thing that keeps her there—seventy-five miles from Palm Beach."

A degree she might or might not pursue. Every time my mother talks about my sister, her voice drops a decibel and she purses her lips. Don't we wonder if Aubrey is more capable than she lets on?

James waits because he and I know that my mother lies about me as well. When she's at cards or shopping at Vintage Tales, she will say, if asked, that I'm not interested in a baby. She'll play up the house we're building instead, what charities James and I favor. I cannot fathom my mother's take on James's strategy, how she would navigate the rumors, the disbelief, Palm Beach judgments and chatter. If this were to happen, my mother would be protecting both her daughters—for their shared decision.

"We've talked about my mother already. We've been through this. Besides, two sisters, one baby—it's irrational. On every level, from how it would happen to living in town *while* it happens."

"You know, your dad might like the concept. He can be narcissistic, someone who would respond to the genetic bond." James is insistent.

"Aubrey wouldn't agree to such a crazy idea, never."

"Aubrey will be giving you the greatest gift anyone can give. A baby! Our baby!" More insistence.

I imagine Aubrey at this hour with Tyler. Prancing to a tune that's favored at the clubs in Miami. "Something About Her," by the Kents, or Everywhere's "Some Other Dude," perhaps. Less classic rock, more indie pop. Lyrics that do not espouse a love that could elevate—take us above the rest. Milling about, mingling with the crowd until their band goes onstage. She's in one of her old Hervé Léger minidresses, which cling to her body, and wearing Pour la Victoire stilettos, purchased at a secondhand shop. Perhaps they'll head next to the Rockcellar, where it fills up steadily, arriving before the second set.

"Elodie, it makes sense. Think about it, the idea of it."

I'm at the kitchen table. James comes close and kneels beside me. His eyes are near enough to mine that his love and appreciation are reflected back at me.

"Elodie, it could work for us. Aubrey is like *my* little sister. She *is* your little sister. We love her. What could go wrong?"

"Do you know what I've learned, James? Something I never needed to know. How at risk a woman is when she is trying to get pregnant. When she is pregnant."

"Aubrey is younger, she is in fine shape."

"I realize that, intellectually. What if she gets sick, what if the baby isn't okay?"

Instinctively, I move away from him, stretching my spine.

"Why not at least run it by Aubrey?" he asks.

Run it by Aubrey? Sort of like shopping for boots at a designer sale together. Do they suit me? Do they suit you? Here, you take them. No, no. You're my sister, you should have them. We could share them. Like that?

My husband comes close yet he doesn't take my hand, kiss my face. I remember when I was in fifth grade and Aubrey was in preschool. We would visit our grandparents in New York and our grandfather would take us to Central Park. The sparrows would flit about and we'd break and scatter Aubrey's animal crackers. We hoped the pigeons wouldn't force their way in, devouring our crumbs. Aubrey begged to touch the sparrows. She wanted to take them with her, while I flinched if they came near our feet, near the trail we had made. Am I not maternal and Aubrey is?

"You'll at least ask her. Elodie?"

Aubrey's profile last night, outlined and in shadow, the sound of the Intracoastal lapping against our new, unknown neighbor's dock. How easily she escaped with Tyler to the life they might have together. How dare we intrude? How could we?

"You'll consider it?" James persists.

"James, listen . . ."

"We *need* to do this."

"Sure, I'll ask," I lie.

Because in the moment I doubt that I will.

CHAPTER 6

AUBREY

At midnight Tyler and I are ushered past the rope line at Pascha's. We shake hands with Marco, the bouncer, and step inside. The club is magnetic tonight—the three tiered dance floors, the scene, the music furiously loud. VIP customers are being seated and served, while those who didn't buy the package are treated like they don't exist. Left of us two "girls" about my age— my sister would call them "young women"—are passing a packet while looking around for someone or something. Everyone who stands, crushed together, is trying to figure out who gets what at this club tonight. Some of the women use their iPhones to check their lip gloss, blush, false eye- lashes. Most have long hair, but a few have bobs or punk cuts. Who isn't tattooed—at least on her shoulder, forearm, ankle? Plenty wear tight, short dresses, short shorts, boots or stilettos. Some seem more in a hurry—like they're at a flea market where the best stalls are emptied fast. They assess the men, perhaps in search of the ones with day jobs, money earners, who graze the clubs at night. These men seem aloof; they hold drinks or beer bottles while walking slowly around the perimeters.

Beyond are those who come only for the show, buy tickets, relish the songs. Plenty like that fill the venue. Their bodies shift impatiently. Despite the AC, the room smells of damp skin, sweat, and perfume. Voices float upward between sets: *babes, rooftop . . . not tonight . . . no jazz . . . white powder, pearls, Ecstacy.*

"Feels good, right? A good vibe," Tyler says. "Sold out."

"Yeah," I say. "They're here for the partying *and* the music. Better than on weekends."

Out of nowhere, more dancing starts. Othello D, the DJ, is moving genres around, reggae, hip-hop, salsa. Soon the group will go on. Dirk O—Tyler's favorite band among his clients, a pop rock group whose music reminds me of Maroon 5. There is this retro feel; they use synthesizers.

Tyler puts his mouth to my ear, runs his hands across my body, and whispers, "I'd like to take you home about now."

"Soon," I whisper back. "We've got a band to play."

Behind him, by the bar, I notice two men, older than the rest of the crowd. Anderson and Douglas, longtime industry guys. They're holding glasses of bubbly water and waving at Tyler. We steer past a group of people and walk across the sticky floor to where they stand.

"Here for your new discovery?" Anderson asks. The neon lights show off his wedding ring and slight double-chin. Tyler has told me that Anderson is the longest-standing music rep on the lookout for new artists in Miami.

"I've known Dirk O awhile. Who thinks they found 'em, you or Aubrey?" Douglas asks. As a scout, he wants only to be a liaison for the recording labels.

I don't like the question or the tone. Could it be that Dirk O really belongs with Douglas? I feel around in my bag for my small angel pillbox and wait for Tyler's answer.

"Aubrey. She's the one—about four months ago. We've been managing them ever since."

More anxiety. I rarely take Xanax, so this pill might be expired. I put it in my mouth anyway and swallow without water.

"Congratulations," Douglas says. "What'd ya think?"

"It's about the guitar," I say. Not about how intimate the music feels. Like it's you alone with the band.

Since Tyler is sometimes quiet with reps and scouts, I smile.

Once the men leave for backstage, we head for a booth. I hold out my pillbox to Tyler. He shakes his head. "Nothing for me tonight."

"Why?"

"I want to pay close attention. What plays best for this band. Sober."

"You already know, don't you, Tyler?"

"Ya. Still, I'm counting on this singer-songwriter part. I don't always find that fusion."

Not that he can't drink a couple of dirty martinis or a few ginger-tinged margaritas and still discern the quality and unrealized talent of the musicians. I'm the one who nurses a wine spritzer the whole night and becomes too loopy to pay careful attention, then wake up the next day with a nasty headache.

Suddenly the lights splattered over the carved-wood

bar seem less intense. I'm calm and kind of doughy, soft. I lean against Tyler and tuck my head into his shoulder.

"Y'know, I bet business doubles by spring. Fucking doubles." He puts his hand over mine.

"Wow, really?" I sound slurpy.

"Yeah, and I'm your boss." He laughs.

"I keep forgetting." I do a mellow laugh. "What a boss!"

"Hey, you're very good at the scene. You have an ear for the singers. Especially the female leads, like Patrice and her all-girl band playing feral guitar at the Clean Laundry, standing room only. Aubrey, you put them on the map."

"A victory. It took a lot of nerve—no, more like stalking. I stalked venues to get them heard." I'm speaking, but my voice is far off.

"So how about if we change that?"

"I'm sorry? Change what?" I'm soft and feathery.

"Change how you report to me. You manage half the bands—the ones that matter to you. I know you'll take on some of the female singers and see what flies. Tomorrow I'll give you an agreement. It makes us equal partners on a company we'll start, our company."

Equal partners. "Why? No, that makes no sense. You're the one who toils away, it's your career."

"Half and half. You and me." He stares at me in a good way, a caring way.

"Equal partners?" I ask. "Are you sure, Tyler? I mean, I'm starting out, really, it's only been a year since you hired me."

I don't mention how women leave this business, the number of men in charge, the hours. I don't reveal how I've been known to flit from idea to idea, that I came upon being a music rep when I saw a posting on Craigslist for an assistant. When the position with Tyler came up, I didn't hold the bar very high. I had no idea he'd be reasonable and civilized, polite. He opens doors for older women; he doesn't cut in line. Now that we're together, I know he is decent all around. He hangs up his towel in the bathroom, takes out the garbage, and unloads the dishwasher. While I expected him to be edgy, given the bands he's drawn to and his music finds, he isn't.

"It's been a great year and we've had some hits. I doubt anyone'll come to town to perform and not ask us to handle it." He slides his right hand under my dress. "You have instincts—you're good. Besides, Aubrey, the papers are drawn up for us to sign."

When Saige, the lead singer for Dirk O, grabs the mike for a solo, I feel like I can be a co-discoverer. I know their sound, their every move. I'm sucked into how nostalgic it is, like music I loved in high school. I listened to Billy Joel, Dave Matthews, the Grateful Dead, Madonna. I loved the raspy sound of Pink. Tyler leads me, pushes through to the middle of the dance floor. We're both so cool, rocking together. The room recedes; we're floating. I could take his shirt off, melt into his chest.

"One more set and we'll go," he says. "I want to bed you early tonight to celebrate."

I bend closer, our bodies welding into each other. Then I remember. "On a breakout night? Aren't the reps from Geffen showing up?"

"Yep, they will." His breath is warm. I breathe it in.

"But will the reps . . ." I begin.

"We got them the gig, it's fine. One more set. Besides, we've got the meeting with Dirk O tomorrow. That's what counts for us."

He moves away from me a step to better see the band. Although he is slouching the smallest amount, his biceps show and he tilts his head toward the music.

Tyler fiddles for the key to the front door, swoops me up, and carries me to the couch near the windows. From the thirtieth floor of this glass tower, the spotlights on the beach are specks. Before my head falls back against his shoulder, I look out at nothing. No stars, no moon, I can't see the ocean.

"You hear it, right?" I ask.

"Yeah," he says. "The waves always crashing."

We kiss on the couch and he undresses me, yanking down my miniskirt, my gauzy blouse.

I touch his immaculately shaved head, trace his jawline with my hands, a three-day beard. How are his teeth aligned like that? I move my hands over his back and down his body.

He stands, I watch him take off his T-shirt and jeans—he's good at it, he's done it all before, seen it all before. Tyler is thirty-seven and had a fiancée six years ago. Two years after the engagement was broken, he had a live-in partner. Beyond those two serious relationships were the others—he's been in demand. A slowly revolving door where the women, one at a time, have moved forward, stepped into the room. They have filled the chair, slept in his arms, his smooth, taut shoulders protecting them. Until he realized, true romantic that he is, that none of them was the one. That was when they sensed a chilliness and knew it was over. There was some sort of conversation and then they left, their scent and human dander gone. I can see them packing their Clarins or La Mer that they kept in the cabinet in the second bathroom—the guest bathroom. Their lace thongs and flip-flops, Stella McCartney mesh jackets or Gap sweatshirts, herbal teas and travel-size Living Proof dry shampoo stuffed into a generic straw bag, a simple canvas tote from the Miami Book Fair. And as easily as they had settled in, they weren't asked to stay. Tyler is a catch if he can be caught. He is the only guy I've not wanted to fix or repackage, ever.

For his every move tonight, my body and mind fall into a chant, a plea, really. *I don't want to be next—I want to be last.* He is asking me to be his business partner; it has to be that we are a match.

My head is on his chest and he's running his fingers across my shoulders. I put my right hand on my heart, then on his heart. I'm on my back, and his hands on the inside of my thighs move upward. "Aubrey, Aubrey," he groans.

That urgency, the speed tonight. Then he's inside me and I wrap my legs around his waist and we move together.

Stuck behind red taillights and truckers on I-95, I turn up the volume for Joan Jett belting out "I Love Rock 'n' Roll" and sing along. I'd be annoyed if I weren't in such an up mood from last night. My goodwill extends to Elodie's plea of an hour ago.

"Could you please, please come up to Palm Beach? I know you're busy with work, this is *imperative*," she begged me.

Imperative. I wonder what that means to Elodie. In our

family, a crisis isn't wide in scope but personal. There isn't much talk about politics or climate change. Nor is there such talk among our friends, it seems. Whatever Elodie has to say, she sounded flat, afraid.

"This is the third time this week that I'm driving up to you," I said.

"I know that, yet I can't drive down, I really cannot, Aubrey."

"I have a meeting in Miami with Tyler and Dirk O at noon," I said.

"With what?" she asked.

"A big meeting. A critical meeting. Can we do this over the phone?"

"I'm sorry, but *please* come," Elodie insisted. "I wouldn't ask if it weren't pressing."

I take the exit that reads SOUTHERN BOULEVARD BRIDGE and turn left toward town. At least in Palm Beach I always feel young. The weird inverted ageism makes the young very young, but it's Mom's crowd and older ladies who rule the place. This compared to South Beach, where I'm close to invisible at thirty-two. Each time that Tyler meets with a new band, these twenty-three-year-old girls appear out of nowhere. Only last week it happened on the pool deck at the Savoy. I bet every time I don't tag along, they lunge at him.

My big sister would be a fossil in South Beach, I realize as I resist the urge to speed while driving east to Royal Poinciana Plaza. When I pull up to Sant Ambroeus, Elodie is sitting on the small iron bench outside the restaurant, beside a gelato cart. In her Milou shift and Hermès flat sandals, she has her blond/brown hair in that half ponytail she's taken to lately.

"What?" I glance at the courtyard filled with pozzetti. Elodie leaps up and we kiss hello. She scans the gold-leaf signage over the double glass doors.

"Look inside. Is it crowded?"

I peer through the glass and see women seated on angular ice-blue-and-toffee leather stools at the bar.

"Sort of. There are people right up front. I can't see past that to the tables."

"We can't go in. I've run into two ladies from the Literary Society and two wives of James's clients, plus Allison Rochester and Betina Gilles."

"Are we avoiding people? I thought you chose a place to *be seen*. And to shop a bit." I twirl my finger toward the storefronts. Zadig & Voltaire for me, 100% Capri for her, Kirna Zabête if our mother joins us.

"We need to talk, Aubrey." Her voice is rushed.

We take off our sunglasses at the same time and look at each other's eyes and eyebrows. We look very much the same today, except my sister is frightened, jumpy. Is that it?

"Want to go to your house? Mom's?"

"Let's get in my car. Or yours."

Elodie points past the collection of bright white or silver Mercedes convertibles. "Over there."

She leads us around the corner and presses the key fob that she's holding in her right hand. Her own silver sedan beeps back. We get in and she blasts the AC. I tug my leopard-print miniskirt down and start checking for a text from Tyler. *Got band Furrow into St. Pete. Want 2 more West Coast clubs.*

I can do it, I text back swiftly. *How is . . .*

"Aubrey?" Squaring up in her seat, Elodie turns to me.

I hit Send without completing my thought. "What is going on?"

"Well, there's privacy here. Unless the car is bugged." She gives a dry laugh that makes her sound old or tired. "Most people are in the stores."

"I mean, why come to shop at Hermès, then stay in the car?" I say. "I haven't done this since that time in college when Daniel practically locked me in his Audi to announce he was dumping me. I was so upset that when I came home for Christmas break a day later, Mom and I sat in her car in the garage while I cried. Then she took me to the Avenue and we shopped at Eye of the Needle. Retail therapy."

"Mom's good at that." Elodie sighs, blows the oxygen around our shared space. Two women walk by and tap at her door. She does a phony official wave, like she's a minor politician and they are her constituency. For once she doesn't explain, doesn't say to me, "They're on my board" or "They're members of the Literary Society."

"I have to ask you something." Elodie holds out her left hand as if she's about to touch my shoulder, then doesn't.

"Sure, what's up?" I'm still curious as to why we're in the car, why her voice is this quiet.

"So we were wondering—I mean James was, mostly—if you could, you know, help us have our baby?" Elodie looks out the window, away from me.

Help us have our baby? For a second, I think she must be making a very bad joke. A joke so strange and perverse that I'm not sure I comprehend the meaning. Could it be that my sister, based on how demanding her life is in this kind of spoiled way, is on hallucinogenic drugs?

"What?" I say.

"I know it's raving mad to ask you. I told James, but he came up with the idea."

"I'm sorry. What?"

"Like I said, James, well, we want to know if you could assist us."

"James? Wait, how? You don't mean I'd have sex with . . . or a test-tube-type thing? Then they put the egg back into you? Or . . ."

Elodie turns toward me. "You know what? Never mind. I should never have asked you."

"Well, you did. So try to explain." I don't know why I'm pushing her, yet I am.

"In a doctor's office. James's sperm, your egg."

I almost say, *I still don't fucking get it.* I don't because Elodie looks like she's a broken bird that has smashed up against a roof after flying in high winds. She survived but is no longer herself. The result is her request, which is unimaginable. How could this possibly be? Does she understand who I am? During the day I book the bands, I'm at the clubs at night, plenty of gigs go until four A.M. What about Tyler, who only this morning held me tight while showing me the partnership agreement. We floated around, swaying while "This Love," by Maroon 5, blasted from the speakers. My any day/everyday life with Tyler.

Tyler and I talk about how lucky we are to be unencumbered. After a trip to the ASPCA two months ago, we realized we can't care for a rescue dog. If we find out on a Tuesday morning that it's Las Vegas by noon on Wednesday, we're there. Tyler doesn't seem remotely interested in having kids. Except his nephew, six-year-old Stefan, is the screen saver photo for his laptop. In the photograph, Stefan and Tyler are at an ice-skating rink in Portland. When they FaceTime, Tyler plays "Puff the Magic Dragon" and tells Stefan he loves him. That's thousands of miles away and at best a yearly excursion.

Then there's Elodie, my older sister, who tied my shoes until I was in third grade, gave me her dog-eared copy of *Little Women* for my tenth birthday, and took me bra shopping before it was necessary. Every adult move she made was impressive, light-years ahead. Today she can't be pregnant, can't have her own baby. Her desperate request proves how much she needs help.

"I know, it's so much to ask," Elodie says. "For you to fork over your body for my benefit."

I sigh. "Elodie, I want to help. I wish I could. I'm not sure I'm the answer, a candidate. I've had lots of lovers. I'm a vegetarian, so who knows if I get enough protein. I've had two abortions, exposure to secondhand smoke, people smoking weed, music so loud at some venues that it could break the sound barrier."

"You would be tested, vetted," she says. "That's not a problem."

Vetted? What about Tyler? How does he fit into this? I doubt I could have sex; even if it's allowed, it would flip me out utterly. I couldn't sneak an occasional smoke, any booze whatsoever, or pop a pill, lug equipment onto the check-in line, take long flights. Who would live this life while pregnant? Who would want to? Aren't I one of those people who says she isn't sure she ever wants children, that the world is a toxic place? There is the greenhouse effect, world leaders scare me, violence is too frequent, and gun control an issue. She would not want to hear any of my reasons.

A valet who works for the shopping plaza comes toward us; he's young and obviously lifts weights. Checking that we are alive, since we're sitting where few would. I flick my hand to discourage him from coming closer, kind of like our mother would do it. Both of us watch him back off, shrugging as he walks toward the other stores.

The car is closing in, suffocating. I hit the button to take down the window, then bang it because it isn't working. Elodie shakes her head. "I've locked it. We have to keep it quiet."

"I need to breathe."

My sister lowers her window an inch, turns on the engine, pushes a few buttons. She's almost whispering.

"Let me at least explain. You would carry our baby, be artificially inseminated." She stops, stares at me. "I know. It's outrageous, right—beyond terrifying?"

"I need air," I say.

"Aubrey, listen." Elodie opens my window an inch, too. I sit up in my seat to catch the breeze.

"I know, I'm worried someone might hear us. Like I said." Elodie looks at the dashboard when she speaks, not at me. "At work I've been looking at these four-year-old children at Reading Hour. Sometimes I get to watch them for years; they move up, to different-age events. I have my favorites. This year there's a little girl named Charlotte, who is four, and boy twins called Gabriel and Aaron, who are in first grade. I sometimes wish one or two were mine."

"Please don't, please," I say. "You do see how confusing it seems. *I mean, yours, mine, and James's baby?* You *are* lucky, you have a great life. I mean, in New York or in L.A.,

I don't think everyone has to have a baby. Do you think this has to do with your friends, Mom and Mimi—with living here?"

"Palm Beach? Social pressure? No, it comes from me, from James. I see friends who have been at parenting for five or ten years and I want the chance, I want to love like that." Elodie seems crumpled.

"I'm not sure about being married, kids. My world is about singers, travel, bookings."

"I know, Aubrey. James and I have been together so long, we want to have a family."

"Why don't you find a surrogate? I've read the ads—they pop up online, advertising for donor eggs. Someone Ivy League, with fine features. A gestational carrier, whatever the recipe is. Someone out of town."

"We don't want to hire a stranger. James wants this child to have our genes. His and mine, which means yours and mine—half our DNA is the same."

"What about you? Is the DNA that important?"

"Well, at first I thought it wasn't, that James seemed to be overstating it. Then I kept asking myself if I would rather have you or someone I don't know, her genes, not yours, meaning ours. Then there's the Veronica and Simon part of it. Dad, I suspect, would totally want this if possible. I've come around to seeing it matters."

Elodie's nose is running. She takes a handkerchief out of her purse. Our mother gave each of us one this past Valentine's Day, from Maltese on the Avenue. The embroidered hearts and flowers on hers are faded—she uses it.

"Wait, I'm supposed to do this for you and James *and* Mom and Dad?"

"That isn't what I said, Aubrey." She pats at her nose.

I put my hands on my thighs and notice how tight they are. A dancer's body, that's what people say. They ask, "Are you a dancer?" Out of nowhere, Elodie appears old to me. No wonder she is putting me in this position, asking me to surrender myself for a year—from start to finish. To be the family savior.

Elodie sighs, shifts her weight around. "I don't know, are you hesitating because of our past? Is it that I didn't want Mom to be pregnant with you, I wanted to be an only child? That's why you're saying no. Maybe you remember, subconsciously, how I wasn't always so nice to you."

"No, Elodie, this isn't some irrational form of punishment. You were fine, I idolized you. You took care of me, protected me. You even dressed me up like a live Raggedy Ann when I was three," I say.

"How about when you were in second grade and wanted to be the Pink Ranger for Halloween and I convinced Veronica it was okay to let you do it. She wanted you to be a witch or Sleeping Beauty," Elodie says.

"The real problem was Uhura from *Star Trek*—wasn't that the next Halloween? Mom so didn't understand. She thought it was too sexy or something."

We both smile for a second, then remember why we're hiding out at a swank shopping plaza.

"Listen." I speak softly. "I don't want to be pregnant. Not with my baby, not with yours. Or with James's." I almost gag when I say the part about it being hers or James's.

I tug at the locked door. "I wish I could do better. I doubt I'll change my mind."

"For a day or two, promise you'll think about it. Please. We would be infinitely grateful," Elodie says.

Does she understand? I can't have her baby because

she wants me to. What Elodie has asked changes us. Like we're underwater and could be washed away.

"Aubrey?"

I half nod. My escape depends on it. My sister unlocks the car and I open my door. The air rushes at me. I know I'll say no.

CHAPTER 7

AUBREY

I park at South Lake Drive and Peruvian to begin the Lake Trail. The western side of the island feels less demanding, quieter in terms of beauty and the open views of the Lake Worth Lagoon. Since I was a girl, I've loved the giant Kapok tree with roots that sprawl strangely and the bougainvillea and ivy—requisite wherever one goes. Within minutes I spot my mother revving up for her "power walk." She's doing body stretches, flinging her arms to the left and then to the right. Next she runs in place, with her fists gently pummeling an unseen punching bag. She starts scrunching her shoulders, then letting them down. She takes breaks to wave to each woman on the trail as she fast-walks or lightly jogs past. Already the scenic path is brimming with those who walk, run, or bike along.

"Mom! Mom!" I march to where she faces the Intra-coastal.

She swivels around to beam at me and stops her routine. Beyond her the palm trees and pink hibiscus appear lush. It has been less than twenty-four hours since I escaped Elodie's car. Hellish hours.

"Aubrey, darling!" We hug. She smells like Clinique Broad Spectrum Mineral sunblock. Because she is in sneaks, she seems shorter than when she is dressed up in at least a two-inch heel. No matter what she wears, it seems that my mother's shrinking.

"Why did you drive up early?"

"To be with you, Mom. The two of us."

"Before my holistic Pilates," she says. "Which has gotten very popular."

"Very popular" translates to "too crowded," but my mother wouldn't say that—it sounds negative, willful, fussy. I shiver for a second. I'm dreading the conversation although I'm the one who asked to meet. Again in Palm Beach and not at my desk.

"So why are you visiting at what must be an ungodly hour if you were out late last night 'covering a band'? Isn't that what you call it?"

Sometimes when I'm alone with Elodie, we laugh about what we call our mother's "rubric." "She's nothing without it," Elodie used to say. Meaning without Dad, without us, without Mothers and Children and her hard work there, without yoga and swimming. Until Mom surprised us by changing the formula after years of straddling two worlds. Announcing it was time, she left her nonprofit six months ago. Instead of being in the field four days a week, visiting families in need, she delved into a rarefied social life.

That's when Elodie added, "*And* the Palm Beach doctrine, especially in season."

She is definitely part of the herd this morning as she starts her ritual, adjusting her sun visor, adding more sunblock to her cheekbones.

"Have you spoken with Elodie?" I ask.

"I speak with her every day. What's wrong, Aubrey?"

Mom takes in deep breaths, exhales in this very style. Her cobalt blue baseball cap has *PBLS* (Palm Beach Literary Society) across it in white stitching. Although she has always been pretty, today her face is angular; her neck has cords that weren't there a few months ago. Among her friends, my mother is the only one who has skipped any plastic surgery. "Botox here, filler there, but not under the knife," she likes to say. Meaning she is undaunted in a clutter of face-lifts, new ones, old ones, redos. Still, her methods could be failing her—isn't that what happens? Whatever, to me her face is always beautiful.

"Let's start," she says. "We'll talk on the trail."

We angle toward the water's edge. Ahead, mothers are jogging while pushing those three-leg strollers. A couple laugh together, pushing their double stroller. Children who look about three or four hold on to the hands of their caregivers—mothers, a few fathers, nannies, grandmothers. What are their fertility stories? Did these women go to bed and wake up pregnant, or were they shot up with fertility drugs and frantic? Regardless, here they are with the morning light like a halo over them. My sister's sadness must trickle into her every move in a place where nothing unpleasant can ever happen. Having not lived here since college, I've forgotten how to work on being perfect. My time in South Beach has blocked it out.

My mother and I fast-walk behind the fancy houses; they keep tumbling toward us, one after another. Moving at a clip, we're almost at the yachts. More sunlight dipping across the Intracoastal, more strangers gesturing at my mother, stopping to speak. *Hello, Eleanor, will your family come for Christmas? Rosalie, how are the grandchildren up north?* The responses quick and short as each party keeps on the trail. Another baby, perhaps six months old, dressed in a pink bonnet, is being wheeled along, her feet dangling. It is her big sister, about seven, who pushes the stroller, while her relaxed mother and father smile radiantly as they pass.

"I read you every nursery rhyme," Elodie tells me to this day, "I pushed you on your first swing, your first carousel ride." I know she did—life was divided into when Elodie was there and when she wasn't. Later she handed me a copy of *Harry Potter and the Philosopher's Stone* before any of my friends knew about it. She took me for my first highlights at Posh Salon, my first pair of stilettos, arranged impressive fake IDs. I wish that she had never asked me to be her surrogate.

"Dad was late for his Thursday game this morning. Can you believe it?

"Oh? Golf or tennis?"

"Tennis." Mom sounds a bit annoyed. "That's why James plays, before he goes to ANVO. You do know that most of the men who go to work start early—"

"Of course." I wait. "Mom, why I'm here, this is sort of urgent."

"Urgent?"

She stops our fast clip. She knows nothing.

"What has happened?" my mother asks as she motions

for us to park ourselves on a quasi-carved bench situated along the water. The wood is smooth and heavy; it reminds me of marble. Contorting her upper body, she looks to the left and to the right. Once she is sure that everyone else on the trail is far off, she leans closer.

"What is it, Aubrey?"

The wind from the west tosses the gulls; they lift higher into the air. It reminds me of being in a plane over Palm Beach, ready to land, just as the announcement comes on about gusts and turbulence.

"Everything is okay." I sort of draw out *okay*.

"Meaning what, Aubrey? Is it about Tyler? Your work?"

"No, no. Not Tyler, work is fine." The swiftest flash of Tyler kissing me in the kitchen at dawn. He was holding our agreement with a playlist, dancing a slow one to "All of My Love'" by Led Zeppelin, to celebrate. Right after a sleepless night, when I decided I had to drive up to see my mother. Tyler didn't press for any details, but he did walk me to my car. That's what makes the Elodie request more complicated: Tyler.

"Does Elodie know we're at the Lake Trail together?"

My mother looks out at the gulls over the docks. "Have you girls had a fight?"

I wish. I wait, count to ten like we've been taught.

"Elodie wants me to be a surrogate for her."

"I'm sorry?"

Mom is frowning beneath the sunglasses and baseball cap.

"A surrogate, a traditional surrogate for her—and for James. I'd be impregnated with James's sperm, I'd—" I stop.

Mom waits.

"I'd be impregnated at Dr. Noel's clinic."

"Dr. Noel does not run a clinic, Aubrey," my mother says.

"That's what you're concerned with, Mom? That it's an office, not a clinic, because clinics are for those less fortunate?"

"I am clarifying, that's all," Mom says.

She's nervous, deflecting, focusing on the wrong part of the conversation.

"Okay. At Dr. Noel's office." I shudder at the very idea of Dr. Noel's anything. "I'd be pregnant *for* Elodie."

"For Elodie? I'm not sure what you mean."

"You know, my egg, James's sperm. Because Elodie's eggs are too old."

My mother's mouth twists, as if she's about to tell me there's been a death in the family—a distant cousin from Pittsburgh or Ithaca, someone she's always loved but hasn't seen in twenty years. She can't persuade our father to travel to the funeral, it matters to her. She has to figure it out.

"Your egg, James's sperm."

She twists her mouth again. "What made you decide on this?"

"Oh, I didn't. I never would have. It was James's idea. The DNA thing, that the baby would be genetically linked to Elodie."

"Is that his reasoning?" Mom sounds angry.

"Totally. He's into the plan. He says it really matters."

"Does he? Doesn't he know how complicated that would be for you and your sister? DNA isn't the only factor."

I shake my head. Mom pats my shoulder.

"The idea of a baby and Elodie's despair and my being

the one, I don't know. Like I'm covered in this layer of . . ." I say.

"Defeat," Mom says.

I can't admit that yesterday I googled morning sickness six times, only to be sidetracked by the aftermath of pregnancy. Descriptions of the forking over of oneself (with saggy breasts, cellulite, and stretch marks) for a sleepless infant, a marriage that becomes sexless. That's the known deal—one's selfishness traded in for a baby to love.

"Yeah, okay, defeat. I mean, I don't want to be pregnant. I'm not sure that I want my own children, Mom."

"Oh, honey, you don't know for certain. You might change your mind. It isn't a decision for today." My mother stops.

"If I do this, I'd be the aunt to my *own* baby—it's awfully hard to wrap my mind around it. Then I see how heartbroken Elodie is. I can't stand that she's like that, either. Every part of it makes me very upset."

"I realize that," Mom says. "I mean, what if you did this, let's say you wanted to for Elodie, and then you fell in love with the baby. It's a big danger. You know, like Baby M."

"Baby M?"

"Baby M—the Mary Beth Whitehead case. Have you never heard about it?"

I shake my head.

"It was a court case that took place in the mid-eighties. About the rights of a surrogate. The woman who agreed to be a surrogate fell in love with the baby, called 'Baby M.' She didn't want this baby to go with the parents who had hired her. It was tragic; people saw both sides of the story. She felt it was her baby."

"What happened?"

"The court ruled that the surrogate, Mary Beth White-head, was the legal mother, the contract didn't hold up. Then there was the 'best interests of the child' application and the father—his name was William Stern, I think—got custody and Whitehead got visitation."

"Jesus. Okay. You see how loaded this is."

"Oh, I do, I do. It's too much to ask." Mom shifts her position on the bench, as if she's stiff from sitting there too long.

I pull my hair out of the scrunchie, pause to let it fly around in the wind before I tie it back neatly. I look down at my lime green Converse sneakers, my yoga pants. I'm neither a twenty-four-year-old babe nor a forty-year-old woman. What is it like for Elodie, with her mansion-to-be and her poetry series, her shoes—she has a collection, a museum of shoes. In Palm Beach it means something. She's interviewed *four* interior designers, including Kimberly Shawn, and decided on Griselda Derrick. Elodie is written up in the *Daily Sheet* at least once a week for her programs, fund-raisers. She and James, a young Veronica and Simon Show, go everywhere. In theory it is already a *fine* life.

"It's strange. We're sisters; that's why she likes it. The DNA thing. James totally cares about that part."

"We know that Elodie has had a hardship. She *wants* a baby," Mom says, "and hasn't gotten it. That's the other side of the situation."

A loneliness blankets me, a kind of hollow feeling that I've known at low points in my life. Except this is coiled with my sister's loneliness.

"You've never been married, never wanted a child. I can't tell you what to do, Aubrey," my mother says in a tone I've not heard since I decided to attend Bard instead of Cornell. Filled with opinions that go unspoken.

"Mom, what are you saying, that I'm the solution? The *only* remedy?"

She comes closer on the bench; suddenly we are more fine-spun than usual, our faces close enough that we skip the whispering. Talking softly works.

"Aubrey, I'm an only child. I never had to share with anyone. I raised you and your sister to be there for each other, to do anything for each other."

Our mother is out of her league, too. She is searching herself. She says in a studied voice, "Aubrey, you know, possibly, I'm not sure, but possibly, you could do this."

A cool breeze circles around us—and no one else on the Lake Trail. The air temperature has dropped, as if a private storm is moving up the coast. Now my mother needs to save Elodie, not me? She starts searching in her tote for the foldable sweatshirt she carries.

She holds up her hand. "Of course, I know how complicated it would be. The entire thing, the result of this favor."

Life has become loaded with requests from the people I love most—those who ordinarily expect little from me. Before this, Dad would simply ask me to show up at a family dinner, to recommend a joint birthday gift for our mother, to choose either Chez Jean Pierre or Café Boulud, then drive north for the occasion.

The Southern Boulevard Bridge is being raised and cars are stopped while boats line up beneath. It must be fifteen after, since the bridge lifts every quarter of an hour. We haven't been together enough time for our conversation to weigh so much.

"Until Elodie asked me this hugest favor, I liked being younger," I say.

"I believe you, Aubrey. Then again, to be *asked, to be*

chosen. Maybe you could at least think about it. How it is about being *the sister, the one*. It isn't James alone, Aubrey. Elodie has been through so much, without a result. When I look at the children—at the Breakers Beach Club, the Harbor Club, those Sunday-night family barbecues—I realize how much I want to be a grandmother. It's been so long since you girls were small. Dad wants to be a grandfather."

"Does he?" I ask.

"*We do*. He and I do."

A flipper—she's flipping. Similar to a friend or a boyfriend who cannot be trusted. My mother's take on it is confusing, surprising. If I wait, maybe she'll flip back, consider my side once more, and stop believing that being a conduit is simple, without consequences.

Taking my hands in hers, she glances toward a Hatteras yacht moving slowly along the Intracoastal. Like she's imagining someplace beyond my sister or me.

CHAPTER 8

AUBREY

Until today, my father has never invited me out for breakfast, alone together at a table. Yet this morning he is meeting me at Java, in the Setai South Beach. Another early-morning plan after yesterday on the Lake Trail. At least my parents are both beauty seekers; neither would waste time in an ordinary space. The courtyard facing the ocean is dreamlike. The breeze lifts the hem of my tie-dyed midi skirt. I tug at the strap of my camisole and walk with purpose toward the maître d'. Beyond him my father is already seated, sipping black coffee, on his iPhone. My father is allegedly in Miami for his new building west of the beaches. Yet it's rare that he personally checks a property; someone else from his office usually does it.

"Aubrey!"

He stands up, "a gentleman with fine features," Mom always says. His hair is salt-and-pepper, thick in front, with that patch of scalp that men get at the crown. Still, he's a father who has broad shoulders, no stomach. When I was at Bard, my roommates called him "an affairable father"— it was over ten years ago, he was even more dashing then. I was upset—I wanted a paunchy father who took you to dinner in Red Hook, while Elodie laughed it off. "He's 'a Palm Beach father,'" she said. "They look good, they work at it."

"Dad, what are you doing in South Beach on a golf day?" I ask.

Today he does a sort of airbrushed half hug and kiss. Probably my father has always been like this and I haven't been in enough therapy to figure it out. Mom would comment he can be "far off." Beyond that, only air-kisses are allowed in public. He's always on my side, and I love that. No matter what I do or don't do. While Elodie and my mother are judging, my father is steady, loyal when I dip in and out of work and responsibility. He says nothing when I drop out of courses, freelance assignments, full-time employment. Although I might want to finish my master's in musicology, I've started other master's programs. One for social work right after college, and three years later I left an MFA program in photography and art when I was midway through.

"I don't remember the last time I was in Miami," my father says.

"Wow, quite something to have you visit," I say.

I slide into my chair and adjust my Panama hat. The sun flits through the open space; a few tourists file in. I smell bacon, and it's making me mildly nauseous. Against my will, I estimate what it would be like to be pregnant for

Elodie and smell bacon. A server—slim, buff, with purple highlights at his hairline and a man bun—hovers over us, holding a coffeepot in his right hand.

"Coffee?"

"No, thank you," I say.

"Tea, latte, cappuccino?" His voice is quite deep; I bet he is an actor. L.A. would be better for that, but I'm sure he's found some venues in South Florida. He could be here for family, secretly glued to a sister or his mother, who are only a ride north or south on the I-95. Sort of how South Beach works for music and for me. The seventy-five miles are close and far, although Elodie and Mom don't quite get why I'm here. I'd like to say to him, *Stick to your plan. Keep the distance.*

"A latte," I say.

A crew sets up lounge chairs around the pool area—hushed and uninhabited by guests at nine A.M. The Art Deco building, originally a Dempsey-Vanderbilt Hotel back in the thirties, is Tyler's spot. He'll come here for a lunch or drinks meeting and comment on the crowd, the atmosphere. Which puzzles me a bit, since the hotel calls itself "bespoke" and rooms with views of the ocean are pricey and exclusive. Not Palm Beach–style luxury, but luxury all the same.

A text bings and my father glances at his iPhone, then scowls beneath his square-frame glasses—prescription glasses that turn darker in the sunlight. He texts back like older people do, his right hand flying, forefinger punching. I shuffle around in my chair, watching the waitstaff. When I'm at a place like this, I make a deal with myself about how I'll get through and be independent. Had Tyler not offered me a partnership, I'd be that way now. I'd be telling myself that if I didn't place enough musicians in the next six months, I could work at a hotel part-time. My family would hate it; they'd make excuses, tell lies in Palm Beach about my "career." I'd do it anyway and try not to ask for anything. Except today I'm thinking instead about a band I'll place called Arnsdale, a female vocalist and her backup, and then another and another. Already we are soaring with Dirk O selling out nightly at Pascha's. That's why it's empty for breakfast; guests who came to hear him last night are sleeping in.

The man bun reappears with my latte. I haven't eaten so early in the day in years. Did I ever? Looking cuter than before, he hands us our menus. It's nice to notice without its being anything more. Life is all Tyler.

"Thank you, perfect." I try to sound light.

"I'll have whole-wheat toast, dry, and scrambled egg whites." My father hands the menu over without saying *please*. Or *thank you*. Maybe in Palm Beach it isn't done. At Longreens, the Harbor Club, Mar-a-Lago, or Trump International, my parents know the staff. They ask about their families—Mom tried to help some of the women who work in the locker room at Longreens through the charity she founded, Mothers and Children. Her goal was access to scholarship money for local colleges for their kids. Two of the younger children had autism and she could help with experts and classes. Then another member heard the conversations and complained that Mom was too intimate with employees. Mom helped anyway.

"Aubrey? What will you order?"

"Pancakes with blueberries and walnuts, please." I hand over my menu and smile.

My father watches our server exit toward the kitchen,

making certain he's gone. The wind kicks up, flaps around our chairs.

"You do know why I'm here," he says.

"I'm not sure." My chest wall feels thin; every second my heart taps an extra beat.

"About Elodie. I know what she is asking you to do for her, Aubrey. Your mother has told me."

Who can trust my mother and father not to trade secrets, including their daughters' secrets? I'm only dumbfounded that my father would drive to South Beach about it.

"Are you considering this for Elodie? Carrying her child, your child, literally." My father's voice isn't often this droning.

"Yeah, well, I've gone over the ways to define a baby I'd carry—impregnated by my sister's husband. Someone who is sort of a big brother to me. It's grotesque, isn't it?"

"Your sister has no right to ask this of you." He keeps scowling.

"She can ask me anything she wants. It's that I don't know what to say."

"Then your answer is no. Is that correct?" Now my father sounds like he needs a cough drop or at least a sip of water. He doesn't move, waiting for my answer. Who knew it mattered to him? Most conversations are with my mother; most problems are snuffed out by her.

"I feel pressured by her request. I wish she'd never asked. I mean, I finally have a life. I'm in Miami, I'm with Tyler, we're booking good performers. I get to be in the music world. A mini music world."

"All the more reason to refuse her. To remind her there are many other surrogates to choose from."

"Wow, Dad, I'm not sure what Mom said. What did she tell you? Why are you against it?"

"I believe that for one thing, Elodie isn't considering you, Aubrey. Your relationship with Elodie after this, with James, too. You will be the aunt and the biological mother."

"I know, I know." The last few days have been an out-of-body experience. I sip my latte, tempted to pour in a sweetener. Maybe I'd better do a real sugar; it's healthier.

"I find it outlandish," he says. "With real repercussions."

"Dad, what is it? Is there something more to this? I looked it up, googled it, it is natural in some ways for sisters to do this. In the nineties it was really popular. There were these stories in a book I found, where one of the sisters was the 'oven'—y'know, she carried the baby, but it was her sister's egg. Then there was this article about a sister who had three kids of her own and felt guilty about her sister. They used her egg and her brother-in-law's sperm."

"I view it as abnormal." My father's tone reminds me of when we were small and he'd be on a business call at home. That steely, dismissive voice.

Abnormal? Before I can argue, say he's biased, he continues.

"Your mother and sister have not thought it through— it's a fantasy for them. They haven't considered what people will say, what they'll whisper through the clubs, up and down Worth Avenue."

"*Worth Avenue?*"

"Anywhere and everywhere, they'll talk," he says. "Mom won't like it. Mimi won't be happy. This might hurt Elodie's work."

"Then Mom will figure it out. She'll find a way with Mimi, what to say. Is that what matters? We're not some divided family, like it's them against us. It's about Elodie. Remember how she was when she miscarried? It was horrible."

The server comes with our food, and although he is well trained, he clanks about our table. We say nothing until he is gone. I wish he could finish the meal with us, be a third person at the table. He could deflect talk of our family.

My father begins to eat quickly, jabbing at the eggs with his fork. He hasn't eaten so fast before, his bites sharp and angled. "Your mother is pleased that you drive up so much. She loves knowing you are nearby. How is Tyler's work going?"

"Great." I pour syrup on my pancakes. I keep squeezing the back of the bottle and moving my hand in circles. Were Mom with us, she would say, "Enough, that's enough syrup, Aubrey!"

Dad is inhaling his eggs. "You know, I've always found the music business interesting, rather seductive. When I was younger, I listened to the Beatles, Roy Orbison, the Beach Boys."

"I know that. Elodie and I were raised on the Beatles and the Stones. Mostly your choices, not Mom's."

"No, your mother favors Judy Collins, Carly Simon."

"Dad, you taught me about music first, and later, when I was at the Academy, Elodie did."

"In the army, music could get you through. Creedence Clearwater Revival, the Animals, Jimi Hendrix." Dad is almost plaintive.

"I'm sure," I say.

"And you're now in 'the business' with Tyler. Booking a lot of bands, is he?" he asks, remembering his purpose for our breakfast.

"Well, yes, he is. I do it, too, Dad. We get bands—not so well known, with lots of talent and potential—into venues in the area." That's my pitch, the one I give to promoters and managers all day long. I breathe in. Why is my father visiting me? I always drive north to him, to my mother. I was there yesterday. With Mom and Elodie, at the Literary Society, after the Lake Trail. He could have been with me then. He's always too busy with his buildings and his cards, his golf and his tennis. I like it better when he is.

"I understand." Dad puts his fork and knife to the side of his plate and begins his fruit salad. I smell the mango—too pungent, too smushed in the center among pineapple and papaya. Overripe. Even at the Setai, this is possible.

"This Tyler, is he the man you are interested in, Aubrey, someone you are serious about?"

"He is."

I'd like to explain that we are becoming business partners, plus how Tyler loves me, but Dad keeps speaking. "He seems to have a solid business, but if he needs something more stable, I have that building out on South Beach Drive, one property in Miami, one in Lauderdale."

"Really?" I am surprised, because my father has not mentioned building management to me before. Is it because I'm with Tyler and he doesn't understand our business? Is it that I'm over thirty and only beginning to settle into work I care about?

"I'd like that, Dad. I mean, Tyler and I are both pretty busy with the music bookings and finding talent, yet it would be more money and that would be useful."

"Absolutely another source of income. However, it does

require time. It is a day job, of course," Dad says. "Could that be done?"

I'm not sure what his implication is—isn't my father presenting an opportunity to me? *I* would like the extra income. Maybe I could manage the building if Tyler hasn't the time. I'm feeling unpredictably industrious.

"Yeah, so it could work. I think we could juggle the building with the bookings."

"Aubrey, we don't know that the offer would appeal to Tyler. And then there can be complications in any pregnancy; you or he might not feel up to this amount of responsibility."

"You mean this is only available to either of us if I do *not* carry Elodie and James's baby?" The restaurant begins to smother me. "Dad, is that what you're saying?"

"It wouldn't be James and Elodie's baby, Aubrey, it would be *yours* and James's, with Elodie posturing as the mother."

Okay, so he's become preoccupied with the baby situation, slightly obsessed. He is not getting what he wants with Elodie's plan; he's being mean.

"That's harsh, Dad, that's not how surrogacy works, how it is interpreted. I'm not hesitating because of that. It's more about superficial things, like it will ruin my body, that Tyler and I will be traveling for work. We have gigs nightly, a relationship to grow. More profound reasons, like it will change everything. I'd be *giving up* my identity, losing myself. My sister's baby in my womb would have to be at the center of my life, wouldn't it?"

"Isn't that enough to say no, Aubrey?"

"Maybe, although I understand why James wants it, why Elodie would want it," I say.

"Listen to me. What I propose is that. . . ." My father sits up, sips his water, and stops speaking. His gaze moves toward the front of the restaurant.

Exhausted guests under thirty have begun to fill up the room. They sashay as they're led to their tables. I notice a second maître d' has been brought on. She wears a lemon color minidress too bright for breakfast, her lipstick too dark; her arms are between a ballet dancer's and strands of spaghetti. Oddly, she is leading my mother's friends Priscilla and Mrs. A. to the table beside us. Our privacy ends; a feel-good greeting is required.

"Hello, hello!" Mrs. A. drawls. "Simon, what brings you to this part of the world?" She rearranges her Gucci beige rectangular frames, smooths her khaki capris, and pats her chrysanthemum scarf. Priscilla is dressed similarly to Mrs. A., except her scarf is a cornflower blue and her sunglasses are the Prada oval rimless style that Elodie and I tried on at Saks. Priscilla fusses with how her scarf is draped, as if anyone cares about her understated "Palm Beach before noon" effect.

Mrs. A. takes in the diners. "What a unique crowd, Simon," she says. "Are they hotel guests? How would you describe them, Priscilla?"

"Eclectic." Priscilla does what Mom calls the "stuck smile"—broad and suspicious. She primps more, maybe realizing she and Mrs. A. are inconspicuous at the Setai, except to us.

"We know you are down south, Aubrey," Mrs. A. says. "Veronica is always saying where you live. How she misses you. Why, she said so last Thursday night—at the opening dance at Longreens."

"How was the dance?" I ask. I'm trying to guess their

ages. Priscilla must be a chunk older than my sister. And Mrs. A. is older than Mom, that's for sure. Mom always says it isn't how old you are in Palm Beach, but that you follow the rules—many rules, to stay in the game. That must include Elodie and her friends—they are becoming part of the ever-present machine.

"The dance was unremarkable." Priscilla sounds disappointed. "I mean the decor, the guests, the menu—of course, that was fine. There were no histrionics of any kind."

"You like it like that, right, Dad?"

"It's my preference." He's impatient; he didn't expect this sort of interruption. With his black American Express card in his hand, he waves to our server, who rushes over.

"We only came to South Beach today for Priscilla's decorator's meeting," Mrs. A. says. "You know that Priscilla is becoming quite the interior designer. We left to drive here at the crack of dawn. We're going to the Michael Smith showroom."

My father yawns.

I say, "That should be cool; he has a showroom in L.A., too."

"Why, here we are and meet *you*," Priscilla says. "Alas, all of us *missing* your sister's breakfast."

"Elodie always has a great event going on. I was there with my mom yesterday. I go when I can."

"That she does."

My father pays the bill fast, like he has my whole life when he has something on his mind. He would leave family dinners abruptly. We weren't to disturb him; our mother was available and he wasn't back then. He scrawls his name across the receipt and stands up. "Shall we, Aubrey?"

"Good to see you," I say to Priscilla and Mrs. A.

"Simon, lovely." Priscilla waves. Mrs. A. checks out my cheapie skirt and how my hair is braided. I know we will fuel their gossip tank within minutes.

My father takes my elbow, as Tyler did only a matter of hours ago. He guides us into the lobby, where we stand in a corner. While we wait for the valets to bring around his new "light gray satin" Bentley and my car—meaning my mother's old white BMW X3, which they've given to me—he lowers his voice. "You should not be obligated, Aubrey."

"Dad, I'm not."

"I'd like you to think about what it will do to this family."

The valet, heady from his short drive in my father's car, comes up first. I see annoyance cross my father's face—he's exasperated with me because I promise to not help Elodie. He is too angry to make it about little things, to find fault with the valet or try to control where his car is garaged at the Setai. After Dad leaves, kissing me quickly, I'm shakier than I've been since I was seventeen and hoping my parents would support my plan for a gap year between high school and college.

The morning crowd grows thicker. Beyond the single blond babes and buff young guys, a mother and her three children cross into the lobby. The daughter looks about eight and is on an iPhone—it might be hers or her mother's. Next a son about five, in bathing trunks and a black T-shirt with KING KONG and a photo of the giant gorilla emblazoned on it, is on a mini iPad. All for the mother to be able to hold her infant, swaddled in a thin pink blanket and wearing the smallest pink cotton cap.

Not that I can calculate the age, but I suspect she must be about four weeks old.

Elodie's never-born child was also a girl. Can anyone rent a baby, make one out of a test tube? Milk-shake it to life?

CHAPTER 9

ELODIE

I don't remember the last time, if ever, that Simon reached me at work and suggested we meet, just the two of us. When his call came through my office line, Laurie, my assistant, knew somehow and paged me.

"Elodie?" His voice was tense when I picked up.

Aubrey. Those late nights with her bohemian boyfriend. "Dad, is everything all right?"

"It is. I'm calling to take you on an outing. Are you free Sunday morning—at the Shelteere, in the gardens?"

I paused. When have my father and I tooled around on a Sunday morning at a museum? Let alone a Sunday in season. Not since my mother stopped pushing her father/daughter hallucination, before I was eight years old, before Aubrey was born.

"I'd prefer the Flagler, actually. For the history, the scale of it. . . ."

"The Flagler it is," he said.

"Let's meet at ten, when the doors open." He clicked off before I could say good-bye. That's how I knew it was a business call.

Although it's not a beach day and a cool mist is moving in, the Flagler is quiet. I try to concentrate on the romantic notion that Henry Morrison Flagler built this Gilded Age mansion as a wedding gift for his third wife (and former mistress), Mary Lily Kenan Flagler. Here at Whitehall, they partied in their graceful, grand public rooms. Next week at the Literary Society, a history professor from FAU will pair with Nadia Sherman, the features writer for *Palm Beach Confidential,* to talk about how the Flaglers created "the season," how their mansion was the birthplace of Palm Beach society. Meaning I should walk into this Grand Hall with enthusiasm, I should admire the massive Doric column close to the front door. If only I could. What is it my father wants?

I'm twenty minutes early because he is never late. My father wins anyway—already there, beside a table with a bust of Caesar Augustus. He waves his right arm to show he's procured tickets. His light blue cashmere sweater is tossed over his shoulders; his nubuck loafers tap against the marble floor when he comes toward me. My espadrilles make swishing sounds as I walk to meet him halfway. Have my father and I dressed for those we might see on the Avenue? Or on South County Road if we stop at Classic Books, then a quick lunch at Surfside? Camera-ready—my mother's motto.

We air-kiss.

"I wanted to talk with you." He ties his sweater in a knot in the middle of his chest. "Let's head this way."

I follow my father into the Music Room. I stare at the marble bust called *The Lady in the Veil*, sculpted by E. Fiaschi. A guard languidly positions himself at the far corner, by the north door. Simon motions for us to stop, freeze.

"You've been going through a great deal." He's awkward, facing out.

With Aubrey, he might have begun with small talk. Were it a family affair and Veronica present, there would be gushing, a warmth blended with scrutiny. More manners or style, more Palm Beach–esque. Not that he isn't polished on his own; it's that he's with me, not Aubrey, not the daughter who pleases her father *without* trying. For the thousandth time, I fail to understand why that is.

I lift my head to say, "It's been hellish, Dad."

"I know and I'm sorry. Sorry for you, sorry for James. Of course, it must be harder on you."

"Do you mean physically, emotionally? I don't know, both James and I have been going through an awful period."

"I saw James yesterday at the club. He was perfectly chipper, telling jokes in the men's locker room."

"He's not happy *with me,* when he's with me."

What fills my head today is what my mother has taught me, her clever tricks, applied to being a wife and/or a daughter. *Be accommodating, willing to compromise.*

"James *is* happy, Elodie. Don't you see where I'm going with this?"

I'm listening to a man whose life is ordered. He spends an hour or two a day on the phone with his office, checking on his real estate holdings. Beyond that, there's the golf, tennis, swimming, high-stakes bridge—compiled on his terms.

"I'm confused, Dad. What are you saying?"

"That James shouldn't be pressuring you to do something a certain way. James has his success." Simon pauses. "What is it your mother always says about couples? Either they grow together or grow apart."

"Dad, James *wants* a child. Asking Aubrey was *his* idea." I feel better telling my father, pushing this fact out into the immense room of a long-gone era. I don't confide that I question why people ache to be parents. Are they afraid of missing out, anticipating a haunting regret down the road?

"That is why you are so pressured, I see. Does James need a child? You two have an excellent life."

"We both want to have a family. We want a baby. You and Mom understand that. I mean, you know what I've been through, in vitro, hormones. You have your daughters. You and Mom have that."

He looks away. In the half fluorescent, half natural light, I see how the lines in my father's face are ridged.

"If this is so relevant, then you should hire a carrier for your baby, a surrogate."

"Oh, I get it, as long as it isn't affecting Aubrey." Welts start—turning to hives beneath my collarbone. "That's what it's about."

"If you and James want this, there are options. No need to push Aubrey to carry for you."

"Push her? I'm not pushing her." My one and only very large denial.

"It won't be good for either of you." Simon straightens his spine.

"Does Mom know you're with me to talk? Does she know you are against it? She *wants* Aubrey to do it for me. I thought you and Mom always agree. Why are you so negative about the idea?" I scratch my neck. I need air.

He sighs and moves one step from me. I imagine him imagining Aubrey.

"James is hell-bent on Aubrey doing it for us. It's the shared-DNA component, that's the thing. At first I was resistant; it was too loaded, too much to ask. Then I thought about it and about you, how you would approve," I say.

"Why, why is that?" Simon stands still enough to be in the military.

"I thought this would please you, that you would be very happy with the Cutler genes being included, that the DNA would be there. That really matters to James. At first I was so worried about this big ask of Aubrey that I couldn't pay attention to the DNA part. Yet I know it connects me to our baby and how that feels."

"Is that the key to being a good mother or father?" he asks.

"Well, not always, but family counts, being related counts."

"Family counts." He repeats this thoughtfully. My nausea returns, almost overwhelming me.

"I'd pay another surrogate, Elodie, a gestational carrier, whatever you need. Someone who isn't related in any manner."

"Are you trying to persuade me against wanting Aubrey?" I want to say, *Are you daring to buy me?* Instead, I lift my water bottle from my Literary Society canvas bag, uncertain how it got past security, and take a few sips.

"I'm trying to help you," he says.

I steady myself. "Aubrey is my younger sister, my blood. We are tangled, in a good way, we are in this *enmeshed* family. Why are you against it?"

I feel the light shift and disintegrate; the length of the Music Room seems distorted. Suddenly I understand. "It occurs to me that you've already gone to Aubrey, tried to talk to her. Haven't you? I don't need anything, Dad, thank you."

A mother and her daughter walk inside and the sunlight returns, streaming into the gallery while the clouds roll out. They are startled to find us there, pitched in the very middle. The daughter is eight at most and reminds me of the third graders coming in for our Nancy Drew series at the Society. I watch them move toward the opposite end, as far away as possible.

"I can't quite understand the depth of your campaign, Dad. Your idea for *my* baby."

The mother's and daughter's footsteps scrape and pad along the patterned wood floor. Are we not out of place in this mansion from a past era, when life had more grandeur? My father is about to take my hand, I feign that I don't see. He tries again.

"Dad, I have to go. I have paperwork for the Society, and James will wonder where I am when he gets back."

"Of course," Simon says.

I head for the exit door, and turn to see if he is behind. His back is to me; he is standing in this "father as stoic" stance. He appears strong, but then I realize that his shoulders are sloping.

CHAPTER 10

ELODIE

An hour later I'm at the Breakers Beach Club, wishing I were spotless, unblemished. I impel my father's words out of my mind, as if I have a flyswatter for thoughts and feelings that are too painful. I move through the terrace, where families—guests of the hotel and members—are finding tables for lunch.

"Elodie, Elodie, over here!" Veronica stands beside Mimi; both are waving their arms in a synchronized motion. They have corraled a row of lounge chairs by the main pool, facing the private beach and coastline.

I wave back, my version, a partially raised right arm, a mild sweep of my hand. At least twenty or thirty members of the Literary Society are milling about. My mother waves more strenuously.

"I know. I thought we'd be in a cabana on the beach." I hear my sister, whispering in my ear.

"Aubrey!" I say.

"I know, startling, right?" Aubrey smiles her brightest, whitest smile. "I drove up after Mom did this 'Palm Beach Sunday in November early season' plea. Something about a family afternoon at the Breakers. Tyler got invited, but my appearance is by command."

"Did he come? Have you seen James?"

Aubrey slopes her brimmed hat toward me. "No, Tyler is with a lead singer called Horace today. I don't know about James. Mom and Mimi expect him."

She's wearing a pastel print bikini with a sheer sea foam minidress over it. Although I've brought my Letarte bikini and cover-up that I bought on the Avenue, the contrast is incongruous. Aubrey is enchanting. I hold my bag closer to my hip and remember my father's defense of my sister's floatable existence.

"I'm so happy to be with you!" My sister hugs me. Has she forgotten I ever asked for help—for a baby I can't carry? No matter what happens, we have asked too much of each other. And gone too far, we supposedly exemplary Cutlers. I should apologize; I should get an emotional eraser and erase everything, including my father this morning. Erase it.

"Ohhh Elodie!" someone yodels to my left as we navigate toward my mother and mother-in-law.

"You are being paged. One of your clients," Aubrey says.

"Society members?" I say. We both laugh at that. A member's voice, even a board member's, won't be so different from anyone else's at the Beach Club on a busy Sunday afternoon. Anyone is capable of an overloud, jarring hello.

"Look. It's Katie," Aubrey says.

Katie, in muted blue yoga pants and a white racer-back tank top, is standing with Zachary. While he is twirling his water bottle, which doubles as a fan, she is tugging on her highlighted hair, gathering it in a loose knot.

"Aunt Elodie!" Zachary runs toward me. "You're here!" He jumps up and down. I kneel to kiss him. He smells like little boy skin dipped in chlorine.

He tugs on my skort. "I'm going to the kid camp! Mom's taking me right over! Can you come with us?"

"That would be fun. I'd love to," I say. "But, Mr. Dinosaur, I'm with my sister, and our mother is waiting for us to have lunch."

"Zachary, we have to hurry. Your friends Charlie and Christopher are waiting." Katie takes him by the hand. "We should go."

"Aunt Elodie, please take me!" Zachary begs. "Did you bring a book for us to read later?"

That's when DeeDee, Katie's mother, arrives. "What a zoo! I've been looking for you, Katie." She turns to us. "The Cutler sisters!" Air-kisses ensue.

"Mom, can you take Zachary over? His friends are—"

"Let's go, sweetie." DeeDee has a firm grip as she steers Zachary through the crowd, back toward the south entrance to the kids' club. He tucks his chin as he is led along, then looks back at me. "Bye!"

"Bye, Zachary!" I blow him a kiss.

We watch them moving swiftly away from the pool area.

"Hey," Katie says. The sweat beads on her shoulders are so perfect, they seem tattooed. "There's a chakra-balancing hour, for the three of us—for energy centers— or we can do the Soul Stretch fitness class."

Aubrey's face lights up. "What time? I'd love either one."

The three of us stand in the midst of two surges—one toward the bungalows, the other toward the Beach Club Restaurant. Off to the right, beside our reserved beach chairs, our mother has one hand on her hip and is holding up a menu.

"We can talk about it, make a plan. I'll text you," I say. "Aubrey, Mom is at a table."

Behind Katie, a tallish, buff man appears. The best-looking father in the Children's Library—with plenty of competition.

"Hi, Katie, Elodie." He is fixed on Aubrey. "I haven't seen you lately. I've been traveling for work."

"Colby, my younger sister, Aubrey. I don't know if you've met her, maybe back in the day," I say.

"When you were a very little sister." Colby holds out his right hand to Aubrey.

She half shakes his hand. "Yeah, I was that. The little naggy sister."

"You don't live in Palm Beach, do you?" he asks.

"I don't." Aubrey looks out toward our mother. "I'm sorry. Elodie, look. Mom and Mimi are majorly summoning us."

"Another time." Colby smiles.

He's not been gone a minute when Katie grasps Aubrey's wrist. "You know Colby Akers is almost a billionaire, divorced not a year. Moved his business to Palm Beach from New York. His girls are with him or the nanny, no one sees the mother around. I mean, *look* at him, listen to him."

Aubrey pulls down on the hem of her mini cover-up and puts on her red-framed RayBans. "Thanks, Katie, I'm with someone."

"Oh, maybe I did hear. You're with someone from Se-attle. Elodie told me when we were at the South Palm fund-raiser," Katie says.

"Portland, not Seattle. He is in South Beach, with me, that's where we live." Aubrey is frosty. Reminding me of how she was with her teachers at the Academy, only half there.

"She's spoken for, Katie," I say. "Besides, this isn't how my sister views the world."

Katie and I air-kiss and I guide Aubrey through the thicket of people standing and seated, ruffling menus, eager to order. I'm sure by now our mother has done the same. She and Mimi have mah-jongg at two o'clock. I glance at my iPhone. James texts that he's winning at sin-gles and wants to have lunch with the other players. It will just be fine for us.

We walk by the factions: nubile teenage girls counting French fries, coeds sipping limeade, summoned home by their parents during winter break. They sport discreet tattoos at their ankles and wrists—a promise of more to come. There are groups of pristine women over fifty who seem rushed to have a kale and quinoa salad before get-ting to the card tables, young mothers with small children and their nannies, their husbands coming in from tennis or golf as the hot dogs arrive. I watch more closely. Some congregate with other couples or grandparents, others are nuclear. *Nuclear.*

"Dad texted. He isn't coming," Aubrey says. "His bridge game starts soon at the Harbor Club. Sort of surprising, right?"

Is Aubrey missing how Dad has been recently? An im-possible situation to have ever predicted, darkening the day. Where can it go, whatever the outcome? I blame both men; James for dreaming up Aubrey as our surrogate, and Dad for begging us to not get entangled. He's become unknowable. I'm not sure I'll miss him at lunch, not today. My hands are clammy.

To get to our lounge chairs, I greet and grin. To my left are a few women from Mothers and Children, the "good doers" who have supported my mother's work there for what seems like decades. To the right is a younger crowd, but older than me: Faith Harrison, Lara Mercer, Maritza Abrams, Betina Gilles, and Allison Rochester, members of the Literary Society, major members. Everyone mixes, everyone buzzes. Most Sundays I am happy to be a part of it. The women talk about the programs; my mother boasts about my influence. Mimi is on her best behavior because she is a guest of my parents, James has won in singles and feels appreciated. Yet today I can only greet my friends from afar, the ones who are settled in their reserved lounge chairs, slathering WaterBabies sunblock from bright pink bottles onto their young children's shoulders and thin, strong arms and legs. I am weighted down, my hair, my body. I'm an outsider rather than the insider my mother trained us to be. I cannot banish the morning at the Flagler with my father—it keeps playing, over and over.

"Girls, girls. I ordered four lobster rolls." Veronica, too, is applying sunblock. Although we are under the shade of an umbrella, she pats it across her forearms.

"Mom, Aubrey is a vegetarian," I say.

"A vegan?" Mimi frowns; her Freywille bangles clank together.

"No, not a vegan, a plain everyday-variety vegetarian," Aubrey says. "I'll order a salad. A goat cheese salad. Maybe some onion rings."

"Of course, silly me," Veronica says.

Aubrey and I trade a glance. This isn't the first time that Veronica has decided that Aubrey ought not to be a vegetarian, that she, as the mother, can will it to disappear. What she objects to is the inconvenience, the lack of sophistication in food choice—or so it seems to her. It means Aubrey isn't like her on this count, not relishing jumbo shrimp or crabmeat, lobster rolls or sushi. I, in contrast, get points for eating every type of crustacean. Definitely at luncheons and dinners in Palm Beach it is sanctioned.

"Let's get a menu and start over for Aubrey," Veronica says.

Her cell rings; she squints, then takes the call. "Hello," she says in her public voice, with that lilt.

Mimi takes the "Sunday Styles" section of *The New York Times* from a nearby lounge chair and opens it back to front. Wedding announcements first.

I put down my bag and gaze out at the ocean and the jetty to the south. I look back at the Breakers. The facade from the ocean is as brilliant as on the westerly side. A legendary castle that hosts Palm Beachers and vacationers.

"C'mon." Aubrey slips her hand in mine. "Let's walk to the beach for a minute."

Behind us, chairs scrape against the patio tile; gossip and chatter add to the noise quotient. We keep going until we pass the Breakers lineup of beach cabanas.

The tide is high and waves hit the shoreline in crooked patterns. Aubrey takes her RayBans off and I take mine off. We squint at each other in the brightness.

"You know, I'm realizing what you need, Elodie, what you've been through, what it must be like every Sunday to see your friends, their children."

"No, no, don't bother with that. We're fine. My request, it's tearing this family apart. No more talk."

"You're my big sister. You saved me plenty of times."

"I know. One time right on this beach. You were about five, not a strong swimmer."

"Right! And Mom and Dad were with their friends, no one was paying attention," Aubrey says.

"I had passed my junior lifesaving," I say. "I thought you'd forgotten what happened."

"Not ever have I forgotten. Sometimes at night before I fall asleep, I can feel how there was an undertow that afternoon, how it was sucking me in. I looked at the shoreline and saw Mom in her purple bikini with that matching sarong. Dad was, like, in the center with the other men. Some of them were smoking cigarettes and two men had cigars."

"Not Simon."

"No, but he wasn't watching me, either. He was talking with the fathers. His head was facing away and I tried to scream. No parent was surveying the beach," Aubrey says. "I kept screaming. I still can feel my throat—how the screaming was too loud and then it got weaker. No one looked at me. Then the wave dragged me down. I couldn't get my head back up to see, to breathe."

I'm there again, in that moment long ago. The sand was a little damp; it had rained the night before until early morning. It wasn't warm enough that kids would jump into the ocean. We had finished hot dogs and burgers at a long table that the Breakers had set up. When they served the ice cream, I started looking around for my little sister.

"Why were you watching me?" Aubrey asks.

"I've always been watching you," I say. "That day I could feel you."

"You must have swum really fast to get to me. It was like I was about to be eaten up by the ocean," Aubrey says.

"I did, I swam like I was in the Olympics. Isn't that what they say about someone compelled to help—to save someone? They have herculean strength in that moment."

"You put your arms around me and dragged me—no, swam in with me. You had me in the tightest grasp. Slapping against the waves."

"Exactly . . . how it felt, you in my arms. Then we tumbled to the shore, coughing, spitting."

Aubrey holds me close and whispers, "I remember."

CHAPTER 11

ELODIE

Before I ever met Dr. Samantha Noel, shades of blue were among my favorite colors. Yet as I arrive in her waiting room this morning, I know it hasn't been like that for a long while. After the first year that James and I started to see her, filled with hope and unable to accept the odds of infertility, I still wore blue. Not now. I get it—mixing sky blue with medium blue with accents of deep blue. Blue as the color of the mind, creating a distance and a sense of calm. It might have helped me along the way, yet it didn't.

I try to settle down while James is at the front desk, speaking in soft tones. The chair is comfortable despite the color. I check for texts and emails from work. I inspect my husband. Will James always win the prize for handsome, sexy husband—regardless of the circumstances?

Case in point: At Dr. Noel's blue pressure cooker, I'm admiring how he walks back to where I wait.

"So we should be next," James says when he returns to the seating area, trying to read my face while he slides onto the chair beside me. "Thoughts?"

His voice stays low. Not that anyone in the waiting room cares; every doleful woman seems to be with a partner or husband. Some distract themselves with their iPhones and iPads, praying this portion of their morning will come and go easily.

"I'm remembering how you came to my parents' house in a leather jacket and jeans when you were in grad school. When we both were home for Christmas," I say.

"We weren't engaged. I was trying to make an impression," James says.

"You did. That's why we're married."

He smiles a little, because lately he isn't sure how to be with me. In the moment he might say something about why he sought me out—brainy while pretty, smooth skin, literary, more empathic than not. If we agree to choose our surrogate from a "catalog" today, I'll make sure she has these features, too. Insurance that while manufactured, our baby will be doubly rich in who we are.

We are called in to Dr. Noel's office ahead of the others in the waiting room. I can't help but believe it happens because we contribute to her foundation every year. While my father suggested it, James takes pride in our effort. Whatever hour I'm here, I'm in a rush to get back to the Literary Society, where fertility isn't the issue.

Dr. Noel sits behind her desk; her confidence is distilled throughout. Her lab coat with her name embroidered on it is a stiff white cotton. Beneath it she is wearing a blush pink shift that is simple and soothing. She has earned her success in a challenging field; we put our faith in her hands. She's wearing tan Manolo slingbacks that my mother would call "classic." I speculate that when she's at a dinner with her husband (most likely a hedge fund guy) she wears something newer, fresher, from Neiman's or Saks on the Avenue. Each time I'm here, I notice the framed photographs on her desk—at Mar-a-Lago, Vintage Tales, Justine's. Although Dr. Noel's office is in Fort Lauderdale (one reason that I chose her), she knows how to get to Palm Beach. Once at the Rose Ball, I saw her in the gardens during cocktail hour and pretended that I didn't.

"Elodie, you are looking well. Much better."

Graciously, she points to the love seat that continues the blue theme of the waiting room. James pushes aside two small medium-blue-and-white-striped cotton pillows.

"Before we begin, I'd like to review the options for surrogacy. There is a traditional surrogacy—sometimes called 'partial surrogacy.'" Dr. Noel adjusts her glasses. "The process requires artificial insemination with the father's sperm. Because of what you are investigating today, I want to remind you that there is no egg donor. A traditional surrogate is genetically related to the baby. She might be a close friend, a sister, a cousin, which has benefits. 'Intended parents' may decide on this, but it can be fraught and emotionally complicated."

I look at James, who is looking at me. We disengage, face Dr. Noel.

"Another concern is whether the surrogate will be able to let go of the baby at birth. And for this reason, I prefer gestational surrogacy. That entails a donor egg and a gestational surrogate. This is a business transaction, a cleaner plan." She pauses, takes a breath. "I wanted to explain both to you."

James takes my hand in his. "Either way, Dr. Noel. We are simply matching someone as best we can, going through what's right for us, for our child."

Dr. Noel keeps tugging on a double-heart necklace—the same pave diamond one that Mimi wears. "Of course. There are screenings and then whichever way you go, you'll get to know your surrogate during the process. I don't believe we discussed price."

I put my hand in the air as if to stop the conversation—I can't listen to the cost of hiring someone to carry our baby. Dr. Noel ignores me, while James, all about numbers, is rapt.

"A traditional surrogate is sixty thousand dollars. The cost of a gestational surrogate is seventy-five thousand and could be more."

I listen, half astonished, half relieved that this is where we are, that it is beyond me. James is jotting things down on a pad with *ANVO* at the top.

"When do we start the search?" he asks.

"In a moment or two, I'll take you to a private library and you'll be set up to begin reviewing both types."

A sharp rap at the door as Dr. Noel's desk telephone rings. I attempt breaths that push my stomach out and suck air through my lungs.

"A moment, please." Dr. Noel ignores her landline and angles toward the door. A second round of rings start. She twists her body back toward the desk and lifts the receiver. "Yes?" A pause. "Excuse me?"

That's when her office door opens. Side by side stand one of the nurses and my sister. *Aubrey?*

James jumps up. "Aubrey? Has something happened? How did you find us?"

Heels rat-a-tat on the limestone tiles as Dr. Noel walks over. She is stricken, confounded. How often might that happen? I wonder.

"All good." Aubrey smiles. "May I come in?"

"Dr. Noel, this young woman has insisted that she find her sister, Elodie Cutler. She barged into—"

"It's all right, Melinda, it's okay." Dr. Noel waves her away. "Please close the door behind you."

"Dr. Noel, this is Elodie's younger sister, Aubrey." James is standing. I, too, stand.

"So I see." Dr. Noel is stern. "Why are you here?"

"I'm Elodie's surrogate. For Elodie and James's baby. I'm the one," Aubrey says.

The one. Dr. Noel, James, and I are rendered dull.

"Elodie?" Aubrey says. "Hello?"

"Are you sure?" James asks.

"For Elodie, I will."

"This is *news,*" Dr. Noel says. "Please, everyone, let's have a moment. Let's sit down."

Although Dr. Noel has surely witnessed more drama than ours, she seems shaken. Glancing at her children's framed faces on her desk, then back in our direction, she says, "You and your sister look so similar."

"People tell us that." Aubrey tilts her head to the right.

"I don't know what to say. I can't believe this." James is beaming at my sister.

"I know, I can't believe it, either," I add.

"We're the new threesome! What have I done?" Aubrey quickly turns to Dr. Noel. "I'm kidding. I know what's ahead. I'm a perfect surrogate."

"Are you?" asks Dr. Noel.

"Well, yeah, I am. I'm with someone, my boyfriend, who doesn't want children, last I heard. No conflict there. Our parents will be happy, right?" Aubrey says.

Our eyes lock. "Yes, I'm not sure about Dad, who ended up caring more about this whole ordeal than anyone."

"Incredibly," Aubrey says. "I am very surprised."

"He doesn't know about this final plan, does he?" I ask.

"No way," Aubrey says. "But this is our plan."

"Now that you've appeared, Audrey," Dr. Noel says, "I think we might use the time left to talk about—"

"*Aubrey,* not Audrey," I say. "My sister's name is Aubrey."

"Our father was hoping for a boy, so he gave me a boy's name." Aubrey has explained her name often over the years. She rolls it out and lets it sink in.

"Let's hear what Dr. Noel has to say." James opens the second button of his starched white shirt. His forehead looks sweaty.

"I wanted to mention the emotional and legal ramifications of a traditional surrogacy. There is a law firm we recommend for the adoption process."

"Adoption? I don't know anything about that," I say. Maybe Dr. Noel likes adding to the fray.

"Not complicated," Dr. Noel says. "The 'intended mother'—meaning Elodie—will need to adopt the baby and the . . ."

That's when I have to leave the blue hues of Dr. Noel's office. James notices.

"Dr. Noel," he says, "my wife and my sister-in-law and I are going to the Starbucks across the street and have a talk. I'll call in to discuss the rundown and finalize plans."

In the reception area we pass the patients waiting to be seen, counseled, saved. One husband leans toward his wife, whispering in her ear. James walks ahead, beyond where they sit, reading their iPhones, issues of *People* and *Star* on their laps. I'm springing along, my step as bouncy as Tigger's in *Winnie the Pooh*. Was it only yesterday that I read it to the three-year-olds at Reading Hour?

The world is rushing by and it's possible I can grab on, be who I was before I had to have a baby. My younger sister has come to save me, save James and me. I ought to warn her against selling her soul to save mine. Except this is the first hope I've had in years. Outside the door, I hold on to Aubrey as I've never held on to anyone.

"It's okay, Elodie." Her body is slender and firm.

"Come, let's go." James leads us. We leave Dr. Noel's office, a triumvirate.

PART TWO

CHAPTER 12

AUBREY

L ook at the waves coming in," Tyler says as we walk on the pool patio at the Four Seasons. "Is the ceremony on the beach?"

I almost laugh. My friend Tiffany, who is having her wedding tonight, is being married indoors, with a party to follow in the Royal Poinciana Ballroom.

"No," I say. "This is the *pre*-ceremony cocktail hour—that's it for outdoors."

"Why?" He faces the ocean.

"Well, when you grow up in Palm Beach you know better than to book anything by the water—the weather changes fast." I don't confide how hair frizzes, makeup slides off your face.

"What a setting, the sky, water, to be stuck inside." Tyler adjusts the cummerbund of his rented tuxedo. While I like that he doesn't own one, I don't want my mother and sister to know. It wouldn't be fair to him, when my father and James each own two or three versions.

"Yeah, except for the wind too, coming from the east. Then storms get stirred."

Tyler keeps looking out at the ocean. The sky is dappled and it's close to twilight. I don't bother to explain that being married between Thanksgiving and New Year's isn't prime time. Tyler wouldn't care; I don't think he'd get it. I never really got it, either; it's just what I was taught, the rules.

"But it will be lavish, that's for sure. My mom calls it 'ever elegant' at the Four Seasons. The year before I met you, I was here for three weddings."

"Three weddings?"

"People I grew up with, winter friends—the ones who came over Christmas breaks and were from up north. They wanted this. I was a bridesmaid at Tiffany's first wedding, eight years ago—at the Harbor Club. She was the first friend to get married and then divorced."

Tyler listens; maybe he's curious, observing another species. "Why?"

"I'm not sure. I was in San Francisco that year. She mentioned he'd run into an old girlfriend. Now he's remarried to her."

"I've heard of that," Tyler says.

"Right. So this time I'm not a bridesmaid, because her new husband, Ethan, has two sisters and a sister-in-law. She wouldn't do any more—it's a Thursday-night wedding. Y'know, more low-key."

"Sure," Tyler says. "Low-key."

The small chip of a diamond post glistens in his left earlobe tonight.

"Like I'm telling you about another form of life on Earth," I say. "Last week at Tiffany's bridal shower at Longreens, her mother handed out these 23andMe kits to everyone, as a party favor, I guess. It must be a fad, people wanting to learn if they're part Neanderthal or likely to sneeze in the sun, predestined for allergies, curly hair. She had extras, so I took two to the Literary Society afterward. Elodie and I sat in her office and spit into our little vials."

"That's a party favor? Are you sure it's Earth?" He comes close and puts his mouth to my ear, holds me at my waist. "What'ya think the band'll be like tonight?"

When the minister and rabbi echo each other, both asking Tiffany if she will take Ethan to be her lawfully wedded husband, I shudder. What guarantees could there be? Living with Tyler is tricky enough, and we are so *not* married. What is it that Elodie has said lately about how the magic evaporates, even with someone like James, and illusion wears thin? After what she has been through, no wonder. I turn to Tyler; he squeezes my hand as the minister has Tiffany repeat her vows: *For better or for worse.* He winks at me. When the two kiss, Tyler shifts closer, our bodies graze.

Tiffany and Ethan march back down the aisle, this time together, wife and husband.

"She looks happy. I'm so happy for her," I whisper.

Tyler nods. "I'm a sucker for feel-good ceremonies."

The two of us sail toward the raw bar while everyone else is lined up for Railcars, Palm Beach daiquiris, or a craft beer. Tyler selects oysters—bluepoints, Kumamotos, and Wellfleets—piling them on a plate for us to share. I blink as if I'm the one from another planet. Already a future anxiety begins: I can't be eating uncooked shellfish once I'm carrying my sister's baby. Tonight Tyler knows nothing—I haven't had the guts to tell him what happened two days ago. He deserves to know; it's that I hope to keep this night separate.

"Hey, Aubrey, am I imagining it or are people staring at me?"

I follow his gaze. I take another bluepoint and wash it down with the fizzy water the waitstaff has been passing around. "Maybe. I mean, I see some of my old friends from winter season, from the Academy. They're looking around—looking at us. Figuring it out, or trying to."

"I bet you were the most popular girl in the class." He smiles.

"I was. So was Elodie for her year."

He swallows his last Wellfleet and finishes it off with the white wine that was offered to him a minute ago. Meanwhile, every girl I once wanted as a friend, prayed would include me, invite me, remember me, watches Tyler tonight. And I'm proud of him, of us. I'd like to make an announcement to this group. *Yes, we live in South Beach. I'm his business partner at Breyler Music, LLC, a subsidiary of Lambent, his company. He started it for us, using the "brey" of Aubrey and the "ler" of Tyler for the name.*

"I knew it!" Tyler is pleased. "I knew you and your sister would be the ones."

"Well, it isn't like that anymore. I mean, Elodie's fine with James. Though he didn't grow up in Palm Beach, he fits in. Meanwhile, Elodie's doing her Literary Society, and as a couple they do that dashing, moneyed thing. Mostly they're with her friends from way back."

"Nice." Tyler is listening.

"My sister had a big wedding," I say. Like I'm confessing, warning him. "At the Breakers. My parents invited everyone in town—year-rounders to snowbirds, work friends, real friends. Their wedding band did love songs and disco—the Bee Gees, ABBA, Elvis. I was twenty-one—I kept thinking how Elodie and James were a retaining wall for each other."

"Plus, you got to dance to that music." He smiles.

"Right!"

I take in the guests spread out and about during the cocktail hour. Every woman in the room, whether twenty-five, fifty, or even sixty-five, is manicured and pedicured, with wavy hair to shoulder-length in shades of blond, brown, and red. No one has gray hair; no one would dare. There is cleavage, including toe cleavage. There are plenty of micro-bladed eyebrows. Not as many diamond or aquamarine necklaces as earrings tonight. Chandelier earrings, oversize pear-shaped dangles made of rubies or emeralds or sapphires. Pearl earrings, too. Mom claims pearls are making a comeback. Every woman is thin and trim. Everyone's dress fits almost too well.

"I like what you're wearing," Tyler says.

"Do you?" I ask.

"I'm not kidding. Why are you giving me a look?"

"Well, the dress, a Hervé, is vintage, say fourteen years old. My shoes, too." I hold out my right leg for him to admire the black suede platform.

"I like how the dress is like a wet suit," he says.

"Oh, for sure it's bandaging me. My mother offered to buy, actually begged to buy, a new dress for tonight. Then Elodie told me to borrow from among her latest collection of dresses."

Tyler nods. How could he know an Oscar from a Mc-Queen? Stella McCartney, Marchesa, a Jenny Packham?

"Shoes, too? Sort of like Cinderella?" He's bemused.

"Totally. She was pushing the same shoes as on that woman over there. See? Attico stilettos. She's one of my mom's friends, Elle Grenier. She's carrying this clutch by Judith Leiber—it's a leopard design, made of crystals."

"Leopard made of crystals?" He's perplexed.

As Jessica Harley, another friend from the Academy, swishes to where Tyler and I stand, I remember why I practically airlifted myself to Colorado after college.

"There you are, Aubrey!" she says. We check each other out in a matter of seconds. She's in her best Blumarine, a quiet sophistication, definitely this year's design. Jessica thrusts her finger in my face. An engagement ring, oval cut, classic, approaching six carats.

"Yes! Now you're the only one left of our crowd, Aubrey," she says.

Whether I am kind of a mean girl and simply say "pretty" in a small voice or I do the princess route and gush over Jessica's ring, I'm stuck.

"Congratulations, Jessica," I smile a demure smile, although my mouth isn't shaped that way. You can't go wrong, no matter how you're dressed, if you are polite but not effusive. Only offer the Mona Lisa smile, no more, no less—Decorum 101 from my mother.

"Jessica. I'm sorry. Let me introduce you to Tyler."

"*Tyler.*" Jessica holds out her right hand while keeping her left in the air, fanning her engagement ring.

He is polite; he smiles for real and shakes her hand, putting me at ease. That's how Elodie describes James. "I can take him anywhere," she says. "I'm always proud, I'm always the one." I know what she means, yet we aren't a replica of Elodie and James by any means. Tyler is an outlier and I'm dissident enough for bringing him along. Except that isn't why we're together; it's just a reassuring byproduct of our coupling. We're together because for once in my life I've chosen rather than being chosen. I *choose* Tyler.

Although few among my old friends would admit it, growing up there were toxic boys in Palm Beach and tangential circles. We Academy girls knew about them. The idea, the goal, was to pretend they weren't tainted and privileged, that they would make catches as husbands. I never could pull it off, go with the veneer; they frightened me too much.

"Good to meet you, Jessica. I'm heading toward the sushi bar while you catch up."

Tyler gives me a signal, then he's fluid, his escape quick—he could be any man in the room.

I take a quick inventory and see too many people I know.

"Jessica, is your fiancé here?"

"No, sadly, he's in Houston on business—this *is* a Thursday night. He'll be back tomorrow. You *do* know whom I'm marrying, Aubrey." Jessica leans toward me. "Tony Baek."

"Tony Baek? Wasn't he Elodie's year?"

"Wasn't he Elodie's boyfriend—I mean like when they were fifteen?" Jessica asks.

"Maybe," I say. "I was only seven, I'm not sure."

"Exactly, he's eight years older. We'll start a family right away." She's making me feel defensive about Elodie, while there's no logic to it. It feels incestuous, not only because Jessica's fiancé was my sister's first real crush but because of how insular it is.

"I should go. Tyler is deep into spring rolls, tuna rolls—he might dive in."

"Ah, yes. Headfirst." After a beat she adds, "He's cute enough. I hear he's a music rep."

"Well, yes, and books bands that we find, indie bands that . . ." I'm tempted to share what I do, construe my work, when Tyler returns.

"Look, Aubrey, Tiffany is coming over. With Louise," Jessica says.

Out of the two hundred guests to greet, the bride is making her way toward us.

"Aubrey, Jessica!" Tiffany says. "Louise and I were looking for you. I escaped the pictures, managed to get some champagne. And find you!"

Tiffany is flawless in that runway model mode. Her makeup, her simple, sleek gown. Her thick hair—she's always had that—is piled high on her head, yet half of it falls down her back.

"Ah, Tyler! You are the one Elodie has been describing to me." She holds out her hand.

"Elodie? When did you see her?"

"On the Avenue, about three weeks ago. She was raving about Tyler."

Tyler and I are surprised, then he seems pleased. The muscles in his neck relax.

Louise follows. "I have heard about Tyler, also from Elodie."

Hasn't Louise always been the quietest, kindest of our group of friends? Tonight she is in navy blue and isn't standing straight, as Mom would notice immediately. *A shame about Louise, the sweetest girl, the best teeth and skin. But too quiet for her own good.*

"Tyler, I grew up with everyone. We were such good friends," I say.

"Got into some trouble, though," Tiffany says.

"Right, you did." Jessica laughs. "Like you missed the first go-round of SAT testing."

"She couldn't help it," Louise says. "That wasn't the best year for—"

"What happened?" Tyler asks. "I heard you were at 'the Academy.'" He takes his hands and frames quotes as he speaks. "I went to a regional high school with some nasty dudes. Some truants. Four hundred to a grade. What could go wrong at a private girls' school?"

We stare at him.

"He's kidding, right?" Jessica asks.

"Well, things did go wrong, very wrong on occasion." Louise pushes her glasses up on her nose. To this day, no contact lenses.

"Basically, Tiffany was stoned, with her then boyfriend."

"Such idiocy," Tiffany says. "And you guys saved me. Called my parents, said I was too sick, had a migraine, couldn't do the test."

"Then she took them the next time and ended up at MIT!" Jessica announces.

"We both were at MIT," Louise says. "We were suite-mates the second year."

"Honestly, Tyler doesn't need to know any more, does he?" Jessica says.

"I doubt it," I say. "Besides, Tiffany has to greet other guests."

Then, without planning it, the four of us make a small circle, our arms around one another. Somehow it feels good to be with my old friends.

"I've got it!" Tyler takes out his iPhone and grabs the shot. "For Instagram."

"Please," Tiffany says. "Let me know."

As quickly as we congregated, they are gone.

"The band's starting up," Tyler says. "'Collide'—Howie Day."

We walk into the dining room, where the dance floor is vast. I look back and see the guests at the carving boards, the groaning buffet table. Rack of lamb, fettuccine Alfredo, and salmon tartare mille-feuille. No one else grasps that the music has begun. My kind of song more than Tyler's, yet we're dancing. Alone, we bend to each other, he twirls with me. A good omen for other heroic feats in the future.

"I'm sorry, Tyler. Jessica can be devious."

"She's your friend. I liked meeting your friends. Old friends, from your hometown."

Then he takes my hand in his and places it over his heart and leads me in our dance. "Look, disco balls." He points to the ceiling.

People are trickling toward their tables, toward the dance floor. I look up at the reflected bursts of light and put my head against his chest.

CHAPTER 13

AUBREY

Being sober means I steer Tyler's Jeep Wagoner for a mile along the A1A at two A.M. We're staying at my parents', not because Tyler liked the idea but because he knew it would be a late night at a wedding, too late to drive back to South Beach.

"Hey, why is the ocean lit up?" he asks. His head is tipped back against the passenger seat and his knees are far apart. He yawns, loosens his bow tie, and unfastens his cummerbund, tossing them both onto the backseat.

"That's how it's always been. The houses, most of them, have owners who light up their beach."

"Between the road and the house?" Tyler keeps looking out at the synthetically lit beaches, made brighter by the full moon.

I wish we had left the wedding earlier. My friends, the

wedding guests, must seem cliquish, too spoiled for him. I don't want Tyler to conclude that I'm exactly like them. Or that I'd conceivably revert to what I've known, be part of the herd. Worse, I wish we had not agreed to stay at my parents' house tonight. Mom will question Tyler about his work and the bands tomorrow. My mother *and* father will fish for information, about his family, his education. They might find out that he has made me his partner. I haven't told them yet, nor have I asked Tyler to be discreet. I'm sure he hasn't a clue why I'd hesitate to tell them. For him it seems obvious that good news is to be shared. It's only that I feel evaluated by my family. That they won't understand completely what we do, or why I've become good at it. Tyler and I aren't on the checklist; I don't want us to be assessed.

In profile Tyler is relaxed, innocent, really. "We've never stayed at your parents', your old house. Your old *bedroom*." He grins.

"Why would we? I mean, we have so few evenings when we aren't at a gig." I sigh. The last time we were both at home, we watched three episodes of *Breaking Bad*. And ate thin-crust gluten-free pizza. I realize how in control I am in South Beach and how out of control I feel in Palm Beach.

"Hey, Aubrey, do you know how many nights we've been together? I don't mean living together, I mean with each other. No separate ways."

"I'm not sure what you're saying." Is Tyler complaining, afraid? "How many in a row? *Twenty-three*. Twenty-three nights in a row."

"And before that you were here in your kid bedroom. You came for your sister one night, some literary fund-raiser. The next day, some lunch for your mother, and she wanted you to be there, was that it?"

That he has counted. "I know," I say.

"Well, I like it. It works," he says.

I pull into my parents' driveway. The hedges cast a darkness, despite the outside lights. "I'm not sure where to park. I don't have a remote for the garage. I left it in my car."

"Hey, Aubrey, while I'm being sentimental, a little romantic, let's go inside. Leave the Jeep right where it is." Tyler leans toward me. "C'mon."

Halfway upstairs we kiss. When we stop to breathe, I stare out the window that overlooks the tennis court and, beyond that, the Intracoastal. Tyler stands behind me. I know he has never played—could I ask him if he might want to learn? Does he watch Wimbledon or the U.S. Open? I could say how in this family, it was mandated that we learn and then play. Elodie and I took lessons at Longreens, where we were taught not only the game but the culture. "Come watch your father," Mom used to say when we were growing up. "He's winning; he's in a tournament. He's number one." James slotted right in; he not only favors singles but is a "fine-enough" player to fill in for our father's doubles matches, too. I twist around and start the second round of kisses.

"C'mon." I hold his hand and we take the staircase side by side up to the second floor.

A flat-screen TV and the Farfalle-print duvet cover—a butterfly pattern from DEA—are the only upgrades in my childhood bedroom. Every other detail in this museum of young-girl dreams is intact from when I left for college. On the bulletin board are faded posters, one of Bob Dylan with lyrics from "Just Like a Woman," a water lilies poster of the Monet painting, a Spice Girls poster, a women's suffrage poster that reads VOTES FOR WOMEN. On the bookcase, beside volumes of Yeats, Elizabeth Barrett Browning, and Wordsworth, is a complete collection of plays by George Bernard Shaw. *Little Women* and *Anne of Green Gables* are used as bookends. Tyler runs his hands across the lower shelf.

"Wow, interesting."

"You don't have to look tonight," I say.

He keeps reading the titles. "Tyler?"

"Okay, next time."

He plunks down on my queen-size bed, the very bed where Tiffany, tonight's bride, and I used to lie together and squeal about the Palm Beach boys. He channel-surfs while I undress in my bathroom, feeling oddly shy. While I scrub my mascara and liner off with what could be expired baby shampoo, the sounds of late-night television ricochet through the room. After a moment, Tyler lowers the volume. I open the bathroom door; he's sitting straight up, propped against those fluffy shams. His pants and shirt are tossed over the chair, the black fabric clashing with the lemony print and peachy pink throw. He's only in his gray-striped boxer shorts, more schoolboy than I've ever seen him.

"Hey." He aims the remote toward the wall and there's that brief whine as the system closes down. He looks at me. "You okay?"

"I'm okay."

I sit beside him. We start kissing again. Kisses unlike the ones in the car, more like the sloppy, untold kisses we first shared, months ago. Tonight that seems important.

He stops, reaches for his iPhone. "What is Love," by Haddaway, starts to play. "Eurodance," he whispers in my ear. He lifts me off the bed and around we go, as if we haven't left the frenzied dance floor at the Four Seasons. Holding our hands in the air, we move in sync, peerless dance partners that we are.

Tyler lowers the lights and leads me back to bed. He lays me down gently; I'm made of gossamer. He pulls on my vintage nightie from VSC, found in my dresser drawer with tags still on it. Sky blue with lace trim. While the song keeps going, filling the room, I might forget what's gone on at Dr. Noel's. My hands are on his chest, while his face is on my stomach, my breasts; we're moving quickly. Tyler is on top of me. I cling to him, shivering. Once the song ends, we hear the tide against the retaining wall, the wind shifting to the west.

"What's going on, babe?" he says.

The moment to confide—to put our relationship at risk for my sister.

"You know how my sister and I were really close as kids? Well, then we grew apart a little. Basically, though, we're very, very connected."

"I know, I know." Tyler nibbles at my earlobe, changing the mood back to us.

I tense up instead of relaxing and he pulls back.

He stops. "Hey, what is it?"

My muscles tighten everywhere; my neck is in knots.

"Hey, hey, Aubrey. It's okay. We'll kiss after we talk." He laces his fingers across my back, taps lightly.

I touch the circumference between his neck and his shoulders because I love it so. I ought to tell him in my room; it's the right thing to do. Where our being together flattens the memories, the history. How it was with Elodie down the hall and my parents in their master suite on the other side of the house. Elodie was planning her future while my mother was juggling her work at Mothers and Children. Always there was the mirroring couple act, the Veronica and Simon Show. For me it was suffocation by a thousand social pursuits.

"We can make a go of this. Of us, together. I really believe it," he says.

The room is dreamy; I've waited for this, waited for him.

"I'm so happy," I whisper. Then at once there is the heaviness of Elodie and James. Of guidelines for their baby, but *my* pregnancy, not theirs, weighing down the world as I know it. I have to tell him this second, so he knows. We're moving fast; he's about to be inside me.

"Tyler, please."

He rolls away from me, waits a beat. I can't tell if he's annoyed, frustrated, finds me a tease, too emotional. The Tiffany mantel clock, a gift from my grandma Renata on my fourteenth birthday, ticks. Christina keeps it running, as if my bedroom is a shrine of some sort, a place that can only turn back time. Tyler runs his hands over my shoulders.

Everything would be much easier if he weren't in my life, if I didn't care. Then giving up nine—actually, ten—months of my life for Elodie wouldn't be as complicated.

"Please, make love to me and later I'll explain."

"Explain what?" His bald head, sexy, lovely, shines from the streetlight that seeps through the blinds. He stands up, puts on his boxers, like a lead singer first on-stage—that minute when the theater dims and the audience pauses for the brightness to follow. "I'll wait until I've heard you, Aubrey. *We'll wait.*"

I start feeling around for my nightie, as if the charm and seduction are being drained away. Tyler kneels down and picks it off the floor. I dress and sit up, missing him already.

"Does what you have to say have anything to do with Elodie?"

He comes back to the bed, turns on the lamp on the Biedermeier night table. We both blink, then sit facing each other. It reminds me of a breakup, a fight, a loss.

He waits, the way my grandpa used to wait for me to tell him what episode at school made me cry.

"Elodie and James. They want me to have their baby, to be artificially inseminated and give birth. My sister, she's been plagued by infertility for years. She has lost babies, miscarried. You know about the last one, but there have been a few. One time the baby had no heartbeat. I can help her, I should help her, except there's you. Us." I look away, toward the wall that had shadows when I was in grade school.

Tyler stands up, cracks his knuckles, walks to the window. From the back, he is an action figure on a billboard poster. I take the cotton-weave throw from the bench at the end of the bed to tug across my shoulders.

"What'd you tell them?" he asks while facing away.

I start rocking my body without meaning to, my knees pulled close to my chest. I visualize us not living together, moving apart, packing up a few things. Mostly I'm afraid of what it would be like without Tyler. Without his energy, his smile, the jokes he repeats—a tendency I usually can't stand, yet with Tyler it's all right.

"I told them I'd do it. My sister—she's been miserably unhappy, she's been too sad for me to bear."

I go to where he stands, to touch his face. He keeps looking out. Then I hold him as tightly as I can. He doesn't move. I try to lift his arms so they circle me. They seem unsteady, not strong and solid, not usual.

"I feel for your sister and for James, what they're going through. My sister miscarried twice before my nephew was born. Must be awful for Elodie."

"That's why I said yes, because it is devastating for her."

"Uh-huh." Tyler sighs, exhales. "Why didn't you tell me what's going on? I mean, I'm at the miscarriage point in this. That's the news I've had."

"At first I thought I'd say no, then I processed it. I waited because it could ruin the rest. I was clinging to us."

I keep looking around my childhood bedroom, murky in the lamplight. "My body will change, sex will be different—it will be safe sex for *them,* for Elodie and James. I can't drink—not that I do, but it's forbidden. I can't smoke weed or an occasional cigarette. Music can't be too loud, when we are at gigs—I'm afraid I might have to leave after a short time."

"It's okay. I wouldn't drink or smoke weed or cigarettes, if this happens. No second-hand anything."

That he would do that, that he would care enough.

"And be okay, in the world you're in, the places you go?" I ask.

"Yeah, it would be fine. I'd make it fine," he says. "I'd start a trend."

We both laugh at that.

Could he be this nice, this decent? The kind of person my mother and sister are always touting. Inherently nice guys are at a premium; sludges and goops are plentiful, easy to come by—wasn't I always tripping over them? Until Tyler.

"You're being very generous, Aubrey. It is an undertaking."

"I know. Mind-boggling."

"Sure, it's a lot. We'll adjust," he says.

Out of nowhere, Tyler has decided to join me on this alien journey. I could warn him, quote the nurse practitioner about waves of nausea, fatigue, nights when the incessant beat of our bands will make me afraid for the baby, for my body. Instead, I listen to the clock ticking while he runs his hands across his head as if he still has hair there.

"I'm sorry," I say.

He leans over and whispers, "I'm not going anywhere. You're not getting rid of me that easy. I might not fit into this town, but I fit with you."

He locks his hands with mine; we're entwined, shipmates. Only the two of us at an inlet where the ocean meets the bay.

The kissing starts again. He is gentle undressing me, charting the rest of our night. A fierce longing begins, like nothing I have ever known.

CHAPTER 14

ELODIE

Beyond the paned windows of the Literary Society, the daylight changes by early January. Some afternoons, like today, clouds dunk and rise, blown by the wind off the ocean. In the past few minutes, a rainstorm has churned up. Palm trees totter and people duck their heads as they hurry toward the main building. Two staff members are putting the finishing touches on the suffragette display. Pictures of Emma Pankhurst, Susan B. Anthony, Alice Paul, and Lucretia Mott are framed and mounted to the wall in the rotating exhibit area of the gallery.

I watch mothers leading their preschoolers and kindergartners after Reading Hour has ended, lulling them toward the elevator on the children's floor. Zachary, Katie's son, runs up to me and taps my hand.

"Aunt Elodie, are the dinosaur books okay for me to take out? Mom says there are more interesting books, but I like the carnivores."

"Of course it's okay, Zachary. I know how much you like *Tyrannosaurus rex,* but let's check out the herbivores today, too."

"Herbi what? Do they have names?" He looks up at me with his brown eyes. Although his hair is cut in a clean, preppy style that Katie loves, today it has grown out. I predict that Zachary will be brainy, alluring, and kind always.

"*Heribivores.* They were plant-eating, not like the carnivores, who ate meat—meaning they ate other smaller animals. The meat eaters are *Tyrannnosaurus rex* and the *Abelisaurus.* Herbivores only ate trees and vegetables. They had names like *Dracorex* and, well, let's see, *Argentinosaurus.*"

"You know a lot!" Zachary claps his hands together.

"I do because of you! I read up for when we are together." I smile at him. "Come, let me take you to Elizabeth, the librarian, who will show you the new dinosaur collection. There's a *National Geographic* book that has tons of information."

I try to engage Katie while she's in deep with the Academy crowd. Their voices thud: . . . *at the Chases, no, only the committee . . . Who is the chair? . . . Aspen, not Vail . . . a better kid camp at the Ritz in Cancún . . . the Arts and Media Ball, the Winter Ball . . . size 6 after months of dieting . . . Yes, Kors from last year . . . only a tummy tuck, Botox for the hair . . . a new nanny . . .* They huddle near the foyer; a few are browsing the stacks with their children.

"Katie?" I motion to her.

She looks over at us.

"I'm taking Zachary with me," I say.

"By all means." She returns to the group, her voice louder. "I only worry with my hours at the hospital if there aren't after-school classes."

Ella Smythe, a disarming four-year-old, lingers by the classics stacks, holding on to *The Dolls' House,* by Rumer Godden. I overhear her mother, Dorothea, discouraging her from taking the book.

"You're too young, Ella. Wait a year or two, darling. At least." She holds a few Amelia Bedelias in her hands. "These are better for today."

Ella does the "good girl" nod and places her right hand on the second book. Although I imagine myself guiding Ella to the sitting area to read the first few pages of *The Dolls' House,* I don't have my usual level of small child/ baby lust. I'm able to admire her while believing I, too, will have a chance one day with my own. I walk back to Laurent Hall.

The thrill of this afternoon—where our guest is the famed transgender memoirist and poet Maisie Natters. I cannot believe she's come to Palm Beach; I cannot believe that members of the Friends of the Society are welcoming her. Now that the reading has ended, women are piling into the reception area, smoothing their hair, reapplying lipstick. Maisie is off at the grand oak desk, ready to autograph, appearing pleased. I see Nadia Sherman from *Palm Beach Confidential* among the crowd. Her photographer is getting shots of the women waiting three-deep for their signed copy of Maisie's latest poetry collection, *Confinement.*

"Ever since you told me about Maisie Natters, Ah've become a fan," Allison Rochester says in her Southern drawl. Her flowered dress is subtle, with a wide skirt. Extremely stylish, of course—in clothes that are not identifiable. "Ah want my daughters to know about her. Ah read her first collection, *Labyrinth,* and was astonished."

"She was my teacher my last semester in grad school." Katherine Harrison, Faith's daughter, joins us. We stand by the oak bookcases, which look darker with the sky dull outside. The rain keeps up. "My friend who was at Columbia with me is in town and we'll take Maisie the airport later."

"You did it, Katherine! You coaxed her to come to Palm Beach," I say.

"Laurie and I did it—*with* you, Elodie."

"Well, it took over a year. And it's true what I said during my introduction. Without you, it wouldn't have happened."

I watch Laurie hover over Maisie, thinking back to the fall, when I miscarried at our kickoff reading. How warm the morning was on the terrace, how afraid I was that the guests would be distracted by the scene I made. Today Lara Mercer commented on it.

"Elodie, here you are, no *flu* this afternoon. Wasn't that the problem? Thank goodness you've recovered."

I smile that Palm Beach smile and move on.

Maisie's silvery hair and black linen dress make her seem very grave compared to today's uniform. Not that anyone is in brightest colors, due to the weather report—pastels are safer. Yet I'm attentive to style in another way—as if I'm seeing it through the lens of Maisie herself. Not about the dress code or who has the courage, as Mrs. A. and Priscilla do, to carry blazing shades (kelly green and hot pink) of Nancy Gonzalez skin bags. Women dress for

women, Veronica has been telling me since I was six years
old. Rather, I view it through Maisie's lens, someone who
has taken drastic steps to present as a woman. However
the female journey occurs, I doubt many of us escape the
demands of looking good, costuming ourselves as a message to the world.

"Fabulous, so impressive." Veronica appears. "A perfect
day to listen to a reading, to be lost in the words. I'm ex-
panding my book list, adding poetry to women's fiction."

"A great idea, Mom," I say. "You're the one who encouraged us to be eclectic readers."

"Agreed!" Mimi echoes. She's behind my mother,
shadowing her. Their jowls have fallen exactly the same
amount, although Mimi has had two mini lifts, lower face.
My mother is into these odd face exercises, which she's
been doing on and off for years. Aubrey and I imitated her
when we were alone together, sticking out our tongues
and stretching our necks in front of the mirror. Then we
howled at how ludicrous it was. Once, Mom caught us at
it and said, "Laugh now, girls—wait until the day comes
when you discover how little elasticity you have in your
jawline and neck."

"Living in Palm Beach," Aubrey added.

"That's right." Veronica had bobbed her head.

A kind of hope fills the room as more fans swirl around
Maisie Natters. What she writes about—women trapped
in the patriarchy until they escape—isn't very Palm Beach
by any means. That women seem moved by her words, her

story. "I am childless and motherful," she read at the end of her presentation.

"Veronica." Adienne Lamsed, who celebrated her ninetieth birthday last week, puts her tissue-thin fingers on my mother's wrist. "You know we admire your daughter when we show up for a transgender poet. I mean, isn't that why we came today? Plus that suffragette section on display!"

"The talent, that's why we are here," says Priscilla, who shows up for everything. She looks up from her iPhone. "Sorry, posting on Instagram. I'm writing, 'We are hooked on poetry and talent.' Hashtagging the Literary Society."

"We support Elodie," Aubrey says. My sister has come in from nowhere. The rain must have gotten heavier, as her hair is wet and flattened to her head. Laurie notices and comes quickly toward us, carrying a clean dish towel from the Literary Society's kitchen. When she hands it to Aubrey, my sister pats at her hair and neck as if she's auditioning for a shampoo ad.

"Laurie, thank you," she says. "The rain, it's loathsome." She smiles in every direction. Her drenched dress is transparent; she is ravishing. Why is she this late?

"You missed it!" Priscilla says. "The crowd stopped whispering, talking through, you know, someone's lecture. They were wowed. And she's trans. A trans poet and memoirist."

"We love Maisie Natters," Faith Harrison says on her way out, back to Vintage Tales. Once guests leave the Society, they'll go to her shop in this weather.

Patsy Deller nods. "Especially when she read about women sleepwalking through life. We're pumped up—it's those lines about the patriarchy."

No one says anything, then Aubrey laughs. "That's right. Exactly."

She looks at me and we exchange forgiveness. She to me for being late and missing the actual program, and I to her for asking her to show up.

Escape is in the air when Aubrey and I leave earlier than I thought possible. An elegant brininess settles over the entire island after the rain.

"I bet there's a rainbow," Aubrey says when she sits down in the passenger seat of my Mercedes. I toss books and files to the backseat. "Sorry, I've just got so much going on at the Society, my car is a slum, or an extension of—"

"Look, there it is! A rainbow over the Intracoastal."

We both look to the west. "It's dreamy," I say.

"Promising." She kicks off her Jack Rogers wedges. They are waterlogged and leak a little on the mat. I remind myself I'm not James and do not make a fuss.

"Where's your car?" I ask.

"I went to Mom's first, left it there. I came today because we should get the pregnancy test results by this afternoon," Aubrey says.

I keep driving. "You mean from Dr. Noel? Did you stop there?"

"I did." My sister opens the windows and starts Sirius radio surfing. Why isn't she saying more? I should ask her the obvious—if she took a pregnancy test at Dr. Noel's, or whether she did a home kit first.

I peer at her. "You might have gained a pound or two.

I thought with your dripping-wet dress that you looked, I don't know, chesty."

"Chesty? Ha! Not likely."

"But do you know anything?" I ask.

She stops at Bruce Springsteen blaring "Thunder Road." A live concert performance with background noise. The song winds down and Aubrey starts fiddling and finds "We Gotta Get Out of This Place," by the Animals.

"Elodie, remember when Mom used to play this for us? Listen, the lyrics are almost ahead of the tune. I was in third grade, wasn't I?"

"Aubrey, why did you drive up?" I pull up to the gate and push the code.

"We're waiting to find out *the news*. I wanted to be with you."

The news. I don't say this has been on my mind nonstop, it is only the first go-round and we don't want to be too optimistic. I don't warn her what a tough way it is to live, waiting every month.

"Oh, Aubrey, thank you. You are so good to have driven up for this!"

The private gate swings open more slowly than usual. It could be the rain. The house that we grew up in looks tired and overused today.

"We should know soon," Aubrey says.

My sister and I make our way into the garage.

CHAPTER 15

ELODIE

Through the living room windows, we stare at the rain slashing the Intracoastal. The ocean is almost invisible to the right, the fog is so low. Aubrey turns on the wall sconces; the room is illuminated in a gold tone. Our parents, such fans of classic turn-of-the-century Palm Beach architecture, have used Jasmine Reese as their decorator. How our mother studied every lamp and side table, every shadow and pool of light. If I had on my blue-light computer glasses, the room would be deeper, a lime gold perhaps.

"Creepy, isn't it?" my sister says. "It's not even five o'clock, and look at the colors."

"I know," I say. "The weather is dampening everything, muting everything."

The rain pounds away at the house and gardens; the

bougainvillea are drenched, soggy. In Palm Beach this heavy a rain is an insult. No one ever quite adjusts.

"It's really odd to be here without anyone," Aubrey says. "Where's Christina?"

"I don't know, probably at Publix, food shopping."

"Why don't they use Fresh Direct?" Aubrey asks.

"Why? Because they want to touch the fruit, push at the honeydew. Have you just met our parents?"

Aubrey's iPhone does that quasi-silent ring; she holds it up. "I think it's Dr. Noel's office." She pulls the iPhone toward her face, squints, holds it out toward me. "The area code—Lauderdale?"

"You're right. It's her office." I'm taking shallow breaths, too shallow.

"This is Aubrey." She puts it on speaker.

"Ms. Cutler?" A woman's voice, without emotion, flat.

"This is she."

"This is Dr. Noel's office. Dr. Noel wanted you to know that the test is positive and you're pregnant."

The entire interior becomes flecked—a precursor to fainting. I watch my sister; she is exactly the same.

"Ms. Cutler? Did you hear me?"

"I did, I did hear you," Aubrey says. We look at each other.

"Please call Dr. Noel in the morning to discuss particulars, how to proceed. Cautionary steps. Next we will call your sister, Elodie Cutler."

"No, no need to call my sister. I will tell her. I'm with her right now. I will!"

She clicks off before the faceless voice with our news insists she must call me.

"It is strange, unexpectedly fast. Elodie. Oh my God,

I'm pregnant!" She sits down on the couch and I sit beside her.

"I know, it's what we've been waiting for. This is it." I look at my sister, my little sister, pulling through for me. I quake, then quickly slink out of it.

Simon's grandfather clock ticks sonorously. We listen as we did when my sister was in grade school and loved the sound.

After a full minute, Aubrey starts laughing. "Our first try! This is insane!"

"Aubrey! Aubrey!" I am relieved, ecstatic. Not only that this part of the process is over so quickly, but that it is Aubrey handing her body over to grow a baby. Plus, we're skipping over a few appointments with Dr. Noel—no more need for statistics, calendar days, ovulation pointers. I am now a bystander, while Aubrey alone has entered the ring.

We come close, hold hands. "Oh my God!" Aubrey shouts.

"I should tell James. Mom and Dad? Mimi? I mean, the *first* insemination. It's hard to believe." I might cry.

Aubrey, pregnant with our baby.

"Yeah, sure. I mean, whatever you want, Elodie." Aubrey strokes her stomach, like celebrities in the magazines once they announce their pregnancy. Something treasured, altered.

We are bewildered, stupefied.

"I know, I know what you must be thinking," I say.

"You do? I'm not sure what I'm thinking," Aubrey says.

"About how much I need you for this and how I've always acted like the perfectionist daughter, the striver, the one who accomplishes whatever she sets out to do," I say.

"Am I that wayward?" Aubrey's voice is sad. The gold light hits her face from the bay window.

"You came through, totally."

We sit together; the rain keeps hitting the windows, the house. "Can I get you a glass of water?" I ask.

"No, no thanks. I'm fine." She comes closer. "I know, let's hold on to our news for right this minute."

We hug dizzily.

"But what about when they walk through the door? Maybe with Mimi. She and Mom will leave the Society together. Mimi always seems to drop by. Dad's bridge will wrap up by around . . ." I'm getting nervous.

"Okay, then we'll tell them." Aubrey sounds calm although we both know this is real news, big news for our family.

"So." Aubrey moves toward the credenza. Photos of our family are lined up as if we are royalty. Baby pictures of each of us that I look at as I've never looked at them before. Then the showpiece—I'm eleven years old, holding my little sister. We are both dressed in white, in this very living room. "Let's do the names thing everybody does, at least among my friends after finding out there's going to be a baby. Let's do names that we like."

She's looking to me to share this, to assure her she's not alone, pregnant with someone else's baby.

"Well, James and I have talked about names every time I've conceived. Up until the point that I would miscarry," I say.

"Oh, okay, maybe not, let's nix that idea," Aubrey says. "Skip it."

Déjà vu. The same apprehension as when I was pregnant

before, yet again. The sense that you can't get ahead of anything, can't make assumptions. I breathe in deeply from my stomach, like every yoga teacher has stressed.

"No, I *can* do it," I say. "Some names I love and flirt with. Like I love Charlotte, but it's too popular. Lily, too Edith Wharton. The same goes for Isabella, India, Mariel, Emmaline, Hanna, Grace."

"India is cool, definitely," Aubrey says. "How about Grace? Wasn't she the prettiest girl but impoverished in that Trollope novel?"

I take another deep gut breath. *"The Last Chronicle of Barset.* Yes, true."

"I like the name," Aubrey says.

I need to look at other names, ones I have never pondered. "What about boys' names?" I say.

We start laughing. "Don't we want a girl?" Aubrey asks.

"Yeah, but in case, you know, the fifty-fifty chance . . . Okay," I say, "it could be Samuel or Baxter, Jackson. He could be called Jax."

"Baxter makes me think of a badger." Aubrey laughs, stops. "Oh my God, what about telling Tyler? I mean, I didn't expect this to be so fast."

"You'll tell him," I say. "I'll tell James. I'll call him."

"Tyler might be traveling some in the next few weeks. To L.A., where there is this one band that he's seeking out."

"You could stay in Palm Beach when he's gone. You can be with us—we have room. Later there'll be tons of space in our new house. You could practically—"

"I doubt I would," she says.

"Well, maybe once in a while, now, since things are changing," I keep at it.

"I like where I am, how I am," Aubrey says.

"I meant in season. While Veronica and Simon are around. James and I won't go anywhere this summer if we're having the baby. Your due date would be mid-September—right? The house will be finished. But before that, James will be here overseeing every move, the foreman, the crew."

While Aubrey will resist the lure of the Cutler clan, I'll want her around. I'll be panicked; I know this deep within me. I'd rather chase a poet laureate and beg her to come to the Literary Society than be responsible for an infant, a helpless infant. As soon as I realize this, I propel the idea out of my head. I should be mature, ready.

"That's not happening." Aubrey speaks in that steely tone she gets when she is about to push back.

"Well, first I ought to reach James. Then call Dr. Noel's office."

I lift my iPhone from the corner of the mosaic-tiled coffee table and go into the den. I take a step that is neither jaunty nor flat, like I'm about to enter a mysterious space. I walk into the marble foyer and cross to the other side. I close the door before I hit speed dial for my husband. The news is good. It isn't like the other announcements; this one has promise.

"Halllooo?" I hear Veronica trilling, above and beyond my husband's eager voice. "Girls? Are you there?" Veronica almost shouts.

"It's my mother," I whisper into my iPhone.

"You might want to let her know, both your parents."

"I'm mustering the courage. Aubrey and I should have

brought them up to speed. That we'd done a round of in vitro."

"Aubrey ought to tell your father," James says.

"I know, probably." I sigh. "James?"

"I'm shocked, really. Jesus."

"Yeah," I say. "I know. Incredible."

"Have you spoken with Dr. Noel?" he asks, sounding less choked up. "Did she mention a first ultrasound? How does Aubrey look? Now we'll worry, is she rested? Is her diet healthy enough?"

"She's fine. Completely."

"We'll celebrate tonight!" Meaning he'll bring home a bottle of Armand de Brignac Gold Brut that someone gave him at the office. I can drink it with him, because I'm not pregnant. I feel pregnant, in this metaphorical way.

"Elodie? Agreed, tonight?" James is ready to end our conversation. Success leaves us breathless.

"Sure," I say. "I love you."

"I love you back." James says it as he always does. Overused, common.

Then Veronica's voice rises again as James clicks off. "I'm here, in the kitchen. Girls?"

I walk into the kitchen through the main foyer and see Christina shaking out our mother's Burberry folding umbrella. I don't see Veronica, who must be in the mudroom, taking off her rain hat and sensible mid-heel beige suede pumps. Aubrey is in the pantry, drinking a glass of buttermilk.

"Aubrey, that could be old, that buttermilk," I say. "You know how they keep milk that is rancid."

None of us has ever figured out why this is true, although it's been going on since we were kids. Christina lets it happen because my mother is insistent that expired milk and yogurt and cream cheese, too, are fine if a week or two beyond their expiration date.

"Oh, don't worry, I doubt that spoiled dairy could hurt our baby so early on. *Our baby!*" Aubrey is digging around the pantry closet and emerges with a box of Mallomars.

"Look at what I found!" She spies our mother beside Christina at the granite island. "Jesus, I thought it was Elodie, I didn't know you were in the room."

"We just walked in. Dad's in the library." Veronica's eyes light up. "Couldn't you hear me calling you? And to learn your news! My goodness!"

Christina, who has four sons in their twenties, starts bobbing her head. "I don't understand." She tugs on her white shirt, then starts tucking it into her white trousers— my mother's idea of a uniform. She looks at us curiously. "Who is pregnant?"

"Christina, it is amazing news! Not for public consumption yet, but Aubrey is having Elodie's baby—a joint effort. I'll explain the entire plan, but I want to find Mr. Cutler first, to tell him."

"A joint effort?" Christina frowns, runs her hands over her forehead.

Aubrey and I look at each other and instinctively move toward Christina. Aubrey hugs her. "It's fine. Elodie and I decided I could help out and it worked!"

"Christina, have you seen my husband?" Veronica asks.

"I'll find him." She smiles at my sister and me as she backs out, practically into the laundry room. Who can blame her—the tension is mounting. We are left with Veronica.

"I'm telling Tyler tonight," Aubrey says. "Elodie has called James already."

"Tyler? Not until we tell Dad does anyone leave this house. Dad has to hear now."

Our mother rushes past the pantry, past the blown-up photos of each of us as early equestrians—maybe I'm fourteen and Aubrey is six—at Wellington. She doesn't, as usual, stop to admire us or our horse, Daisy Dragon. Named by Aubrey and allowed to stick. Instead, Veronica glances for one second at the wall where a shot of her with Simon at the Arts and Media Ball is framed. Then she edges toward the front entrance to the house.

We hear her voice as it lifts and then descends.

"Simon?" I imagine her tilting her head at that unhealthy angle. She does it whenever she is preoccupied or afraid.

"Let's go," Aubrey says.

We follow our mother. Simon stands by the library, appearing tired. He has his iPhone in one hand and his iPad in the other.

"What is the noise about?" he asks. "The market is down. The Dow is at—"

"We're about to announce our big news!" I say.

"Can you wait until after I make a call?" Simon asks. He holds up his iPhone as if it has special powers. He's stalling, isn't he?

"It cannot wait, Simon, please." Veronica is speaking to him as if he needs to read between the lines, as if we are too covert.

"Big news!" Aubrey says. "Momentous."

Despite that there are enough rooms to sit in for our conversation, we stay in the foyer.

"I'm pregnant, Dad!" Aubrey announces.

I like how happy she sounds, how direct she is. The announcement rattles around the unfurnished space. I watch our father's face and the face our mother takes on for our father's sake.

"Why, it's sensational, isn't it, Simon?"

Her staunch smile, her social smile, preserved for events outside the home. Why would she need it here? Simon doesn't react.

"Simon? The baby, the girls. Aubrey is pregnant. It worked!" Veronica says.

Without looking at us, he steps back.

"Dad?" I say.

"I had no idea things had advanced to this degree. That the insemination had taken place."

"Your father has his deals, his buildings on his mind," Veronica says. "I didn't give him a running commentary."

"What has happened has happened quickly," Simon says.

"Yes, it's miraculous—so easily," Aubrey says.

Simon looks ill, that food poisoning or seasickness kind of ill.

"Of course this baby will love chocolate, play every sport, be a genius, and have great hair, Dad," Aubrey says. "A Cutler through and through."

Our mother claps her hands. "I am delighted! We are delighted! Aren't we, Simon?"

Aubrey links arms with our mother and me. Veronica leads us to where Simon stands and tries to lure him into our finite circle. He hesitates and then his cell rings, an acceptable distraction. He gets to duck out.

CHAPTER 16

ELODIE

"Y ou know," Veronica says three days later as we trace our steps from the master suite to the nursery in the new house, "the timing couldn't be more perfect—and it is simply gorgeous."

She contemplates each room, mesmerized by the progress. I value how emphatic my mother is. She and James are the ones who share the house project. I am the thread, included in texts, emails, and supposed verdicts regarding the paint colors and flooring, hardware, including vintage Sheryl Wagner doorknobs. The antique claw-foot bathtub found on 1stdibs.

"James is a genius," she says. "For the estate section—with historic homes, Sims Wyeth, Mizner, John Volk—yours is slightly courageous. Quietly lavish."

I frown. I recognize how diligent James has been about the balance between young, innovative, and traditional.

"I know. Look at the double-height beamed ceilings and where there's going to be a fountain," I say.

I'm doing my best while again there's that gnawing feeling about the entire project. I'm trying to call to mind why I was game, why I said, Sure, let's build a very big house. *Build?* Wouldn't it be arduous enough to purchase one and do work on it? Then I do remember. I was miscarrying. James wanted a fancy house. I owed him, didn't I? Because I kept losing our babies, it was my fault, I had failed us.

"Wood floors everywhere?" she asks. "Wide planks throughout the house, including the kitchen?"

"Yes, we are, throughout."

My mother isn't a fan. I'm sure she believes it's not Palm Beach enough, there should be limestone as well, at least. For her sphere, the old guard, that is the case. The ones who prefer marble floors, cream-and-white living rooms.

"James is fine with it. Homes have bare wood floors nowadays." I am polite.

That Aubrey is pregnant muddles my brain. Why aren't we talking about the baby? I suppose because the news is new, there is a wide veil of confusion.

Then Veronica says, "Well, we must insist that Aubrey comes next time. Especially for the layout of the nursery. A layette from Baby Mirth on the Avenue and a Caravan crib by Kalon will be lovely." Her head is turned toward the Intracoastal when she speaks.

"Did you say Caravan crib?"

I hear Griselda Derrick, our interior designer, before I spot her. "They're sustainable, made of natural materials." She sounds eager, hopeful. I want to say, *Relax, it's a crib.*

Instead, we bob our heads as a greeting and dive into the decor.

"You'll be pleased, Elodie," she says. "The baby's room is going to be tranquil, delicate."

I try to imagine Griselda's life, single, living in Palm Beach Gardens and proud of it. Her home, known for the right taste and wrong location by Palm Beachers, has been photographed for its aesthetic in the *Daily Sheet*. She's sought after and certain, and when she shows me a swatch for my home office, for the master bedroom, the dining room, it isn't about what I like. It's how she expects the house to be. Although James and I have hired Griselda, it is my mother who appreciates her the most.

"She's innovative," Mom likes to say. Mimi seems incredibly gushy over her, too, although she has described her as too pretty to hire, too young-looking. Griselda always carries around fabric swatches, color themes, and samples of hardware. Today she's superpeppy because my mother is with me. When we are alone together, Griselda and I, it's rougher going.

"Mrs. Cutler, Elodie! I raced through a few things to find you, and voilà!" She pushes her aviator sunglasses over her crisp blondish brown chin-length hair as if they're a headband. She is wearing bronzer on her face and her arms and legs and has missed a patch of skin on her neck.

"Today I thought we'd concentrate on the kitchen." Griselda takes her melon-colored leather-bound notebook out and frowns at something.

"Lovely. The nursery, too, if not today, next." Veronica smiles almost slyly. "Soon."

"Really? I didn't know that was the sequence. I didn't prepare any swatches for today," Griselda says.

"The kitchen, then. A very large kitchen," Veronica says.

A wind kicks up from the east, as it has almost every afternoon for the past few months. Because Palm Beach is a tropical climate, it begins to rain in little pellets. Veronica is tugging her portable straw hat farther down to cover her hair. She opens a hunter-green umbrella that has *Palm Beach Literary Society* in white letters across the bottom. She attempts to cover us both while rain splats against it.

"It will be installed next week." Griselda opens the same umbrella. Did I give it to her?

"A Viking oven," she says. "The eight-burner Wolf range is the most exciting part."

I can't stand it. I look at my cell. "Excuse me, I have to check in . . . work-related." I move away, toward what will be the eat-in area of the kitchen.

"Shall we continue?" Mom asks Griselda.

"We ought to wait for Elodie. I have questions about the island in the kitchen. I'm imagining that for guests or a charity event, the flow would be—" Griselda says.

"Oh, don't wait for me on that." I raise my voice to let them know. "My mom can weigh in."

"Elodie," Mom says, "you don't mean that! We'll wait."

Although I hope never to boil water again, I hang up quickly.

"Griselda, I don't mean to be rude, but I don't want to cook. Not anything."

It's the first time I've seen Griselda perplexed. "Your kitchen! Most of my clients would be thrilled! You have top-of-the-line—"

"Of course she does. It is Aubrey who loves to cook. When she comes over—"

"When she has the time," I say. "And remember, she is a vegetarian."

"Of course I remember." Veronica is pinching my elbow.

A second after that, Griselda's cell rings to Stevie Nicks's "After the Glitter Fades." Bending toward her shoulder, she says in an inviting voice, "This is she."

Veronica puts her mouth to my ear. "Things are moving along, Elodie. The house is going to be luminous, a curated house. Aubrey is pregnant. You will enjoy every part of your new life."

I move a few steps away. They're right: Most women would be elated, not squelched.

"Mrs. Cutler, Elodie?" Griselda comes closer. "That was my latest wallpaper contact—in London. By tomorrow we'll have samples for the bedrooms and for the nursery suite. They can be delivered to the Literary Society for Elodie to see soonest. Once chosen, we'll do a special order." Griselda cheerily glances at her watch. "If only I didn't have to dash. I was only dropping by."

"We have to leave, too," I say. "Don't we have a six-thirty?"

The rain stops as we walk outside. Veronica takes off her hat and rolls it up neatly. If ever I have felt a rush when I arrive and a pang when I leave, there is none of that now. I am devoid of the sensation that inanimate things seem alive. This house does that for James. Veronica is definitely identifying with the very walls as they are constructed. She places her hands on my forearm and Griselda's forearm and beams. I haven't seen my mother distracted for a while.

"It's glorious, Elodie, Griselda, totally glorious," Veronica says.

A few gulls caw overhead. Griselda is half running, half

pirouetting to what will be a paved circular driveway in several weeks. When she is halfway down the path, she turns and shouts, "Oh, Elodie! I meant to congratulate you! What amazing news. We'll do the nursery next—that's our timetable!"

Is Griselda speaking to me when she calls it amazing? Of course she is. But ever since "the news," I have this sensation that I'm hearing words through some barrier. Or it doesn't hit me right—what is being said. Or it's like a staccato hammering. I remember those jackhammers on the streets of New York City when James and I lived there. You'd be walking along, talking, without hearing or being heard. Maybe a salient point was made, maybe it wasn't. Either way, you couldn't hear, so you couldn't react.

I do the familiar smile and wave, code for so many versions of reality. "Sure, all good." I smile wider.

After she slides into the front seat of her tidy white SUV and pulls out, Veronica and I stand beside each other, facing the A1A. Cars are speeding by; there is a hum that I've never heard before, like it's the turnpike, not an ocean road.

It could be the twilight that makes Veronica too fatigued, how the hour belongs to neither of us. Both of us should climb into our cars and head to our next destination.

"Elodie," my mother says, "could I see some enthusiasm, please?"

CHAPTER 17

ELODIE

At dusk the Turquoise Go super-yacht is about to sweep along the Intracoastal. We, the guests, are at the Grotons' first party on board their new purchase. The celebration of their son Seth's engagement to Tabatha Langley is festive; people are jubilant. Both families are longtime Palm Beachers, and "yacht people." Still, everyone is astounded by this current brand of boat—an aqua hull that blends with the water, the five decks, eighteen cabins. The glossiest Palm Beachers would admit that the Grotons' treasure is the sleekest of boats. No one bothers with views to the west when they walk on board. What is a sunset compared to exploring a forty-million-dollar, 253-foot yacht?

"Otherworldly," I say to James, who is dumbstruck.

He is too busy scouting out the forward deck to answer.

Around us, Pamela Groton is flitting, hailing guests like it's an assembly line as we pile onto her mega-yacht. Although I've not read Emily Post lately, I believe the etiquette is flipped tonight, since the Grotons are hosting, not the Langleys. Aren't the parents of the bride expected to host the engagement party? Except perhaps when the groom is in the stratosphere in terms of net worth. I doubt that any of the two hundred guests care who pays. Pale Martini, a local party band that both Aubrey and Tyler know, is starting up a few feet to our right. The lead singer announces he's about to pay homage to Bon Jovi.

James, a step behind me, says, "We'll dance." We share a smile, mostly because it's an easy night. It isn't about the Literary Society or a private party hosted by a client of James's. We are mere guests. Thanks to my sister, the millstone of being barren is lifted. As a couple, we are almost weightless, for the first time in years.

"I'd love that." I mean what I say.

James leads us toward the dance floor. The Bon Jovi sound is amplified; couples in their twenties and early thirties twist themselves to "It's My Life." We bend, buckling slightly to a slow dance when the singer puts his mouth close to the mike for "Bed of Roses." Since it is an engagement that is envied and perfected—a family party—I spot my parents to my left. My father is stuffing his face with mini crab cakes while shaking hands with people. My mother, at her best in her Lela Rose dress and carrying a vintage Gucci clutch, is taking inventory.

Across the way, Aubrey and Tyler are affixed to each other. Mrs. A. seems focused on my sister and Tyler drifting along the margin of the dance floor. Aubrey is more incandescent, more lustrous than ever, her hair tumbling out of a pile-high hairdo, her legs longer than anyone else's. Yet it is Aubrey's body profile that has gotten Mrs. A.'s attention. My sister has a bump and her breasts are inflated. I know, although she's hiding it well, that she's pregnancy seasick. The steady waves of the Intracoastal tonight are revolting to her—I sense it. Only she and Tyler are dancing cheek-to-cheek; he, in fact, is holding my sister up.

What a relief that I'm not the one carrying a baby—this thought seeps into my consciousness. Aubrey, meanwhile, conveys little. If she craves bananas or gags on once-adored dishes—ravioli with butternut squash, crème brûlée—or has a baffling rash on her upper back, she isn't confiding anything. We don't sit around laughing at how her inner thighs already appear padded or she craves sleep by eight P.M. When I mentioned her reticence to James yesterday, he shrugged husband-style. "We have a plan in place, don't we?" he asked. Yet when I look in the mirror, it is a divided reflection—what I have endured, what my sister is sacrificing.

Conversations rise, voices mix, those that are overly confident with those that are muffled. *PT—a frozen shoulder . . . skiing Deer Valley . . . acupuncture for six-year-olds . . . twins everywhere . . . purchased two tables . . . in the* Daily Sheet *. . . member guest tournament, . . . the bridal registry.* I lead James past the cluster, only to meet the Veronica and Simon Show joined by Mimi. They have moved themselves to the sofas and lounge chairs of the upper deck.

Veronica is speaking in her serrated-knife voice. "I'm

not sure how this happened. When I see the husbands or husbands-to-be that Tabatha and her sisters Linnie and Rainey have found . . ."

Simon, taking in the night, speaks up. "Aubrey seems pleased to be with her old cronies tonight."

"Do you believe that, Simon? Aubrey *grew up* with both Tabatha and Seth. The yacht is *swarming* with her old friends," Veronica says. "Were she that smitten with the group, she wouldn't be here with Tyler."

"Tyler is an entrepreneur. We just aren't familiar with his business, what the music business is about." I look to my father when I say this. He nods slightly.

"I'm referring to a more known, more conventional form of happiness," Veronica says.

"A merger in a marriage!" Mimi adds. "That's a goal."

Beside me, James stiffens, holds his head higher. Although he is cautious in engaging in these sorts of conversations with my parents and his mother, Aubrey is dear to him.

"Mom, please," he says.

"Aubrey has chosen another path." I, like my father, defend her.

"I know what Elodie means. Aubrey isn't a Palm Beach girl who has angled for tonight," James adds.

"That's enough," Simon says.

Aubrey has her back to us, her arms only half raised to Bono's "All I Want Is You." It is Tyler who faces us without any idea what the topic of conversation is. Gliding around the dance floor, neither has had a drink. How protective he is of her, that she doesn't slip and fall, that no one accidentally crushes too close.

As I observe her, James slips off to the aft bar, returning with two highball glasses. I practically swig it. A tray of cheese puffs is passed to my left and I grab one while James is being offered mini beef Wellingtons from another tray. As he lifts two, one in each hand, the server almost twirls away from him. I turn slightly, take my cocktail napkin with *Tabatha and Seth* printed in a bright blue, and spit out the mushroom that was not named by the server as part of the cheese puff.

"Shall we do a tour?" Simon holds up his glass of Grey Goose as if it were a hurricane lantern. "Let's take the elevator."

One floor below, guests clamor for the sushi bar and raw bar. My mother offers her unreadable face. If she is still thinking about Aubrey and what's next, she doesn't concede this. Instead, she moves toward her friends from the Mothers and Children board, where she is most welcome. My mother-in-law finds the widows and divorcées, snowbirds from New York and Greenwich, and heads in their direction. Their voices are raspy or too high, rising over the slap of the waves, clearer because of it. *Dalton, no, then Harvard . . . acupuncture, that was what saved the day . . . a mini lift, neck and jawline . . . No, no, thermage if you are under sixty-five . . . not real estate, a hedge fund . . . the best* Traviata *since 2004 . . . at the Norton until the end of February . . . one red Birkin left . . . a third granddaughter . . . a newish husband . . . only a Labradoodle . . . the Miami City Ballet.*

"I'm going to the bathroom." I hand James my half-empty glass.

A crew member leads me to one of the two VIP state-rooms, since the other bathrooms are in use. As we take the central staircase up, icicles fall over us in a trickling effect. At the top of the stairs, she is texted and holds up her hand, then pauses and walks off to the side. I ought to tell her I've had too much of the Boozy Tea and can't wait much longer. I find my own way.

I expect the stateroom to be empty and for the crew member to be right behind me. Instead, I'm alone. I hear crying; someone is sobbing and another person is consoling her. Although the lights are low, there is mood lighting on the walls. The decor is white and turquoise, including the bedding and chairs. On the floor by the coffee table are my sister and Tabatha, the bride-to-be. Aubrey has her arms around her.

"Elodie! What are you doing?" Aubrey asks.

"Peeing," I say. "I came with someone who works on the boat. She's right outside the door."

When Tabatha pulls away from my sister, she is crumpled. Her emerald green tulle dress is decaying. She's gazing at her Harry Winston six-carat oval-cut solitaire, which she showed me at the Literary Society months ago. The ring catches light in the darkened room, sparkling wildly. Jumping up, Tabatha sniffles.

"Your little sister, she and I were remembering the things we did at the Academy when we were sixteen," Tabatha says.

"After, too, when we started college and came home for break." Aubrey stands up. "So much reminiscing, maybe too much, Tabatha."

"Well, you were great friends, egging each other on," I say.

When they stand together, I realize my sister has been away from Palm Beach for ages, enough time to no longer be a threat, no more a fish in the bowl.

"Definitely, besties." Tabatha snorts in a small wad of mucus. "I'd better get back to the party."

"Me, too." Aubrey doesn't look me in the eye. "Tyler is probably searching the ship for me."

"The yacht," I say. "Probably."

Tabatha slides beyond me easily, then smooths her dress around her hips.

"Can you wait a minute?" I ask my sister.

She shakes her head. "I don't think so. I'd better follow her."

The sun sets a fiery orange more to the west than usual for late January. The entire guest list congregates by the starboard bow on the second deck. Rory and Max Langley stand behind their daughter, while Pamela and Robert Groton are behind their son. Although there isn't a woman on board over fifty who hasn't had her face improved or a total redo, both Rory and Pamela are newly minted. They are chiseled—maybe that is why neither woman is smiling. The affianced are far from each other and I realize I've not seen them together the entire night—not on the dance floor, not to mingle, not to party.

Robert Groton steps forward. "Everyone, welcome. Welcome to the Turquoise Go. My wife, Pamela, and I are delighted to host you." He clears his throat. "Each of you has been invited to celebrate the engagement of Tabatha and Seth. Their union, their marriage, their hopes for a future together. What should be a very celebratory occasion."

People begin to shift their weight, cough, glance at one another. They wait for Robert Groton's pause to end.

"However, it isn't a celebration. Until the final hour, we believed—that is, Seth, Pamela, and I believed—that Tabatha would sign documents on behalf of herself and Seth, my son."

Gulps from the guests. Mumbling, a muffled epicenter. The men drink up; the ice in their refills clinks. They tap their Gucci loafers against wood flooring. The women are confused, forlorn. Robert Groton waves his hand.

"Please let me go on, let me explain." He sighs. "We, both sets of parents, had high hopes for this couple. Love, privilege. A future. But Tabatha and her lawyers, if not her father, maybe her parents, cannot come to an agreement. They cannot come to terms that work for the marriage to go forward."

Rory Langley steps up. In the starlight her face is refined, incredibly honed. Her hair has that keratin sheen. Tabatha, actually all three daughters, look like her. She smiles regretfully, winces. "My daughter isn't comfortable with what is being asked of her. That's what has occurred. To put it plainly, Tabatha won't sign the prenup."

"There won't be a wedding." Robert Groton obscures Rory. "Tonight is a party on a boat. Nothing more."

Tabatha, without turning away, begins to cry, heaving, bereft, and Seth leaves his parents to console her. His mother stops him. "Seth, no, no. Not now, not again." Seth is constrained by his mother while Tabatha looks out over the guests, weeping.

"Please, please, everyone, have more to eat, to drink," Robert Groton says. "The evening is young."

Two distinct line surges begin. The groom's side beelines for the Grotons, to voice their support, promise to stay longer, lap up the ambience. The bride's side is already scurrying to get off the yacht, only slightly short of a stampede. Veronica and Simon have a dilemma; they are friendly with both sets of parents. After a pause, they congregate with other couples who have the same decision to make.

Aubrey's arm is looped into Tyler's. That's when it registers that she is not well; it's as if someone has made her up with the wrong color foundation. She has a greenish gray tint to her.

"Leave or stay?" James asks.

"Leave. Aubrey looks sick; maybe she's seasick," I say.

"That was a minute ago." James points at Aubrey, who is throwing up into a small bag.

She is discreet, off to the side, while the stampede is at the center of things. As Aubrey keeps vomiting, a soupy sadness descends. A blasted hope that is palpable. Beyond, gossip boomerangs through the air, soon to be carried off the Turquoise Go to the outer reaches of Palm Beach, then across the bridges to West Palm Beach and north to Palm Beach Gardens.

Tyler, behind Aubrey, sturdily steers her our way. They are coming to where James and I line up to leave the yacht. Maybe my sister isn't wrong to be with this man.

CHAPTER 18

AUBREY

"Look." Elodie holds up a Stella McCartney designer sneaker. "I love the colors—great effect." She points to a white Gucci bee-pattern sneaker. "Or?"

"I don't know." I'm trying to imagine my near future in flats or sneaks with billowy dresses to fit my billowy body. Boots on a cooler day. "I have plenty of sneaks."

"I'll get these for you, Aubrey. James and I are in your debt."

"Well, hello there." Tiffany's voice flutters toward us from the escalator, located beneath the fabric butterflies that hang from the ceiling. As a child, I was petrified of this swarm of butterflies and would beg my mother not to go to Neiman's. Saks, I told her, was better.

Tiffany jumps off and rushes toward the shoe department. "Why are you two shopping at this hour?"

"I might ask you the same," I say as we air-kiss. Her face is puffy; she looks heavier than when I last saw her, at her wedding.

"I'm buying Aubrey a present." Sweet, Elodie does sweet. Probably because Tiffany's family, including her grandparents, are patrons at the Literary Society.

Tiffany grabs the sample Burberry sneaker. "I'm avoiding brunch at Longreens or the Harbor Club and shopping instead. Do you like the leather with the plaid bit in the middle?"

"Nice," I say.

Tiffany moves on to the white Veronica Beard sneaker.

"I don't think I've seen you since right after my honeymoon. I thought I texted some pictures. Thailand was incredible. We booked a boat to the tropical islands from Phuket; we did the Krabi jungle tour. . . ."

Scrolling through her iPhone, Tiffany offers pictures of her with Ethan at every junket. Both of them are in straw hats and carrying backpacks.

"Look at the color of the water. Aqua!" Tiffany says.

"You know, we have some terrific books in the travel section of the Society on trips to—"

"Elodie, Tiffany has just *returned* from Thailand," I say.

"No, that's fine," Tiffany says. "Ethan and I want to do another adventure soon. We will come in and look around the travel stacks. Sometimes it's better with a real book."

I feel like Tiffany is watching how I move. I hold my sweatshirt to my middle, loosely.

"Hey, how is your guy, Aubrey, the cute one with the twang?"

"Tyler," Elodie says.

"Wasn't he booking bands?" Tiffany asks.

"He's good. He's still doing it," I say. A fair question, because in sixth grade Tiffany and I shared plans for our futures, a canvas of life as it should be. I resist the urge to ask her if the second husband is the charm.

"Aubrey?" My sister holds up a Tretorn espadrille. "These are no big deal, very cute, useful."

"I'm fine, I can wear my Nike Airs, my Lululemon tie sneakers."

"For what? What are they for?" Tiffany asks. "Are you and that cute guy Tyler traveling somewhere?"

"Not really, not much past South Beach," I say.

"We're improving Aubrey's collection," Elodie says. "Sneakers are a rage."

Already Tiffany is preoccupied with the array of sneakers, stilettos, platforms, turning over a few to check the price. She is a far cry from the night of her wedding; her ponytail is straggly and she has dark roots. She holds up a Gianvito Rossi ankle-strap pump and a Balenciaga color-block sneaker.

"Life is changing—I'll do low heels, but I can't resist the high ones." Tiffany starts taking pictures of the sneaker selection. "Jessica's meeting me—Sunday was the only day she could manage. Her work, her schedule—I'm more flexible. Anyway, she'll steer me clear of any shoe that isn't sturdy."

Sturdy. Elodie and I know before we are told; of course we know. Elodie nods, while I watch Jessica come off the escalator, beneath the butterflies. Tiffany starts beckoning her.

"Jessica! There you are!"

Jessica is waving her hand with her solitaire as if we are still greeting one another at Tiffany's wedding. She does an air-kiss, my left cheek first, then my right. Next she does the same for Tiffany, then Elodie, whom she hardly knows. The overhead lights are too much. I need water. Ice-cold, refreshing filtered water.

"Aubrey with her big sister!"

"To shop—we're on a spree." Elodie saves the day. "But we've got to move on, head down the Avenue."

"Jessica, tell them you're going to steer me clear of shoes and clothes that won't work while I'm *pregnant!*" Tiffany horse-whispers across the shoe department.

Her voice practically crashes into the wall on the other side of the building and bounces back to us. I look away from my sister. How many times has she had to hear this from a friend over the past years?

"What news!" I do as I've been taught: I'm brief, polite enough, excited enough.

"Yup, impregnated on the riverboat," Jessica knows.

"A happy accident. We wanted to have some fun alone together first. Not that I care. I mean, being a newlywed, it's not that great," Tiffany says.

"On to what's next on the marriage checklist," Jessica insists.

They've had the conversation before.

"Congratulations," Elodie says with that edge that means we are exiting. To be authentic, she pulls out her iPhone. "The time, it's slipping away. Do we want to look at dresses—decide on sneakers later?"

"That's best," I say. Holding my sweatshirt close to me, I shrug. Meaning I must follow Elodie. I always have.

Elodie and I don't speak until we cross the Avenue and are in a large dressing room at Saks. In the double mirrors, we are counterparts. I sit on the chair facing her. We fit as if we are a Chinese box or a puzzle, echoing each other's shapes. Except that already my body is unlike me, as if a stranger has invaded the space and is churning up to take charge. Although I dread it, I also am inexplicably placid, marveling at the baby inside.

I kick the tired-looking pumps on the ground to the side, the pair provided by the store that everyone wears when they try on dresses.

"Not sure anything in this pile will work," Elodie says. Obviously she's a quasi-pro. "I grabbed a few things."

"They might be too tight. You see how I'm getting. Worse, how some days feel."

"I know this isn't logical, but I feel how you feel. Like I'm a sympathetic weight gainer. I'm exhausted, too—the baby is always *there*," Elodie says.

My sister linked with me—as best she can be.

"Oh, that's so supportive. Don't worry, it's a pipe-dream pregnancy," I say.

Elodie smiles. "Try these, what I brought. Nanette Lepore, Marni, a Milly dress."

I pick up the first boxy top that she's collected. "Can you believe that Tiffany is having a baby, too? Maybe she and I can go to natural-childbirth classes together."

My sister recoils. "Maybe not such a great idea."

"I mean after the news is out," I say. "She is my friend."

"That's the sticky part. I mean, why rub in how your pregnancy is unconventional. By any standard, that's the case. In a town with your childhood friend, who is pregnant naturally, it feels odd. Too odd."

How uneasy Elodie is. I resist telling her we need to be overt, sanguine, our usual selves.

"You could come, be with me for whatever is ahead. And you'll be at the delivery."

"We'll figure it out. Dr. Noel can recommend some childbirth classes in South Beach, too." Elodie is more composed now. She starts handing over flower-print dresses and tops. "Want to start trying these on?"

In a millisecond, I pull on a navy romper and admire how it looks. I'm sleek except for where my abdomen is already stretched. I'm supposed to say *womb,* think *womb.* I can't do that, not today. My sister watches, eyeing my smooth "bump."

"I'm glad we're alone, the two of us," I say.

Both our iPhones ding. In the reflection, I laugh. "Not that alone; Mom is obviously looking for us."

A second ding. "Let see what she wants, because I'll either go straight to South Beach and Tyler can swing around to pick me up or I'll go later in an Uber." I kneel down and take my phone out of my bag. Elodie is already reading hers. "Is it from Mom?"

"She said to read her email. She's sending it now. With a list of maternity shops in West Palm."

"Why? We're not doing that, are we?" I say. "I'm starving. Let's go to Ta-boo and get lunch."

"Yes! You must eat. Chicken Milenese, key lime pie," Elodie says. "Let's decide if Veronica has any ideas worth . . ."

I scroll through my emails. "Nothing yet from Mom."

My sister is reading. "Wait, one came in for both of us, this second. I'm reading it. Skip Mom's list, you'll do better right where we are."

I read my screen. "Did you also get an email from 23andMe?"

Elodie does that brainy, nerdy scowl. "Yes, I have one, too. The results from the DNA testing, they're in."

"I'm really hungry." I put the iPhone down. I take a small can of Pringles potato chips out of my bag, eat a few, handing a few to Elodie.

Elodie ignores me. "Maybe you should check yours."

I open my water bottle, drink in gulps.

"Aubrey, please read it." Elodie's mouth is thin, like our mother's mouth gets when someone is in grave danger or has died. When she cannot deliver the "headline."

"Okay."

The fabric on the beige love seat scratches my thighs. Elodie is on the chair across, fixated on her screen. I'm feeling queasy, almost in an air sickness mode. More that I'm in dread of what she'll find.

"Elodie, if it's a surprise, I don't want to look."

"The DNA, the report," Elodie says.

"So do we carry a bad gene? What is it?"

I suck in what air is around us. She's holding her phone like a weapon she can't put down.

"That isn't it. Not from my test," she says.

"What do you mean, your test? Wouldn't our tests be similar for being carriers?" I ask. My sister isn't looking at me. She's hunched over, reading or rereading her screen.

"Elodie?"

"The report is that we aren't full sisters. We're only half sisters."

I do a fake Palm Beach laugh, like the women in Elodie's library circle do when they don't agree on the writer's tone or style.

"Stop," I say. "Stop."

"Here, give me your iPhone. Go into your emails first, then log in to your 23andMe account."

The fluorescent lights are too bright. I hold my phone closer to my face, tap the screen, then pass it to her.

She starts reading my results. "Yes. Exactly. *Half sibs, half sisters.* Mom is our mother, but Dad, he's . . ." Elodie is crying. No gulps or heaves, quiet crying.

My sister, who hardly ever emotes, who has always warned me not to get upset too quickly or cry out loud. When I was in tenth grade and weeping over J. P. Ellias, who liked Beezy Blanchard better than he liked me, Elodie practically shook my shoulders. She said to me, "Here's the key. Don't let anyone see how you really feel, don't let anyone know what bothers you."

Elodie keeps at it; now she is heaving, too. "Aubrey, he's your father *or* my father."

"You're scaring me. He's *our* father. The tests, they make mistakes; maybe they get ruined when the kits are shipped or past an expiration date." I am crying, too. "You are so smart, like Dad is."

I have this dread and fear, a sickly sense I won't survive. This must be what it is like when someone falls down the elevator shaft of an eighty-story building. Plummeting, spiraling downward, the shock of it. The same kind of shock I had when I was biking with Elodie two years ago. We stopped short on the Lake Trail and I flew over the handlebars. Tossed through space, I realized how everything veers, how the life you know is about to be snapped up, snatched away. Then I landed and had a broken wrist and had to have stitches on one knee and one elbow. "Lucky you," Mom said while she sat in the ER at South Palm Hospital with me. "You are very fortunate."

"We *know* she's our mother," I say.

Dad has to be our dad, I tell myself. It becomes a mantra, thumping around my skull. I need a wand to wave, some method to stop what's ahead. I stretch my arms over my head for a second, as if I can vanquish this crazy shit.

"Aubrey, listen."

Elodie has stopped crying. She comes to where I'm sitting, her legs against mine—we are that near. "I'm trying to sort it out. What I'm wondering is if you and I could both have fathers who aren't Dad."

Dad belongs to us and we belong to Dad, I want to yell. But this investigation is moving at record speed; I can't be tearing up. My sister isn't going to fuel my wishful thinking; my hope versus what she needs to learn has to clarify. She pats my thigh while scrolling through her iPhone. I cannot stand how businesslike she is.

"Before we were born, then when we were little, Mom was so pretty, so stunning. She had an affair, I bet," I say.

I imagine our mother floating around her own life, sorry for something, pining for more. Hasn't it always been a little like that? Yet it isn't partially amusing or slightly curious anymore, not after today. No longer is it about Mom's style. The questions now are: What has she done? What does she know?

"We have to find out what happened," Elodie says, making her a mind reader.

"I know. I was just thinking that."

More dread and fear circle around me. I can't judge if the windowless dressing room with its lack of daylight is too much for me or if they've temporarily stopped circulating the air. I inhale more deeply, try those breathing exercises everyone raves about. I try to envision myself in a safe place. I hold on to the corner of my sister's skirt. The room hurls, turns gray. I might faint.

I put my head in her lap and she pats my head. Outside the dressing room, there are voices; more women are coming into the area. Yet we can't leave. Where would we go?

The salesperson named Deedee knocks at our door.

"Excuse me, how are you girls doing in there? Is there anything you need?" Her voice is singsong, from another galaxy.

"We'll be out soon," I say.

"Of course," Deedee says. "Let me know what you've chosen and I'd be happy to assist you."

Her footsteps back off.

"If Mom had an affair and got pregnant, was it with me or with you?" I whisper.

Elodie shrugs. "Maybe we're both because of an affair."

"Two affairs? That's madness. Who *is* our mother? With Dad nowhere in this?" I say.

"I don't know. I don't know. . . ." Elodie puts her right hand to her right eye and tugs on her eyelashes.

I touch her elbow. "Don't do that."

"Where is Mom? We should go to her wherever she is," Elodie says.

"She's in a card game at Mar-a-Lago."

"Let's try Dad," Elodie says.

"Dad? I'm not so sure; besides, he's at tennis or golf." I stare at the screen of my iPhone, at the 23andMe site.

"Let's go find him," Elodie says.

"No, not Dad. Mom first," I say. "Before anyone else."

"Why do you want to protect Dad? Why spare him?" Elodie says.

"Because we have to go to Mom first. It seems a better way to find out," I say.

So unlike my sister—how her eyes are darting about. Like a damaged sparrow's. I hold her against me.

"Who cares who our DNA father is? These are *our parents. Dad is our dad,* Elodie," I say.

"I care," Elodie says. "I have to know."

Deedee knocks on the door again. "Excuse me."

"Out in a sec," I say. There's sand in my mouth, dry sand; my stomach hurts.

Elodie straightens up. "Okay, so, maybe we shouldn't do anything until we look around their house, search for papers. There have to be documents in Dad's safe."

"Yeah, I agree," I say. "Can't we ask Mom, though?"

"No, Aubrey," Elodie says. "I doubt that. Look at the conspiracy. Look at how we were never told anything. That means no talking to James or Tyler. Or anyone else."

We stand up and face ourselves; all that is the same isn't quite the same. Only half the same. My sister and I have been halved.

"How do we know that 23andMe is right? That it's not their mistake? We might call them up," I suggest.

"Yes, we could try that," Elodie says. "For me, I'm certain, absolutely certain that what we learned is correct."

How can she be positive? My iPhone bings. Tyler is texting. *You joining me?*

"Tyler is waiting at Mom and Dad's for me to head back to South Beach. We'll go through our work schedule in the car," I say. "This whole week is busy with bands, some new singers."

The idea of Tyler in my childhood bedroom or my parents' den, their kitchen, their house is like being on a film set; nothing is authentic. Whoever it was who ran my hands over his chest this morning and kissed him seems to be missing, maybe gone.

"Let's leave." Elodie is not herself. She is practically sobbing, dissolving.

Hey, Tyler texts.

I stand up taller, text back. *Yes. All right if I stay longer with Elodie?*

The little bubbles show before his text comes in: *Ok. Sure.*

He's such a good sport that I decide to deliver the news in small pieces. In an hour, I'll text that I'm tired and I'll be staying with my parents or my sister. Trading in a night at the clubs for the quiet of Palm Beach, of family. *Family.*

Elodie and I walk to her car. The air is infected with deceit.

CHAPTER 19

AUBREY

Elodie, Aubrey?" Mom's voice does that trill. "What are you doing?"

"Mom, we texted," Elodie says. Both of us stand outside our mother's dressing room.

"Ah yes, texted." Mom opens the door and her closet is a crazy salad, meaning she is late. She does that bird peck with her head, since she can't kiss or be kissed—it would affect her cinnamon-colored lipstick, or an earring might be knocked off a lobe. Our mother is easiest on the Lake Trail before seven A.M.

Mom steps out. We stand in the wide hallway at the top of the stairs. "Dad and I are off to cocktails at the Norrics', then the Bergs' for a dinner party."

"We know," Elodie says. "You told us."

"Plus, we have an app with your calendar," I say.

"Girls, is everything all right?"

I squeeze Elodie's hand and she squeezes back. In a flitting second, we see how the Palm Beach machine at its finest affects her.

"Fine, Mom." Elodie sounds calm.

A dampish air penetrates; the Carrier air-conditioning that our father highly values isn't kicking in. I look up at the Arthur Merton Hazard painting beside the Antoine Blanchard. My entire life, I have known these as our mother's selections. Since today is not a normal drop-by, my mind fills with doubts about snooping in their home, deeper doubts that our father isn't our father. How could he *not* be? Don't my sister and I have our height from him, our acrobatic nature? Our fingers are long like his; the three of us sneeze in the sun, not so our mother. When her hair frizzes in the humidity, Dad's doesn't, nor ours. If he taught us how to think, how to achieve excellence—and Elodie clung to those lessons more than I did—aren't we *his* to teach? What about being disciplined enough to work out every day? He set the example with his fifty push-ups every morning, a habit from his army days.

"Elodie, don't you and James have some sort of plan for tonight?" Mom asks. Her voice for a millisecond is persistent and worn. Her forehead is not moving because she was at Demi Dexter's office ten days ago and is freshly Botoxed.

"Isn't your night a busy one?" Is our mother asking why we are there?

"James is taking Raphael, who works in his office, to the drinks part and I'm meeting them afterward, when Aubrey heads south," Elodie says.

"Ah, I see." Now she is pleased that everyone is set in place.

Elodie's gaze is on me, then on the paintings. I resist reading my iPhone to know the exact hour. We have a tight plan if Mom and Dad would only leave the house. Another pang of doubt—we shouldn't be doing this. Isn't it obvious how our phenotypes (having looked it up yesterday) play out, how our family is divided—and it makes sense? I resemble Mom with our right-brain responses. Mom breezes in and out of events with her social skills on high alert; everyone calls her a delight. Few would say that about Dad, who is more remote, despite his appeal. I, too, like Mom, am on the friendlier, warmer side of the family; we are maniacal about pleasing. Not so Elodie or Dad. Elodie is left-brained, like Dad, a brooder, someone who stews first, speaks after. Neither is cozy but they are dignified. They're both foodies, they know about wine. Why are we second-guessing? Elodie and I have made an egregious mistake in believing the 23andMe tests.

"You girls are entitled to be alone together. I'm hoping the wardrobe for Aubrey is coming along." She beams at us.

"It is," I say. "You look nice, Mom," I add, nervous, sorry.

"That she does." Dad emerges in his Peter Millar button-down shirt and Brooks blazer—he wouldn't dare not look like this. He kisses Mom's head—he's that much taller. Until now, I've always been grateful that Elodie and I got our height from our father. Except thanks to 23andMe, our lifelong belief is smashed to pieces.

"We should go, Veronica," Dad says.

Elodie nods. "Yes, Mom, first in, first out at every party. Isn't that what you taught me?"

"She taught me to be on time," I say.

I glance at Elodie. Were we raised with disparate messages?

"Girls." Dad faces us. "Are we holding you up?"

"We're going through old dresses." I hope to be convincing. "Then I'll go back and Elodie has her whatever."

"Ah, finally emptying a few cupboards, racks of old clothing." Mom smiles. "Clothes can be sorted and added to the pile that Elodie began a few weeks ago. There is a RealReal pile, a Goodwill pile, and a Housing Works pile."

Dad places his right hand on her forearm, as if she needs to be steered toward the door. Maybe he always leads her. Tonight we know they're a posturing couple, secret keepers. Our parents have lied our entire lives. Doesn't that make every step false? I stop myself; that might not be fair.

"Are we nothing but the repository for your remnants, shoes, and purses?" Dad says.

"Only a man would say 'purses,' not 'bags.'" Elodie laughs a half-genuine laugh. Mom winks. I wink back. For a millisecond, it's as it should be, the smiling Cutlers in Palm Beach.

Dad looks at his tank watch, then gives us a longer look. Does he know what we're about to do? That would be impossible. "We're off." He checks his watch again. "Veronica?"

Above them, the crystal chandelier that they bought a few years ago to "brighten things up" flickers. Together they whisk down the curving staircase. Seriously, they're sharing every step. Their togetherness strengthens with time and age. Who are Elodie and I to question that?

"You'll put on the alarm when you leave, Elodie?" Dad asks.

"I will, Dad."

My sister would know about the alarm; she would know that after our mother swerves across the marble entryway, there is a one-minute lag before the heavy front door closes. After another lag of about forty seconds, then the purr of their Bentley as it cruises down El Brillo Way to the A1A.

"His office first," Elodie says. I follow; the low lights are sickening. Again, I'm nauseous.

"Elodie?"

She pauses at the doorknob. "Want me to get crackers, ginger ale? You have a ghoulish hue, I mean to me. Others would say you're fine."

"No, I have saltines. I carry them everywhere. I wanted to ask before we go in, before we raid Dad's office, why we were never allowed inside when we were little."

"When *you* were little," Elodie says. "I was old enough, but Dad was strict and Mom said nothing. She said to leave it alone. She said there was nothing for us in Dad's office."

We both sort of snicker over that. "I hope that's the case," I say.

"During the season, you used to beg Veronica and Simon not to go out. Sometimes I'd cancel plans or ask friends to come over so you weren't left alone with Christina."

"Yeah, I know." I take a saltine from my pocket and start nibbling, knowing no one is allowed to have food in this part of the house. "No bread crumbs, no Hansel and Gretel, I promise."

"Finish it here," Elodie says, "in the hallway."

Standing together in the low lights, I polish off the crackers. I want Elodie to wave a wand, make the 23andMe reports vanish.

"We should never have done the DNA test."

"I don't know about that." Elodie is staring at me. "You know what I remembered when we were outside Mom's dressing room? How you would go in there when you were four, maybe five while she was fussing and rushing to go out."

"I loved it. Remember how she would let me try on her necklaces? There was her David Webb necklace with malachite, and then she'd let me teeter around in her highest heels," I say.

"Oh yes. I was busy getting ready to be with my friends. You used to come into my bathroom in time for the makeup and hair," Elodie says.

"Yeah, well, the night I broke Mom's black-and-white pearl necklace—you know, the one Dad bought her in Paris—I ran into your room for cover."

Elodie frowns. "Dad was pissed. He said Mom should have given you toys, not her jewelry, to play with. No one actually got upset with you. *Ever.*"

"No, no one," I say.

We both laugh. Elodie touches my wrist. "Let's go."

Our father's office is a library within his library. A holy place in this house, including the books that are his taste only. None of Mom's or our collection—Edith Wharton, Margaret Atwood, Kate Atkinson, Kate Chopin—are on these shelves; they are in the library on the first floor. History books, including titles by David McCullough, Candice Millard, and Nathaniel Philbrick, are lined up in alphabetical order. Does every man in Palm Beach do this? Does

Tyler like books enough? Not these books, which some-how increases my queasiness. The other men who have similar books to our father's are Tiffany's and Tabatha's fathers, and James keeps talking about the library he'll have in their new house. Another male library/office that looks like it's been photoshopped. Same color wood, titles, the order of it. But our father is in this room every morn-ing from seven to eleven, mostly. Working on his newest buildings, expecting his managers to report in. Followed by a round of sports, then the Veronica and Simon Show by evening.

"Their life, wow—they don't dare buck a trend," Elodie says.

"I know. Decades of their secret. I feel terrible for them."

"For them?" Elodie's eyes narrow.

"Well, for us, too, yeah, but they *had* to protect their se-cret," I say.

"Or chose to," Elodie says. "Don't you feel that, too, Au-brey?"

Across from the bookcases are framed pictures for the family story. There is the day that my parents brought me home from the hospital where we're haloed together. Elo-die and me at Wellington for my first riding lesson—she's helping me put my helmet on. A surprise birthday brunch for Mom when she turned forty, at the house. Dad stands behind her on the terrace, cumulus clouds and the Intra-coastal behind them. Elodie is holding my hand, her head tilted away from us.

"I know they've lied to us," I say.

"How about to the world?" Elodie touches Dad's impec-cably neat desk. I wonder if he could work as a private de-tective or for the FBI.

"I've never been in here without Dad," I whisper.

"No, I haven't, either. Why would we?"

"It's creepy." I look at the other side of the wood-paneled wall. Framed newspaper articles about Dad's real estate ventures over the years, pictures of him winning a golf tournament at Longreens, another at the Harbor Club. Our parents at every black-tie opening dance, surrounded by their inner circle. More of this manifold fiction has to be on my sister's mind, too; her eyes are still narrow.

"Let's go through the usual papers first." Elodie opens Dad's left desk drawer. She practically tosses out their passports, global entry cards, membership cards for clubs wrapped in a rubber band. "Predictable."

I tap at the hidden door that covers the safe. "I know the combination."

"You do? How come?"

"Dad once gave it to me years ago. I doubt he expected that I'd memorize it," I say.

"Mom doesn't have it," Elodie says. "Dad gives her a watch, a ring, one of those necklaces, earrings when they go out—that's how they do it. She kind of orders it up."

"Completely freakish," I say. "I don't know how we can be searching. I swear I'll have nightmares."

"We know enough to need to know more," Elodie says. "No nightmares, I promise."

She checks her iPhone. "Shit. James is texting about to-night. We're due at a dinner at Justine's. Now he wants me to show up at the Storeys' for drinks first, a business thing. Let's hurry up."

My hands shake. I'm more nauseous. I check my phone, since Tyler has our night planned. First we're going to T-Bar to hear a male vocalist whose music combines country with hip-hop. Although Tyler has told me his name, age, about his current songs, it's a blur. From there we're meant to hear my latest find, Larina L, a singer with a clear voice who does retro/pop. I heard her at Grapevine, a karaoke bar, a week before the in vitro. "You've been excited about her for months," Tyler said last night. Instead of being brave and texting him this minute to suggest he go alone to both gigs, I decide to wait. There is a slight chance that I'll feel better when our spying is over, that I'll rally. I push aside my latest angst, that amplified music could hurt our baby.

My sister comes close enough for us to kiss. She places her arms around my shoulders and pulls me in. "I know, I know."

The lock is stiff and strong when I start turning. A trespasser, an interloper, I move the numbers to the combination. With the third number, a seven—Dad's favorite number—I open the heavy metal door. Jewelry boxes and Redweld folders are neatly arranged. There are so many of both. To the left are Dad's papers, orderly, categorized. There are promissory notes, stacks of cash—at least ten or fifteen thousand dollars' worth that look freshly minted— stocks, bonds, documents for the London condo. Across from these is Mom's jewelry, what she trots out for the opening dances and fund-raisers.

My sister takes our father's reading glasses from a small tray and puts them on.

"We should try to find our birth certificates or see if there is some hidden stash of something. Some reveal." I feel dirty.

Elodie takes a color-coded file and opens it on the desk, scooping a manila envelope out of it. "It's dated 1974."

I panic, my heart thumps. It can't be good for the baby.

"Or maybe we should quit, just not do this. I mean, we're snooping around and—"

"Not yet." Elodie has the envelope in her hand; small welts are starting on her neck. "For now we keep going."

I take the envelope from her as if I'm interested. Once it's in my hands, it feels radioactive. "Let's put it back," I say.

Elodie is surprised. "Why? No, we're not." Then she takes it from me, forcefully.

"Aubrey, we have to. Nothing should take long, I mean, we're in the damn vault."

"I'm sick to my stomach," I tell her. "Seriously sick." Too sick to fight my sister.

The French antique mantel clock ticks annoyingly— possibly it is the loudest of the clocks in the house. Hasn't it ever bothered my father when he is working?

"I'm cold," I say. "Tyler must be waiting to hear from me."

"Only a few more minutes." Elodie rubs my arms, like a mother would—absentmindedly, caring. She's rooting around, moving papers cautiously. "We'll get you more saltines or green tea the minute we're finished."

The librarian in my sister is systematic. She flips through a Redweld from when our father closed on two buildings in Jersey City in 1993. Although I was little, I remember how much the deal mattered, how hard Mom said he worked to make it go through. More real estate files. Elodie puts them back and finds another Redweld with our birth certificates. She opens them like she's wearing plastic gloves. "There's nothing. Both of us were born at New York Hospital, both times Veronica and Simon signed."

"See?" I say. "It's all good. We should go."

Elodie rereads the paperwork and folds them perfectly. "I don't know, I don't buy it."

"Elodie," I say. "We're *their* children. There is no other father in our lives, no matter what you find."

The song "Who'll Stop the Rain" begins over and over in my head. Musicians my father has played for us for decades. Bruce Springsteen, John Fogerty, the Doors. Is Linda Ronstadt like the only female vocalist he played besides Carly Simon or Carole King? Next up is "L.A. Woman"; Jim Morrison's voice fills my brain.

Elodie forges on. "We'll see what else there could be."

Photos of the long dead, including Mom's aunt Clara, and Dad's uncle Charlie, are in the second file.

"Don't you remember Mom going through pictures with you? She did with me." I start sleuthing through the photos, as if we're spies for a happy cause. "Remember Dad's aunt Aurora?"

"She has nothing to do with our search," my sister says. A five-by-seven-inch envelope falls out of a folder marked "Miscellaneous." Elodie takes out a photograph of our parents at a table with three other couples. The men are in army uniforms.

"Okay, so this reads on the back that it's Philadelphia in 1970."

"I have no idea who these people are," Elodie says.

"Could Dad have been on leave? Mom looks pretty dressed up. See how young they are."

Elodie roots through the envelope again and pulls out a card. In her loopy half script, half print, Mom had written "August 18, 1974. Simon, I love you."

She hunts around in the folder and finds a slip of paper, part of a letter, torn off.

"This is from Dad," I say. "His handwriting is always in tighter letters."

"He isn't a natural; even a line or two on a birthday card is awkward."

Elodie hands it to me. "What's this? '. . . as long as we know. By February we'll . . .'"

"Weren't they married in March 1975? There has to be more to Dad's letter."

Elodie's fingers flash along. "Jesus, there's got to be something else."

She hands me the folder; I touch it like it might ignite. I shake it and what's left spills onto the floor, another envelope, a few photographs. First one of our very pregnant mother standing in front of a fireplace, our father scowling at the camera.

I read the back. "You, it's you, Elodie, in 1978. Mom wrote 'We are a family.'"

Elodie takes it from me. "I've never seen it before, have you?"

"I've seen this one." I lift it up. Our mother is very pregnant with me. She stands by the Seventy-ninth Street Boat Basin in New York. Elodie, who is eight, is looking over the water, waiting. Our father is smiling.

"That's the same as the one in Mom's Christofle frame. By her nightstand. Jesus," Elodie says.

"Elodie, please."

"Something was awfully wrong," she says. "Maybe there was an affair, no joke. See Dad in that first picture—he looks furious."

"Two affairs," I say. "Maybe by the second time he was better about it."

Elodie claps her hands together; then I do. We begin to laugh heedlessly.

"Fucking off the charts," she says.

We stop laughing; we are horrified, petrified.

"Maybe she loved your father more than she loved mine. Or Dad hand-picked him?" Elodie is rattled.

"Don't, please, don't." I cover my face. "That's *deviant*."

"Maybe that's why Dad favors you. You know he does. No matter what I achieve, he's delighted with you, Aubrey."

"He doesn't favor me, Elodie, he treats me like the one who needs help. For you, it's effortless—whatever you do. So Dad, really everyone, expects it of you. I sort of float around. I mean until recently I did."

My sister starts to pace while she listens. "It must have something to do with the real father—something that's always there for him. Because Veronica doesn't hand us separate 'parcels'; she never has. She's fair and she *sees* who we are."

"I guess she doesn't have to," I agree. "We're *hers*."

Again the clock ticks, interrupting us. There is this density between us—we've uncovered a principle that both divides us and makes us whole. Elodie is shakier than I am.

"It's okay," I say as she stops to pick up the Boat Basin photograph. She turns it around in her hands.

"Besides, we look similar." I keep talking. "We both have long legs, a good profile. Mom talks about our widow's peaks."

"Not exactly the same. You have voluminous hair," Elodie says. "Your nose isn't quite like mine and you're longer-waisted."

"I didn't say we're twins, I meant we are alike. You have straighter teeth. You score higher on standardized testing," I say.

Elodie is pacing. "There's a lot more to know."

"Aren't you . . . aren't you slightly angry?" I say. "I mean, no one told us, we've been told nothing."

"Slightly? I'm enraged."

I nod. "At least we have each other, we're in it together."

We stand, not believing what we know or what we imagine. There is a vague scent to the room—like a man inhabits it. It is fragrance free and almost fresh.

"Can we close up and, I don't know, take a few days, collect our thoughts?" I ask.

Elodie gathers everything together. Next she reorganizes the files—she could be a professional thief. She closes the safe door, twists the lock.

"We need to talk with Mom," she says.

"We will," I say. "It's just making me so sad. And what have we found? We could wait a little before . . ."

A bile begins in my stomach and burns through my throat until I throw up. It lands on Dad's desk, the wood floor, and Elodie's Gucci mules. I'd like to apologize, I can't stop. I keep on—as if the entire hour is being reenacted through my body as vomit.

"Oh my God! Aubrey!" Elodie holds her hands over her face. "Oh God! Run to the bathroom!"

"Too late." I slow down. "I'm sorry."

I wipe my mouth with my hand. Elodie pushes Dad's tooled-leather wastebasket toward me, but I'm finished. She plows through her bag to come up with a small pack of tissues. As she pats my face and mouth, I'm afraid I might start vomiting again. I still feel wretched. My sister puts her cool hand on the back of my neck.

"All right, we should clean up and get out, if you're okay—if you're finished."

"We need Clorox wipes and I'll wash up."

"The office, we have to fumigate it." Elodie checks the floor. "Before anything else."

After the scrubbing and Lysol spraying, we're both terribly late. While she texts James to blow off the first stop, I'm panicked about how the room will smell tomorrow morning. I start spraying more Lysol, wiping over and over again the spots that were hit the hardest.

"Dad will know," I say.

"We've scrubbed that room five ways. Please, don't worry."

The vomit that left my body has cleared my head. It would be unfortunate if our father were to intuit that someone had invaded his inner sanctum. I swat the thought away.

"Are you well enough to get into an Uber?" Elodie asks. "You could stay with me or with Veronica and Simon."

"I'm okay, and Tyler is waiting." I do feel better than I've felt in days. I can pull it off.

Elodie is near me, a sign that my quick shower and change of clothing has helped.

"Tomorrow. Tomorrow we should try to see Mom," she says.

"Except this South Beach–Palm Beach commute would sicken someone who doesn't have unending morning sickness."

Elodie listens to me for a moment, but she's keyed up. "Aubrey, we have to speak with her."

I nod, praying I'll feel well tomorrow.

"Fuck their lies and pretenses," Elodie says.

I hold my head higher than usual, in need of fresh air. We leave our parents' house together.

CHAPTER 20

ELODIE

Around our parents' pool at seven in the morning, it's the chirp of the whippoorwills that bothers me, a playlist gone wrong—that is, too strident. There isn't much moisture in the air, more like Santa Monica or Bermuda than Palm Beach. Or maybe the climate in those far-off places includes morning dew and dampness. Places we went as a family on spring breaks that seem far off and slippery, too long ago to recall vividly.

My mother and Aubrey are at the steps; Veronica is dipping her toes, delighted that it's the three of us. If she is suspicious, if she knows that we were in Dad's office and Aubrey left a vomit trail, she isn't revealing it. Aubrey's pregnancy—that has to be the topic for her, the baby-to-be. Isn't that enough spectacle for one family?

Veronica points to the round McKinnon and Harris

table, where she's placed raspberries and blueberries, cashews and walnuts.

"Let's sit at the table. I have cold brew." She is proud that she's gotten it right. "Will that be okay for you, Aubrey? I'm not certain about caffeine and I can't honestly remember what the rule was back in my day."

"I'm fine," Aubrey says sweetly.

I wrap my sweatshirt around my waist while Aubrey pulls up her hoodie.

"We could go inside, where it's sheltered. The wind— honestly, the house is better. Dad has to leave soon," Veronica says.

Dad is inside.

"We're happy outdoors." I point to the periwinkle curved outdoor sofa. "We can sit there."

"Exactly," Aubrey agrees. The bougainvillea and ivy rustle in the wind. I look around for a spot where there are no squalls, then plop down on the left side of the half circle.

"Good idea, Elodie." Aubrey smiles brightly. "That'll do."

Our hands brush as we settle in close to each other. My sister tugs on my palm for a second, squeezes, and I squeeze back. Our mother sits in the middle; we flank her. I realize that she's holding something.

"Girls, I bought these yesterday, for both of you." She takes out two copies of *What to Expect When You're Expecting.* "It's the bible."

Aubrey and I do not trade a glance. Veronica, satisfied with her endeavor, hands them over.

"Thank you, Mom." Aubrey's voice is very low.

I put mine on the ground.

"Did you want to meet to talk about if it's a girl or a boy? Do you know yet?" Veronica asks.

Aubrey smiles less brightly. "Well, Mom, we could talk about that."

"Aubrey." I stop her. "Mom, we want to tell you something."

"Yes?" Veronica squints at me. "Is everything good? Is the baby okay?"

"Yes, yes, the baby is fine," Aubrey says.

"Then I'd like to talk about how to present *this* baby." Veronica sighs.

"Present?" Aubrey asks.

"Women, you know, friends and those who are not quite friends, are talking already," Veronica says. "About Aubrey. Is she pregnant? Is she married? Mimi hears it, too."

"Why doesn't anyone come right out and ask?" I say.

"Well, that's not how it's done, Elodie, you know that better than most people. Look at your job, how nuanced every move is. The delicacy of situations."

"There has to be a party line," Aubrey says. "Why can't it be the truth?"

Veronica looks very troubled. "How would that sound? Would I disclose how my daughters and James made a decision?"

"Yes, Mom, that would work," I say. The wind blows my ponytail around my face. I cover my ears for a second. "That's a good idea."

"Fine." Veronica sounds annoyed or disappointed. We have failed her at coming up with a brilliant strategy that would change the circumstances.

I walk to the table and bring back the macadamia nuts, holding out the dish to Veronica and Aubrey. Veronica waves them away, while Aubrey takes a few. I sit back down.

"There is something else." I'm staring at my sister.

More gulls circle, caw at us. "I'm sorry?" Veronica says. "If you girls have time before you head out to work, that's fine with me."

"There is time, Mom." Aubrey's voice sounds foreign, wrapped in bubble wrap.

Aubrey and I lean in toward our mother. She redistributes her weight, coughs a Miss Havisham from *Great Expectations* sort of cough.

"Did I tell you that at Tiffany's shower, right before her wedding, they gave out 23andMe kits?" Aubrey asks.

"23andMe kits? What are those?" Veronica's mouth moves very little when she speaks.

"They're this popular DNA test," Aubrey says.

"Ah, yes, I do know." Mom runs her tongue across her front teeth.

"Well, I took an extra box that day to give Elodie. We decided to take the test."

"The results came in," I say. "That's what we wanted to talk about."

"What Elodie and I have in common as sisters," Aubrey says.

Now Mom rotates her head on her neck like she's been planted on Mars; if she looks out to the west or the east, she'll be saved. I know she feels ambushed and not courageous. "I see," she says.

Aubrey is stiff, lifeless, reminding me of how she was at the Academy before her exams.

"We'll show you, Mom," I say.

Choreographed, actors in a melodrama, we both reach into our bags and hold up our iPhones at the same moment.

"So how it works is that they send you the results, the findings." I scroll to the 23andMe website, log in.

Our mother is pale—paler than she used to be winters in New York City before Aubrey was born. Her sunglasses hide half her face; she's immobile.

"What we learned is that we, Elodie and I, aren't full sisters, we're half sisters." Aubrey pushes her screen toward Veronica. "You can read the percentages. *Half sisters.*"

Veronica is unable to acknowledge Aubrey's iPhone. I hold mine out to her. "Here, on my phone, Mom. It's the same information, same website. I'm on my account."

She won't take it; instead, she swishes her hand at us. "That makes no sense, girls. There must be some kind of mistake. Misinformation."

"There is no mistake." My voice is soft, but I feel like shouting.

"I have no idea what you mean." Veronica smooths her hair back and lifts her shoulders. She doesn't want to hear a morsel of what is about to be said. She speaks as if we're delivering news of someone's poor behavior, a disappointing fund drive for Mothers and Children, a quasi-toxic acquaintance around town. As if all that lurks beneath in Palm Beach is known to her. She is aware that no woman is ever blissfully married, totally satisfied. That women make do, we are acrobats. That's all.

I'd like to bellow, *This is about a paternity lie. Yours and Dad's fucking lie.* Instead, I say in my civilized Literary Society workday voice, "Mom, please, stop. Look at my screen. Or look at Aubrey's."

"Mom." Aubrey comes near; their heads practically tap each other's. Their necks both crane, that scooped-out hollow we all have between our collarbones is obvious. "Please tell us. What is it?"

More of our almost identical profiles, jawlines, cheekbones—how can that be?—the three of us are some variation of Aubrey's desperate plea. Different flavors and methods of sadness. Mostly we have trapped our mother, which doesn't seem possible. It's nightmarish how alone she is with us. Except Aubrey and I *have to know*: our mother matters less than stripping her artifice.

The alligator float that my parents keep in the pool to stave off the birds starts to bob wildly. Veronica hugs her arms around her waist and says nothing. A siren goes off—unusual for Palm Beach at this hour. Perhaps someone is in an ambulance, unexpectedly ill, being rushed to South Palm. The seagulls come in for another round, flying overhead, nose-diving in the wind.

"We have to know," I say.

"Elodie." Aubrey's voice is sharp. "Please."

"No, no, it's okay, Aubrey," Veronica says.

She is very quiet; we tuck our heads to hear her. "No one was going to know, to learn anything, ever." She sucks in the air, smiles like she always does before she makes an announcement. "And yet here we are."

"Know what?" I ask.

Aubrey puts her hand on my wrist, squeezes hard. *Stop,* she mouths without speaking. *Stop, leave her.*

"About this." Veronica's posture, how stiff she has become, is concerning.

"Mom, it's okay." Aubrey puts her head against Mom's shoulder. "You don't have to tell us."

"No, let Mom *tell us,* Aubrey, that's the whole idea," I say.

Aubrey gives me a look—I am the bad sister who drives the bargain, needs the information.

The gulls start dropping shells on the patio, which always annoys our parents, especially Dad. Clumps of cumulus clouds blow overhead and off to the north.

"Mom?" I say.

"About Dad. Dad is . . . Dad couldn't . . ." Veronica puts her hands over her mouth. Aubrey and I squeeze nearer.

"What happened?" I ask.

"I don't want to upset Dad." Veronica straightens up, pulls away from us. "That is requisite—a must."

"Sure, of course," Aubrey says. "Elodie?"

I pause. "Dad? Is he that fragile? What about *us*?"

"In some ways, yes, Dad isn't strong, He's been short-changed, cheated. I have always kept this secret for Dad's sake *and* for yours. I didn't want Dad to feel less, to feel diminished. It's that he couldn't have children of his own." Our mother wrings her hands. "We might have adopted—I don't know. I wanted to be pregnant. I made this deal with him. I didn't want to miss out. My friends were having babies."

Veronica's eyes fall on me. "Elodie, I know you understand that part, how it should be your child—somehow. In a marriage, the idea that a baby would be related to at least one of the parents."

"I don't understand," Aubrey says. "Why couldn't Dad have children?"

Veronica frowns. "I have thought about Dad's situation—especially when you miscarried and when you girls made your plan."

Your plan. I ignore how she is choosing to frame it.

I ask, "What went on?"

"When Dad was in Vietnam, he was exposed to Agent Orange, a chemical. Or some element, a toxin. There have been studies—it turns out that it may cause sterility. Servicemen came home who were exposed to something and found out they'd been affected. No one knows for sure exactly when, where, or what caused it."

Our father, secretly maimed? Someone who stands tall, who commands people in his company and wins at every game. While he is one half of the Veronica and Simon Show, he seems the heftier half. When she carries on about opening dances, kickoff balls, what echelon of giving they must be at, how "the Cutlers" are listed, he decides. When someone, be it the Snefts, Bettins, or Chases, trade up their nine-million-dollar home for an eighteen-million-dollar home—or higher—he is Zen-like, disinterested in her social ambition. He has said, "This is what we have, Veronica, this is how it will be." He who owns the gold rules, Palm Beach 101. Isn't that it?

I'm going to choke. I swallow, take out my iPhone, and start googling Agent Orange. An article on CNN's website pops up first. Aubrey is bending over as if she is nauseous again. I watch, feeling detached *and* entrenched—just as Simon must have watched Veronica when she was pregnant. Suddenly our struggles, our ambivalences dovetail.

"Dad and I are alike," I say. "About this—about having a baby. He *must* have identified with what I went through—how could he not? He was lobbying for us, he was antisurrogacy. Then we find out he's *not* our biological father."

"He is our father, he raised us," Aubrey says.

"How many times have you been with Dad alone?" I ask her. "How many times has he held you? I mean, it isn't like it happens very much for me."

"Elodie, stop, please." I don't think Aubrey notices how she's smoothing her hand over her stomach in this round motion.

"No, Aubrey, tell me."

"You mean overall, since I was young?" Aubrey asks. "Including those summers at the Bridgehampton Candy Kitchen for ice cream? Well, if you count . . ."

"I can tell you how it was for me. Mostly it was before you were was born or when you were little. Horseback riding at Wellington—that went on until I left for college—a fourth-grade tennis clinic at Longreens, or once waiting for him at the Cricket Club, sitting in the clubhouse reading *Great Expectations*. I graduated summa from *Princeton* and he didn't say much. It keeps going—sometimes it's like I'm not in the room."

"He does it how he does," Aubrey says. "He's *our* father."

The Simon piece of the Veronica and Simon Show is hurting both our hearts. Our father standing tall, fractured within.

"The game has been changed," Veronica says. "These kits, these companies. Stories of lost, then found half siblings, full siblings, children given up for adoption. Dad and I didn't dare discuss it. I could feel it, I know he could, too. We've been worried."

"Kind of like Sleeping Beauty and the spinning wheel. As long as there's no wheel, there's no problem," I say.

Aubrey considers this. "Like that, yes. But why didn't you tell *us*, Mom? I mean, you had to realize that more and more people are using donor sperm, a donor egg, that Elodie needed help."

Veronica ought to say something mollifying, but she

doesn't. Instead, she says, "Do you know how painful this is for Dad? That's why."

Again, a defense of Simon. Aubrey reaches for our mother's shoulder and Veronica pulls back. My sister looks at me, perplexed. I reach for her hands, cool, smooth, comforting. I imagine Dad on his private beach—as I saw him last weekend when I was jogging. He thought he was alone; he was hunched over, his back humped a little.

"You found a sperm donor," I say.

"We did," Veronica says. "Back in the late seventies, the early eighties, it was a swear-on-your-life secret. Your father has this fantasy that either of you could be his, maybe both of you, by some miracle. Mixed sperm, both times. The men, the husbands, they were told that."

"Mom's right, it must have been tricky for Dad," Aubrey says. "I mean, his work, his rental buildings, he has those employees who *love* him, while he knew he had failed."

"Dad is respected in Palm Beach. This can't get out, we have to be loyal to him," Veronica says. "A place that makes your father proud of himself, among other successful men; a lifestyle that helps to forget—I owe him that."

I look at Aubrey. She's chewing on her right thumb, which she hasn't done since I bought that sickly nail solution when she was eleven. I used to put it on when she was asleep at night, and she stopped gnawing at her cuticles.

"Well, I mean, the gossip. How the Lestats clawed their way back. Did anyone ever truly forget about Faith and Edward Harrison? Look at Faith now, spending half her time in Delray. Remember when Maria T. fled town with her boys? Your mother-in-law talked about it an entire season."

Scandals—one of this type would be juicy because it isn't the usual sort. Unlike prenups that don't hold up, husbands who lose the money, affairs, mistresses, illegitimate children, false identities.

Aubrey tips her chin, as if she's considering the significance, as if she's not thought of it before. "I read a book—a study—about secrets and how women do it, keep them, lie carefully."

"You get used to it," Veronica says.

I have never seen her so raw and real, her pleasant breeziness shattered. Not when her own mother died. In the circles where the Veronica and Simon Show travel— Palm Beach, Sag Harbor, Aspen, New York City—their secret was airtight for decades. The length of our lives.

Again, Veronica reaches out to take Aubrey's hand, to take my hand, too. Her fingers are bony; they've aged since we sat down. This isn't the moment to ask about the sperm donor, what she knows about Aubrey's, what she knows about mine.

"Dad's ego, how he needs to be strong to his daughters. Never a failure."

"If you hadn't married Dad, you would have had other children, yours with another husband," I say. That would apply to James, too. Had he had a fertile wife, he'd have what he wants, readily.

"Yes, other children," Veronica says.

"Other lovely children," Aubrey says.

Veronica is doing that stare she saves for funerals and other bad news. "You are my children; I can't say it enough. You are my children with Dad. There's a path, our path. I'm asking you girls to consider his feelings. You both have partners. Consider it." Veronica holds our hands too tightly. "You *cannot* tell your father that you know, please, girls."

"Well, good morning." A wind gust blows our father's voice into the semicircle where we are locked together. His greeting is palpable even though he is still four feet away. Watching one another, we must have missed his entrance. Tugging down his tennis hat on his head, Simon reaches us.

"There you are. I didn't know you both were coming for breakfast." He speaks quietly.

Aubrey begins to check her iPhone. "Dad! Hey!"

"Hi, Dad," I say.

"It's a high-velocity wind until noon," Aubrey says, holding the phone up, attempting to defuse the situation. I try to measure how her voice carries toward him and away, blustering in every direction. Was he able to hear us?

"Simon." Veronica gives him a capable, Palm Beach smile. As polished as she is, the scene challenges her.

"Please join us. Before we go indoors."

"Absolutely. I will." Our father walks to the curved sofa.

We ought to get up and keep pretending. Yet both Aubrey and I, who move at our own paces, are identically stuck. Trying to fathom what we know, our parents' commitment to each other, to having children, to what festers beneath. We are immobile.

"Great, Dad." Aubrey lets go of Mom's hand first. She draws out "greeeaat" and gets up.

Simon is watching us, exactly the way he watched me the night I married James. From afar, although it is momentous.

I remember how Veronica and her sister, my aunt Lett, unbuttoned every silk-covered button on the back of my gown when the wedding was over. Then Veronica, in a motherly whisper, said, "Be vigilant. This is the end of one dream. You'll have to start another."

CHAPTER 21

ELODIE

Not four hours after the poolside chat with my mother and my sister, it's as if I'm wading through four feet of mud. The incessant wind off the ocean whips around the island; on the west side, the Intracoastal is frothy. Mrs. A., Priscilla, Cecelia Norric, and Lara Mercer waltz into the Society, searching for the latest fiction and the Distinguished Lecturer Series spring calendar. Snowbirds file in, complaining that the weather has diminished their perfect Palm Beach day. Any weather that isn't optimal proves successful for the Literary Society, as it does for the merchants. Several women race through the stacks of new titles before heading over to Neiman's and Vintage Tales. I am displaced, an alien on my own soil, seasick, lost, sorry. *Agent Orange.* Every gesture, every step today is to get myself into my office to wildly google the effects, to understand my father's plight.

"Thirty-five new sign-ups," Laurie whispers. "Mostly for the breakfast series."

"That's great." I attempt to be myself—whatever that is. The members' conversations—their voices—often a soothing mantra for me, are disquieting, piercing.

"Are you all right?" Laurie is eyeing me. "Have you eaten something that doesn't—"

"I'm fine," I lie, close to telling her that I need a day in bed with three Milky Way bars, an iPad, and an evaluation of who I am—beyond the reveal of 23andMe. What were the "controls" for sperm donors forty-one years ago? Was it like dress shopping at Bloomingdale's? I'll try this; no, that. I want a child with a high IQ, a short nose, an athlete. How it works today. I know instinctively it wasn't like that when my parents chose my donor, if he wasn't assigned to them. I'm not sure about Aubrey's donor, whether eight years demanded another method.

"Do you want something?" Laurie drifts past the reception area, costumed in her weekday gray-sky "uniform," a navy print McLaughlin shift and Jack Rogers wedges.

"Such as?"

"Well, we can't open a bottle of wine, but maybe a Fioricet?"

In her hand she is carrying a small mosaic pillbox and holds up a round blue pill.

"And not the generic."

"I don't know what you mean, but no thank you." I shake my head.

Laurie presses her lacquered fingernails into my palm. "You seem distraught."

"Isn't this for migraines? I don't have a headache."

"One time, Elodie, try it one time. It will help," she whispers. "Whatever it is, you are not yourself today."

Exactly right.

Across the main entrance and great room of the Literary Society, life is per usual on a buzzy indoor day in season. I smooth my thumb over the tablet. *Agent Orange. Our father not our father. Aubrey and I half sisters.* Aubrey, visibly pregnant, jounces around my mind. After our mother's statement this morning, I want our baby plan to be disclosed. Practically advertised—proudly advertised. Anyone in town who has questions will be told about our decision. No secrets or reproach—not after how corrosive the masquerade has been for our parents. Suffocating both of them, playing a mind game with Aubrey and me.

When I swill from my small Perrier bottle, the tablet bounces down my throat. Within an hour, I am floaty, disengaged, my thoughts muted, forced downward. Rain starts hitting the paned windows in the Great Room. Although the lights are on, there is this dim quality filtering in from outdoors.

"The valets are slow at the Jade Bar, don't you think?" James asks as he steers his BMW along the A1A. "A pain in the ass. I should look for parking up the street."

"There's no easy place nearby," I say. Although it is seven hours since I took the Fioricet, I hardly recognize my trained "willing to endure" wife voice. I resist shouting, *Who gives a fuck how or where we park. You've no idea what happened today with my mother. With my family.*

"Don't fret," I say instead, my tone upbeat.

What would Aubrey say to a husband about deficient valets at a restaurant? She wouldn't, because she hasn't got that type of person in her life. She wouldn't, because parking is more egalitarian in her world, in South Beach. Or so I imagine. *Aubrey, my pregnant half sister. We share 25 percent of our DNA. Our baby is at 12.5 percent.*

"Happy to be celebrating?" James asks as he steps on the gas.

Sworn to secrecy with Veronica and Aubrey, I'm trying to be appealing, collected. "I wouldn't speed. Around this bend, there are police and—"

"It's our anniversary; maybe you could stop worrying." James slows down slightly.

"You've seemed exhausted these past few days—that's why I booked this. You like the Jade Bar."

"Thank you for making a reservation. I do like it—I like the idea of it," I say.

"Well, we might run into a lot of investors if they're over forty-five, maybe some Literary Society members," James says.

"This is the first place your parents took us when we moved to Palm Beach. It had just opened and it was impossible to get a table. Somehow Simon managed to get us up front, best table there is. I like it because of your father."

I look out at the ocean view as it slips into twilight. The hole in my being, the dread of what Aubrey and I learned today, is unrelenting. Trailing up and down my body, squeezing my heart, swelling my tongue. How my father never talks about the war—now we know why—it weakened him, made him less. How pictures of my mother pregnant are sparse or tucked away, along with the few pictures of my father in uniform. The Veronica and Simon Show is a ruse, a cover-up, an escape from their lonely secret. The one that has determined my life and my sister's. Every choice we have made, including where to live, friends, men. Men—yes, my husband. It is a fortunate perk, a by-product, that I love him, since in part I chose him to please my parents, chose him because he fit in—Ivy League, tall, ambitious. His fussiness—over cars, couches, houses, sports—is familiar to me. Without effort, James belongs with the Veronica and Simon Show more than I do. In truth, I've been contorting myself to fit their mold, to please their fantasy since I was eight. I'm tired.

There is one car ahead of us in the valet lineup and James has worried for nothing. Within minutes I'm whisked out of my seat by a young, fast-moving man who needs to park the car pronto. The frenzy is over. James claps his right hand over my left wrist and we walk inside.

Dipped in the orange and darkened woods of the boutique hotel, the Winchester, is the Jade Bar, a jewel within a jewel. James and I come here for our more precious occasions. When he mentioned he'd reserved a table for tonight, I realized it was our wedding anniversary—an event I have not missed in the past. Beneath the soaring ceiling, we pass the dance floor. The music of Madonna, John Mellencamp, and Dave Navarro graces the clubby, posh surroundings. Aubrey would be pleased with the lineup, Aubrey, who is at the center even when she is off to the side.

"Elodie? C'mon." James holds out his hand.

Tonight James must remain clueless, an uninformed husband. I pray the dinner can be about us, pre–baby lust, when life flowed as a couple. Before our function was making babies and there was a glaze over anything else. When we were curious beings who promised each other a future with or without a child. At what price is a baby craving? "No one can know," Veronica said five times this morning. "Girls, promise me, no one tells anyone, not James, not Tyler. Not a friend, no one." We pinkie-swore, made it sacred.

The captain, who is not the usual one, steers us to our table. We pass some clients of James's and he gives them a confident, not too warm smile. They seem pleased and wave at him as if he's a minor rock star. The crowd is diverse for Palm Beach; that alone is worth noting. Two women from the board of the Literary Society, Chandra Vive and Brenda Pearl, greet me eagerly. I smile as if I'm happy. Happy to be here, happy to see them. We keep moving into the room; I don't believe I've ever gone so deep into the Jade Bar. To forgo a front table is unlike James, unheard of by my parents. Perchance my husband and I will have a real conversation tonight, perchance we will be able to hear each other if we sit away from the groove.

Our banquette is covered in tea green ultrasuede. James puts his arms around me while I look into the bar room where the young, trendy beauties cross their long legs. Along with an older crowd, women who are too sunburned, men with elaborate comb-overs. James is more handsome than when we met. His hair falls on his forehead in the same clumps and his features have matured. He has a face that shows thought; the crinkles around his eyes are surprisingly becoming. He stares at me more profoundly today than thirteen years ago, more willing to appreciate me. In his white starchy button-down shirt and navy blazer, he is rather stiff and old-school for this place. My black dress might skim my body, but it's mid-calf, not mini, and my tan suede booties might be high heeled, but not five inches high, not notable in a sea of younger women in stilettos. There's nothing trendy or artistic about us except our ability to admire the Damien Hirst on the wall. I can't imagine the lives of the others, but I understand my own existence very well.

"You and James are regal," Aubrey used to say. Not anymore does she admire us. Lately she's been busy, working with Tyler, being pregnant, carrying a full-term baby. Her means to an end is real, something I never sensed about my own pregnancies. The baby, our baby. No matter what Aubrey and I learned today, I walk with a lighter step, imagining how life will be for the three of us. Our baby on a swing, at the beach tossing shells, being read Dr. Seuss.

"You look better than the night we met." James speaks under his breath. The candlelight flickers.

"I was thinking that about you."

And I'm not sure where to put it. Where admiring each other's appearance, based on memory, belongs in our multilayered lives.

"Better than ever." He is truly enthused.

"Is that a line?" I wish this could satisfy me. It used to.

"Maybe. It's how I feel," he says.

"I'd say the same thing back at you, James." In this brief second, I'm there with him, I'm flattered.

I tug on my hair clip, and my hair spills out around my shoulders. The last time I wore it down was two months ago. Then, suddenly, I can't focus on James and me. I feel ill. Worse than morning sickness or a stomach flu—it's bottomless, bilious. I am proof of the con—Aubrey, too. We are shocked by what we now know, followed by pity for our father. Add that our mother and father are deceivers who cling to their story.

The server brings two fluted champagne glasses to the table and pours into James's glass. Since we're not spontaneous or gushy, I wait. During the pause, I'm not in this room, I'm with Aubrey and Mom, wherever they are. "Not our biological father," Aubrey whispered after the mystifying news. "Not our biological father." Her voice was sharper, higher as she spoke. "Did he ever love me?"

"Aubrey, please don't, please stop," I said. Because I felt as awful as she did. Because neither of us could bear to know.

James, proud of this night, tastes the champagne, nods his approval. I reel myself back to our banquet, our dinner. "Celebratory," I say.

"The baby," James answers. He hands me a jewelry box, an innocuous box, not one marked Graff or David Yurman. A small navy leather box with gold trim. "Open it, Elodie."

I unlatch it and look at a multi-stone heart ring. Not a Vhernier Freccia, which is the rage, or a David Webb Geodesic Dome ring. Not what one would find on the Avenue.

"Try it on." James takes my right hand. "For this period of our lives," he says. "I hunted it down, I didn't consult Veronica or Mimi. I called a few shops. Out of town."

How funny, how daring. As if we could exist under glass. I hold it up in the dim light of the Jade Bar. Pink and green stones, diamonds and sapphires sparkle in a cluster. Somewhere between vintage and trendy. He slips it on. "Do you like it?"

I keep staring at it. "It's perfect."

"We've been talking about a baby for so long, we never focus on much else. I know years ago you didn't want an engagement ring—and how our mothers convinced you to have a solitaire, to *want* one, so maybe a baby ring?"

"Maybe Aubrey's having a girl." I turn the ring toward me. "Or a boy—there's blue, too."

"Either way." James smiles. It's awkward, being together happily, knowing what I know. If I could separate out the Elodie of Elodie from the Elodie of the Cutler family, it might be easier. Aubrey could separate herself out and finesse this—she has that knack.

"Nights in White Satin," by the Moody Blues, becomes a few decibels louder. A favorite of mine, not as much for James. Although it is the song he played the first time we ever made love. That day, I thought if we left each other, I'd fade into oblivion. As someone who slotted from one boyfriend to the next in college, meeting James in New York, a month after grad school, was already more "adult." He waited, he didn't pounce upon me like the others. We went to dinners for a month before he began to kiss me, undress me. His patience made me want him. He was mindful of me, meticulous.

"The song," I say, "it's so unlike the Jade Bar."

"Do you remember what I said to you that night when the song was playing?"

"Yes, I do," I say. "You said you would be the last guy, not the first. You announced you'd be around for the 'duration.' And I thought, *Duration? Hmmm.*"

"I am! I am the guy who stayed. That was thirteen years ago, Elodie." James actually laughs.

"You called me 'sweetie.'" I stare into his eyes.

"Will you dance with me, sweetie?"

James comes to my chair. I stand up. The ring captures what light is reflected. He holds me close, dating-style. There is no talk of building a house that consumes him, and I'm not obsessed with my writers, with the next poet on the docket at work.

"Elodie." James tucks me toward him. I'm Penelope to his Ulysses. He's come back from the war, the Sirens' call, the vagaries of the sea. I've been waiting, years on end. The longing on both sides for us, how it remains, what we ourselves couldn't have predicted. Sated by my husband's reappearance, at last.

I put my right hand up to his left shoulder and again the color stones catch the dimness, brighten this patch of James's blazer.

"Elodie, what is it?"

"I'm okay, James," I say.

"Are you?"

"With you, yes."

We slow-dance without moving our feet, folding into each other. The tile is cold beneath; my shoulders are cold, too. His arms around me are almost a shawl, a blanket. His neck is completely perfect and I want to sniff it, sniff his skin and feel the smoothness. James leans down for a kiss, a public kiss. How out of character, as if he left his brains at the new house, at the construction site this afternoon. While I'm kissing him back without proof or reason, a chill runs through me. In the middle of our return to each other— after what feels a very long time—I'm planning tomorrow. When I'll call my father, then my sister and mother, to have an hour together. And I'm tugged to the Cutler side, despite how I love James. No other conversation matters.

CHAPTER 22

ELODIE

In the luxurious anteroom of Mar-a-Lago, my sister and I face south. To our left is the ocean and to our right is the putting green. Aubrey adjusts her sunglasses, shaped like hearts, squints into the room, and tugs on her Zara print dress. The print is very like the flowered Erdem that I notice on both A. J. Barker and Linnie Langley, except it's not. Women are coming through the doors. Aubrey might know a third of the guests, maybe a quarter, from growing up in Palm Beach. For me, it's a roll call.

I'm tapped on my elbow by Mimi, reminding me of how first graders in our Wednesday-afternoon Reading Hour approach me.

"There you are." Nearby, the scent of musk, which should be outlawed, hovers. Mrs. A. is holding on to Veronica's wrist while she speaks. Other conversations surround us.

Not in the city in June ... her third marriage ... downsizing, auctioned the art ... gutted the house ... not on her guest list ... I read it the day it came out, the writing ... liposuction ... Yale, I heard ... miserable grandchildren, thankless.

Mimi and I air-kiss while Veronica edges out of Mrs. A.'s grip.

"Girls!" Veronica is beside us, vibrant, her social graces in full throttle. Has she been bonged on the head since yesterday's conversation took place? She is impeccably outfitted in a navy-and-gray tweed Chanel dress and a Davidor bangle bracelet. Aubrey frowns when our mother does her wide, although not widest smile. She's adept at shifting gears, compartmentalizing her life. I yearn to be distracted, to have my mother's talent for escape, her ongoing need for society.

There is the first line surge and we spill onto the alfresco patio to find our assigned seats. Sunlight sparkles; there is hardly a breeze. The high winds of yesterday are forgotten; they never occurred.

"What I've missed is lunacy," Aubrey whispers to me.

I purse my lips; we can't jeer *and* be part of it. "Eh," I say.

"Aubrey!" Jessica and Tiffany pile behind us and say her name together.

"Hey!" Aubrey smiles, more air-kisses.

"What are you doing here?" Jessica asks.

She is consummate for a luncheon at Mar-a-Lago, with her five pounds of hair pulled into a messy ponytail or bun, indicating that a stop at the Blow Bar is planned for *after* the luncheon. No one under forty has her hair coiffed; only women over fifty care.

"I'm in Palm Beach a lot these days, when I'm not booking groups," Aubrey says.

"With that guy?" Tiffany asks. She, too, has that unkempt long hair. I put my hands to my head, where every hair is tucked into a neat ponytail.

"Yes," Aubrey says, "still that guy."

"Wow." Jessica checks out Aubrey's face and the rest of her body. "It's been a while. So it's serious, finally a man who gets your attention?"

"Must be some kinda guy," Tiffany says. Her eyes move toward Aubrey's middle, since she, too, is expecting a baby. A normal-pregnancy baby.

A slithery panic rises in me. We, my mother and I and my sister, although she's certainly more blithe, have miscalculated the luncheon today. Aubrey's bump *could* prove a feed for the Palm Beach gossip machine. I try to catch my sister's eye, my mother's eye. Mrs. A., standing in the center of the patio, takes a knife and raps her fluted glass filled with a virgin Bellini.

"Ladies, ladies. Welcome, all." Mrs. A.'s two-headed tiger Cartier bracelet glints in the sun. Allison Rochester and Rita Damon stand with her, both in shades of violet. They are too chic to be uniformed yet they are uniformed.

"Please be seated with your group," Allison, an ideal host, says. "If you haven't yet claimed your place card, I know the chart by heart."

The guests clap, do a weak laugh, and move toward their assigned seats.

"Doesn't Mom seem all right today?" Aubrey asks. She is behind me on the walk to the tables.

I face her, my fingers on my lips. "She's pleased we're both here."

Aubrey gets it. "Of course. It's great that we are."

The furtive and not-so-furtive glances keep going. I can virtually touch how word of Aubrey's pregnancy will travel in every circle. Especially with the present lull in local stories and a deliberate avoidance of any world news. Aubrey and I are up next.

Veronica is settling in at Ina Coles's table, as she does every year for this midseason Mar-a-Lago luncheon. Seated next to Karenna Tapper and Nan Payton, our mother is doing a hawklike inventory and misses my wave. When her gaze circles back to Ina, who is watching Aubrey, I know she knows. I try but fail once more to get her to glance in my direction. I am furious with myself. Am I not the elder daughter, *schooled in* the Veronica and Simon Show? Could I, could we, truly be this ill-prepared, this unpolished? I look at my friends, who glom on to one another, perhaps in search of the next gabfest. Our mother's friends could be unpredictable; they might or might not be supportive. That will be followed by Mom's and Mimi's ability to deal with being iced or judged. Or both.

Far to the right, my sister, still standing, texts me a heart emoji. *Love the playlist. The beat.* She would notice the playlist—ABBA, Cat Stevens, the Rolling Stones. Is she kidding? I sidle into my seat between Katie Kutin and Linnie Langley, nodding to Mrs. A.'s nieces from Boston. I entertain having a glass of wine. Any voodoo or potion to pour the old me back into my veins, the one who seeks out members of the Literary Society at these gatherings.

Beyond who wears Valentino, Oscar, or Chanel, wedges versus stilettos, platforms versus kitten heels, more Manolo than Louboutin, Jimmy Choo alongside Stuart Weitzman. Beyond the urgency of a Dior, Balenciaga, or Vuitton bag. It is about wardrobe as a lead to heavy hitters, women who might double their contribution to the Society. I don't have it in me today to work the room.

"How is Zachary?" I ask Katie.

"Wonderful. He wants you to come over to do a hundred-piece puzzle."

"A hundred pieces? I can do that," I say. "And then a game of Clue. He loves that game."

The taller Boston niece is fanning herself with the calligraphied menu. *Chicken salad with avocado. Lemon cake, chocolate cake.* Across the table, there's talk of the Academy, small children, how orders at Neiman's for the spring collection have already started. If I felt set apart these last few years without having a child, I will soon be set apart for another reason. My child will be brought into the world in an unconventional way. Unless there is a surprise reaction and what I'm doing is a trend, it won't be welcomed in Palm Beach. Isn't that what our parents were trying to tell us when Aubrey was inseminated?

"White baby roses!" the other Boston niece says. "They're ambrosial."

"Ambrosial," Linnie, Katie, and I repeat, as if we're saying "Amen."

The first course is brought to us, slivers of smoked salmon with caviar and crème fraîche. A bread basket of whole-wheat rolls is passed. Everyone refuses, except for me—I take two rolls, one with walnuts, one without. Linnie is staring at my sister, who is standing with Jessica beside their table. Together they are looking at their iPhones, Aubrey is showing her bands, gigs, photos of Tyler.

"Well, your sister—look at her," Linnie begins.

"I noticed, too, Elodie." Katie becomes syrupy. "I suppose everyone is wondering what Aubrey will do."

"Do? About what?" I ask.

"Evidently she's . . ." Linnie's voice trails off.

I'm about to play with their heads, act as if I don't see Aubrey as they do. Then I notice fifty feet away that my mother is in distress. She bends her neck like a maimed egret. I jump up, holding my iPhone.

"Excuse me," I say. "It's work. I'm being texted by my assistant, I'll need to take the call."

I practically hopscotch on the terrace to get to my mother's table, en route to a good spot for cell reception. Other conversations stream from Rita Damon and Mrs. A.'s corner, moving like a symphony, rising music, soft sounds, large sounds, through the air. *Look at her. Whose baby? Veronica and Simon . . . A Breakers wedding? Poor Elodie . . . over forty.* Am I the only one who hears it?

With purpose, I stand behind Veronica as Dory Rainee, who is talking to Mimi—Mimi? "Did I blink and wasn't invited to a wedding? Veronica at last with a grandchild!" She makes eye contact with each woman, then puts on her bifocals for more drama. "Look at Aubrey."

I bend down slightly. "Mom, one question?"

"Of course, Elodie."

I watch her rise gracefully and we step to the side. Aubrey comes to us and says, "I feel like I should have brought a billboard to answer everyone—or held a press conference."

"We ought to stop the talk," our mother says. "Agreed?"

"A great idea." I smile the smile my mother has mastered, leveled at everyone.

Veronica gathers herself; she will not tolerate another word. Nor an overt or covert glance. She claps her hands together. The sunlight behind us is like latticework.

"Excuse me, ladies, may I have your attention? I'm sorry to interrupt the luncheon—I ask only for a few minutes of your time."

My sister and I shadow our mother.

"I have heard talk today, questions about Aubrey, my younger daughter. What's going on? Is she actually pregnant? Is she married? I want to offer the entire story—and be brief. After miscarriages and heartache, Elodie has asked Aubrey to be a surrogate. The baby, their baby, is due in the fall. That's what I thought you should know," Veronica says. "And perhaps it's a first for Palm Beach."

Aubrey and I step up. Our shoulders touch our mother's.

"Does anyone have a question?" Aubrey asks.

The entire patio of women seems to have fallen under a spell.

Allison Rochester holds up her glass. "To the Cutler sisters, who haven't come together to one of our winter lunches for many years. Isn't that true, Veronica?"

Mrs. A. is standing with Allison. "I believe it is true. And they are very welcome."

I raise my glass. "To our gracious hosts."

Aubrey is radiantly pregnant. "Thank you for including me. I am happy to be part of this."

Gulls, warblers, herons, the birds my sister and I have known since we were children, circle above. For now, any shreds of gossip evaporate into the ether.

CHAPTER 23

AUBREY

I pace back and forth in my parents' formal living room. The couch and love seat are so fresh, it's as if they've just been delivered from an upholsterer. Has any of this room ever been used? I keep pacing, counting steps.

"Aubrey, stop." Elodie walks in through the patio doors. "Please, you're making me anxious."

"I am making *you* anxious? I don't know why we have to keep the drama going. Mom is reeling from lunch two hours ago." I try to glare at her.

Mom appears, kicks off her medium-heel nude Manolos, collapses on the couch. "I agree. Haven't we had enough for today? Can't we just be pleasant?"

"I can't skip talking to Dad, we planned it," Elodie says.

"And you, Aubrey?" Mom asks.

"I don't know, I don't," I say.

Our baby somersaults. Although I've not told my family, I've begun to call her Grace. *Baby Grace.* As dire as this family moment is, my mind wanders to the Lake Trail. I wish I were there now, finding other pregnant women to walk with along the southern end. We could trade notes, cravings for Reese's Peanut Butter Cups, lemonade, chili peppers. They might think it's my baby.

"I can go either way," I add.

Dad walks into the living room in his tennis whites, holding his Prince racket. Mom is about to ask that he place the racket in the mudroom. Instead, she opens her mouth and closes it, looks off toward the garden. The colors of the hibiscus are vivid, life aglow outside these glass doors.

"Simon, perfect timing, right on cue." Mom sounds strained. "With the girls, together again."

"On cue! High praise." When Dad smiles, his teeth seem more spread out and whiter than they used to be. Or maybe I never noticed his teeth before.

I am ill, not a lingering morning sickness, but something soupier, heavier. Obviously, he didn't hear us yesterday morning at the pool, luckily. Or has decided to be stoic. *Stoic.* I feel sicker. Elodie stands up, leans against the far wall, silhouetted, her hands on her hips. Exhausted, as no one is on an ordinary afternoon.

"We wanted to speak with you," she says.

"Sure," Dad says. Then he frowns. "What happened at the luncheon? Is Mimi around, too?"

"No, no, she stayed. She's in a card game at Mar-a-Lago." Mom is grim.

Dad sits on the end chair, while Elodie is on a chair that is parallel, completing the set. I decide to stay on the couch beside Mom, although the beige fabric is scratchy through my dress. Was life always like that—my hypersensitivity to anything tactile, to smells, to sounds?

On the Intracoastal, boats steer by slowly. Sunshine sparkles over the water and a family on a Sea Ray navigates the strait. Happy travelers, a family without secrets. The clouds move in.

"What's going on?" Dad puts his right hand over his skull, where his hair has thinned the most. He's very handsome. How could he *not* be my father—what is it called on the websites, my "bio father"? She's so pretty, our mother. How could my sister and I—such high-end offspring—*not* be theirs totally, the result of their union?

Don't Elodie and I have Dad's lankiness, the heavy ash brown hair he had when he was younger? What about his eyes, which can be brown or hazel? For all the eye shadow, eye powder, and clever eyeliner in the world, Mom's eyes aren't as tantalizing as Dad's. His whole style, how he doesn't get unnerved or surprised. He calms us down; he has that humor, that IQ. I can't stand that he isn't our father, our biological father. I don't believe it. Too many fairy tales were read to us, after that we were expected to read too much literature. This has to be a story, a fable, *not* what really happened.

"Aubrey and I have gotten results from the 23andMe tests," Elodie begins. "The tests we took because we were given the kits. We wanted to know if we carry any dread disease or . . . I don't know. I swear, I can't remember why we took the test beyond curiosity. What I can't get over is what we found out."

For some reason, I'm watching Mom rather than Dad. She stands up, maybe to go to Dad, toss her arms across his shoulders, comfort him. Instead, she assumes an odd pose, bending at her waist without breaking. Like a dancer—like the swan princess in *Swan Lake*. In the version that we know—the Miami City Ballet rendition that she took us to each year—the swan princess is a victim and a heroine.

Mom almost stumbles, then sits back down. "Simon, no one planned to take these tests. I didn't know about it until . . ."

His face is red, redder—he's never red, only tan. He could be having a stroke. I take my iPhone out of my pocket in case I need to dial 911.

"What happened?" His voice is husky.

"We want you to know we know." Elodie speaks as if she is introducing a controversial author or poet for her winter series. She is concise; she enunciates. Is my sister hopeful that this conversation will be positive, that every member of our family will be all right afterward?

Mom pushes her hair off her forehead. The air is too warm, stifling. "I'm not equipped for the tumult," she says.

"Okay, all right, let's try to parse it out." Dad remains red. The kind of power—that presence he has because he is my father—is missing. He is diminished, shorter, less than eager to be with us.

"Parse it out? What would that be, Dad? Would that mean the part of you that I've had in my life and the part of you that Aubrey's had while we never knew anything?" Elodie asks.

"What are you expecting me to say, Elodie? What is it that you're after?" he asks.

Except he has not spoken to us in such a gravelly voice before. His eyes have a flash to them, as if he's very angry, possibly afraid.

"Simon, we don't have to have this conversation," Mom says. "Ever."

"You and Mom are amazing parents. We're not trying to ambush you," I say.

Elodie stares at me, counts a beat, and asks, "Why did you keep it from us, Dad?"

"Girls." Mom's voice is also gravelly. "Dad was a lieutenant colonel."

Dad walks to the window.

"It took years before I got in touch with my troop, my friends from the war. No one talks about what went on. Two of the men have no kids; one had a daughter with spina bifida." Dad speaks very slowly. "The herbicides, the exposure. It wasn't your mother who had the problem. She . . . we . . . wanted a family."

"So we were conceived because Mom wasn't happy," Elodie says. "And it had to be a secret."

"She wanted to be pregnant," Dad says. "Isn't that understandable?"

"Please stop talking about me like I'm not part of the conversation." Mom twists her wedding ring. "Please."

"How about you, Dad? Was it going to make you happy?" My sister sounds too harsh.

"Elodie, don't do this. Dad loves us, we're his daughters," I say.

"I thought I'd have a boy, one boy," Dad says. "It's what I expected."

"Ah, it must have been disappointing. All those sports,

booked solid," Elodie says. "Tennis, winter ski trips, swim meets."

"Exactly." Dad keeps looking out the window, as if the view is new. He and Elodie should be on the same side, considering what Elodie and James have done. Instead, Dad continues. "There was your mother's agenda, too, for her daughters—dance lessons and dresses, certain friends."

Her daughters. I look at Elodie, who isn't reacting.

"I was tested for practically three years. Meanwhile, the pressure to have a baby was awful. It was destroying our lives," Mom says.

"Your mother had to have you, both of you," Dad says.

Your mother. Maybe Elodie is right on some level.

"Elodie, it's fine. We got to be born." I defend them, soapy as I sound. A song starts in my head about no one asking to be born. Saige, from Dirk O, wrote it, and Tyler said she sang it last Thursday. The first night we agreed I shouldn't go to a club, that I should stay in, get rest.

"Of course I'm grateful, I am," Elodie says. "But I don't understand the long-festering secret. You were watching me with my miscarriages and saying nothing?"

Our mother sighs. "You saw with Aubrey today. Sure, some people are accepting, but others are arbitrary."

"It was a different time. We were encouraged—advised—to keep it quiet. People weren't doing this as commonly as they do today," Dad says. "Then with the DNA tests, the stories in the news these past few years, your mother and I began to think about it again, after decades."

"There was a chance you might find out. I would tell Dad at night; I'd say I was afraid," Mom says.

"How about with me, Mom? I would have felt less alone, less a failure. Y'know, more identified with Dad," Elodie says.

"It isn't quite the same," Dad says.

"Why would you say that? Why isn't it close enough?" Elodie's voice seems too loud for the living room.

"The circumstances. Your problem, my problem," Dad says.

"You *were* pregnant, Elodie," Mom says.

"Mom!" Elodie says. "The babies weren't viable! What don't I know about infertility and in vitro treatments?"

I want to protect him, my polished, honored father. My elegant parents, living a lie, choosing the lie. I run my hands over my "bump" for about the sixth time in the last half hour. I promise myself I won't be rattled by this, I won't let it affect my cortisol levels.

"Your mother and I are a team. We were engaged before I went to Vietnam and married three months after I got home. In Philadelphia, at the Bellevue-Stratford."

I nod; I always nod when Mom or Dad talks about their wedding. We've heard the ingredients of their romance our entire lives. Mom's family was distinguished, Dad's less so.

"Why two different donors? Do you know who they are?"

"Elodie, please!" Mom says.

Dad's voice is strained. "Because Mom miscarried with the first donor on the second and third go-round."

"You understand—you are almost eight years apart," Mom says.

"Elodie, look at what Mom and Dad went through to have us. Isn't that enough for you?" I say.

"I'd like more information," Elodie says.

"It isn't to be talked about beyond these walls," Mom says.

She practically wraps herself around Dad, who, while not moving, does an invisible wrap back. Their entire life together, they have been cocooned. And good at it.

"I have tried so hard, Mom, that's why." Elodie is shaking her head. "Striving to be like Dad. I felt, I don't know, that something was off."

"Off?" I tilt my head. "Elodie, this is stressful." Baby Grace pounds and punches.

"Look at what fabulous daughters you are. What Dad and I did was the best decision of our lives," Mom says.

"No, Mom, please hear me. *Something has been off.* I kept wondering what I had done, why no one was quite enthused enough about me. It didn't seem that Aubrey felt it as much."

"I didn't," I say.

Our father is listening, but for Mom, this deserves only a moment. She purses her lips. "Elodie, this isn't necessary."

"Mom," I say. "We might not agree. Still, let's hear Elodie out."

Dad comes to where Elodie stands by the dining room. In the past few minutes, he has become another man, weakened, sorry. What people mean about "before and after" news is announced. News that can't be tossed or ditched, forgotten or changed. There are the dusty shades of eggshell paint and gentle lights—the living room too tenuous for our conversation.

"My only request," he says, "is that this isn't disclosed to anyone. That our secret, your mother's and mine, is yours—our two daughters' secret. Sealed, sacred."

What about James? What about Tyler? Will we not tell them? I can't be sure. I'd like Elodie to ask about that, yet when I attempt to get her attention, she looks away.

"I understand, Dad," she says.

"Should we hold hands and swear to one another?" I ask.

"We won't enforce that," Dad says. "Your word is your word."

The room bleaches out; nothing but the four of us fill it. Our mother lifts our father's hand to her cheek. "I trust my girls."

"You know that for me"—Elodie moves a foot away from Dad—"it's fine to respect the secret. As long as you know how I feel about the truth."

"How is that?" Mom sounds polite.

Again, my sister seems as if she is at the Literary Society, about to introduce a speaker after she makes one important point.

"This truth, for me, changes my life. Someone opened the gilded cage and let me fly out."

PART THREE

CHAPTER 24

AUBREY

The crazier the glue of my family gets, from our three-way baby to the DNA insanity, the more I come back to Tyler to be safe. Not that he knows it, because the secret keeping has shut me down, subdued me. I miss Tyler when he's beside me. Tonight, after the damn traffic on 95 South, I'm back. At Keats, a small venue in Miami, I listen to musicians talk about their songs. I push what happened with my family this afternoon in Palm Beach out of my mind. Tyler and I have a young soloist, pop rocker named Celeste, who is first on the roster. We sit with her family and friends, who are overly enthused about her standing in front of fifty guests listening to her gushy tunes.

"I wish she'd sing and they wouldn't talk," I whisper to Tyler. He holds my hand, lets it go. "Right, but afterward she does a set at the Bowery at eleven. Okay with you? Not too late?"

"Tonight?" Not only the hour but that I can't manage much more today. Then I've been around so little, he's been running the business. Celeste, with her reddish waves and flower tattoos, her short jeans and boots, she's mine. I found her. Before I became pregnant, before I had to show up in Palm Beach almost daily. Why do I risk disappointing Tyler, not my sister, my mother?

"Yeah. It's tonight." He's patient, I am able to choose.

"Let's do it."

Celeste starts off with a Melanie song, "Candles in the Rain," a song that my mother used to play for Elodie and me when she drove us around after school. I was only four, Elodie was twelve, already very cool. Mom wore her hair in a bob that frizzed in the Florida humidity. At least it was her real hair color and texture. Music played on cassettes, Melanie and Leonard Cohen, Tim Buckley and Joan Baez. I doubt that other mothers with girls at the Academy had the same taste.

"What're you thinking?" Tyler asks.

I am so tightly wound. "About my mother."

"Yep. I bet."

I want to confess: *Here's the scoop about my father, about my sister and me.* Except we are sworn to silence. Do Elodie and I get to carry it around like our parents, buried for innumerable days?

The night long, I'm sleepless. I keep wanting to wake Tyler, to confess, despite the promise. It would be opening a door, taking the lie into another room. It would be wrong. Besides, with Tyler it's precious—living together, working in the same office. I'm not sure spilling the family story is wisest. I thought when I moved in that he was the one with ghosts of lovers past, a dense history. Yet what I have is a pile of damage that can't be fixed.

At four A.M. I get up, ready to go to the living room to scroll through emails. I'll check what was posted about Celeste on Instagram after her performance tonight. Tyler hears me, senses my moving around. He's half asleep, but his voice is clear.

"Hey, Aubrey, try to get some rest. Tomorrow is the ultrasound."

Why do doctors' offices affiliated with hospitals favor a shade between celadon and mucus green for their walls? Tyler looks brighter and sharper against this background, while I am wan. Worse, as if I might take on the same hue as the walls. A far cry from Dr. Noel's designer digs for desperate women, an office Tyler has been, thankfully, spared.

"You're pissed at Elodie." Tyler speaks quietly.

"I am." I don't look up from the paperwork, myriad questions I don't feel like answering: marital status, spouse's name, occupation, spouse's occupation. "She's planning to meet me."

"Could be that she's struggling," Tyler says.

"Are you making an excuse for my sister?" I place the pen inside the clipboard. "My sister, who has gone AWOL?" Can anyone comprehend how alone I am, *waiting* for her to show up.

"Have you heard anything?" Tyler asks.

"Texting. She and James are both supposed to be here." I am almost relieved to be alone with Tyler. Still, she's very late; they're very late. A foursome, when it should be a two-some. The two of them or the two of us. Baby Grace flips and turns.

"Before this began, she was—"

"Ms. Cutler?" A technician comes to the front desk. She's tall, young, and has curly dark hair. Her name is embroidered across the front pocket of her white shirt. *Aida.*

Tyler and I stand up together. Aida is about to say something, then decides against it. Our vibe, our ersatz family–concocted baby, some signal causes her to open, then close her mouth. Her cover-up is a stilted smile. Maybe Tyler smiles back and I miss it, lost in what's next.

"Come with me, please." She turns into a hallway. We follow her.

Where is Elodie? Were Tyler not with me, I'd feel thrown to the dogs. He squints at the monitor, although I'm not hooked up yet, while I change. Dr. Lieber, studious, probably Elodie's age, walks in. Aida dims the lights.

"Ms. Cutler." Dr. Lieber holds out her hand.

"Yes, I'm Aubrey Cutler." Why do I sound tinny, unconvincing? This can't be my life.

She's reading the chart. Without looking up, she says, "You are thirty-two years old and this is your first pregnancy. You are, let's see, in your twentieth week. Approximately. Please, lie down."

I do the clumsy climb onto the table and Aida opens my

blue hospital gown at the front. The smooth half model of my stomach, my uterus, is a mound, a petite mountain. Beside me, Tyler tenses up, like he's made of batter board.

The ultrasound whooshes and clacks. Tyler watches the machinery with the kind of fascination he has when a lead guitarist brings out a B. C. Rich.

I whisper, "I'm glad you're with me."

Aida gives him a look and he backs away from me. She squirts glop on my stomach and starts moving the wand.

I should be glued to the screen. Instead, I'm worried about when Elodie will fucking arrive. Is she at the Literary Society, bossing Laurie around, yessing women who drop by to collect a book on hold? Has she simply cut it too close with traffic, the Southern Boulevard Bridge up every quarter of the hour? Then again, there's the chance she's rushing in to rush out. A scheduled coffee—despite our scheduled ultrasound—with one of her friends, an über-mother who deposits her eight-year-old daughter at the Academy and selective after-school activities. That friend would have a hedge-fund husband or a lawyer or doctor husband whose field is significant. The type of friend who will fish for the nitty-gritty of my pregnancy. A friend who might say, "Elodie, you've no idea how children impact a marriage, what a quagmire it is, the schools, other mothers, the children." Then Elodie could add to what swirls around town—what she knows from the Society, albeit she hasn't any children. Yet.

"Dr. Lieber, can we wait a moment?" I ask. A trickly qualm begins. Doesn't Elodie want to do the mother thing, see her baby?

"Excuse me?" Dr. Lieber has taken the wand from Aida

and starts circling it around in the air. "Mr. Cutler, what are we waiting for?"

"I'm not Mr. Cutler," Tyler says. "I'm Tyler Brickland."

"I apologize, what an assumption," she says.

"My sister and her husband. The baby is hers. I mean, it's my egg, her husband's sperm. I'm a traditional surrogate," I say.

Tyler puts his face near mine. In the darkened room his teeth glitter. I hold on to his thumb.

"Well, I'm certain you've heard from your sister. Close relatives, relatives involved with the baby, aren't often late." Dr. Lieber, sounding hurried, motions to Aida, who rubs more glop on me. I don't want Dr. Lieber to conduct the procedure; I'd rather have Aida do it.

"Just one moment more?" I ask. Tyler takes his cell phone and begins texting. Dr. Lieber shakes her head. "We should begin, I'm afraid."

For some reason, I wonder what this doctor is wearing beneath her lab coat, if she has any children of her own.

"When your sister arrives, she arrives," she says.

The plan is set with or without Elodie. I get it: The baby is the baby.

"I'm heeeere." Elodie smiles as she stands at the door— one she's pushed open herself. Her sunglasses serve as a headband, holding back her shock of hair. Hair we thought came from our father. "It's happening," she says. "Tyler, you've come."

"I did." Tyler moves toward the shelf in the front area,

where he put his backpack. The room seems more green-ish. I don't see his disappointment, but I know it.

"James is parking," Elodie says.

Tyler moves his gaze from the screen to Elodie and back. Elodie starts to watch.

A knock on the door, because James has arrived and, unlike my sister, he's polite; he's asked someone to lead him to us. A woman technician steps back and James slides into the room; he's taking his seat in an amphitheater.

"Just in time." A guest at a party, one the others waited for.

Dr. Lieber frowns. She's collected, with her smooth red-dish hair and lavender-framed glasses. I want her to patch up the situation. A stranger with a wand.

More glop is spread on my stomach by Aida, who then moves to a kind of switchboard. Dr. Lieber and she look at each other, speaking in code. A swooshing sound gets louder, keeps going. "The heartbeat, that's your baby's heartbeat." Dr. Lieber digs the wand in a little. "Here we have your baby."

"Can you tell the sex?" Elodie asks.

"Wait, Elodie," James says. "Let's not—"

"Is it visible?" Elodie asks.

"Before I tell you, please confirm you and your husband are in favor of—"

"We are, we are!" Elodie says.

Dr. Lieber moves the wand with a heavy hand.

"A girl," she says. "Yes, you're having a girl."

A girl. I knew it. *A girl*. Elodie and I both suck in our breaths and watch our baby float through the space that I've given her. She has far-apart eyes; her mouth is open. Her face is diaphanous; her arms are wings.

"Oh, my God, Aubrey!" Elodie says. "A girl! A girl!"

"Oh, my God," I say. Elodie pushes to be near my head.

"We wanted a girl!" I say. "Look at her!"

"She looks like us, doesn't she?" Elodie says. "She's got those thin arms, full lips. She's long, isn't she?"

I watch her flip again. "Yes, like us."

"A girl. A little girl. She's beyond splendid." Elodie sounds teary, uncommonly emotional.

Baby Grace. I knew it.

Tyler is captivated, the sloshing heartbeat, the arms batting about inside me. "James, my man, a girl!"

"A girl!" James holds up his hand to high-five Tyler.

"I can't look for some reason." He rubs his wrists, as if he has gotten poison ivy but doesn't remember being out in the field.

"What are you talking about, James?" Elodie is taken out of our shared trance. Undercurrents begin; James shifts out of our circle.

The baby keeps going, dancing in utero.

Dr. Lieber stops, lifts the wand back into the air, where nothing can be recorded or reported.

"I've not had an entire family in my ultrasound screenings before." She sighs. "I'm going to have to ask that two people leave, for the moment. There can be places traded in a few minutes, but four at once is disruptive."

James's attention is obviously diverted, perhaps influencing Dr. Lieber's decision. He shuffles his weight; he's listless in a packed room with a screen and churning sounds.

"It is crowded with four, not two, of us," Elodie agrees. "James, if you want to get some air, I'll find you in the waiting area later."

"We should go, Elodie, you and I," James says.

"Elodie, please stay," I say.

"James hates the sight of blood," my sister says.

"No one is bleeding." Dr. Lieber is back on track.

She moves the wand. Baby Grace's face looms closer.

"The room is too close, too warm—that could be the problem." James is at the door, still watching the screen. "Not enough circulation."

Elodie walks over.

"Tyler, maybe both of us should leave," James suggests.

"Sure," Tyler replies, but he is transfixed. "That'll do."

"I don't know what's come over me," James says.

"It happens, doesn't it, Dr. Lieber?" Elodie composes herself.

"Well, on occasion." Dr. Lieber is gliding the wand.

"Elodie?" James is at the door.

"I'll step outside with James," Elodie says. "I've had a good look. I'll come back in. Swap places with Tyler."

My sister comes to me, puts her mouth by my ear. Aida and Dr. Lieber bristle; she ignores them.

"Our baby is everything, isn't she?" I whisper to my sister in that strangely pitched voice we concocted when I was five. No one else could know or understand why we do this.

"I hope so," Elodie says.

I hope so?

Elodie is watching the screen. "She is incredible."

She squeezes my hand, then she walks to James.

The baby that is our baby, no one's baby, everyone's baby, keeps at it. So like a ballerina that Tyler is enraptured.

"Smitten, are you?" Aida asks.

"That we are," he says.

As if directed, the baby somersaults onto the screen, her eyes similar to ET's. Her tiny fist clutches the other fist. In this frame, no one counts except the three of us.

CHAPTER 25

ELODIE

An hour after Aubrey's ultrasound, James and I aren't able to speak in the car. In silence, he drives us to the Gardens Mall. I have never been here with him, although several times I have come with Mimi.

When he parks, he turns to me. "What are we doing?"

I've told him already, but we're both so thrown by our baby on a screen, I want to be patient, considerate of both of us.

"Papier Bliss to get the proof for the baby shower. My mother said it can be sent or emailed, but since we would be nearby, she asked me to stop in."

"Why is it crowded on a weekday?"

I want to shout, *Stop talking minutia. Let's talk about what happened at South Palm, why you left the room.* Instead, I speak slowly.

"Retail shopping is popular. It's a nice mall. Your mother likes to come. She doesn't mind driving up here. She walks through the anchors and the smaller shops. She says it cheers her up."

I admit, it's fun to go with her. We usually get frozen yogurt with walnuts at Bloomingdale's.

"Okay, fine." James turns off the engine and we get out without slamming our doors. He squints in the sun, maybe at how large the place is, and we start walking into Nordstrom. "I've got to get to ANVO. How long will things take?"

Air-conditioning and muzak blast at us. James reads the directory as fast as possible. "C'mon," he points.

I'm following him, he won't even walk in tandem.

"What is it, James?"

"Yes, I'm fine," he says. As if we don't know each other and there's no reason he needs to be polite or friendly. I want to cling to him, ask for an emotion, say it's not my fault that my family is spilling everywhere. That the ultrasound might have freaked him out for reasons I'd like to learn is a separate issue. Although it adds to the utter chaos, triage of the Cutlers.

A woman who works at Papier Bliss is expecting me.

"Your mother called; she was very specific. You must be Elodie," she says, handing me the proof.

She's in her fifties and blond, with rimless glasses. I am too loaded down to conjecture her life, her passions, as I usually do with strangers. I'm absorbed with what to say next to my husband. In a numb manner, I thank her and carry the envelope outside to where James stands, reading his iPhone.

"Want to look with me?"

He shakes his head, and I know he is working with his office. I walk back inside and sit at the table, where people look at samples of countless invitations and announcements. I'm too queasy, too upset to check the proof. Veronica will need to see it in any case; a pass from me won't matter. Again I leave the shop, nodding to the woman, whose name is Mary.

James isn't right beside the storefront anymore. I spot him wandering through the main corridor. Could a shopping mall be adding to James's odd disconnect, how desensitized he is? When he looks around, I smile cheerfully and signal that I'm coming to where he is.

"Ready?" James asks. "It's very busy at my office."

His upper lip has a line of perspiration. His jawline, which I admire, is undefined; his entire affect is flat. Maybe carrying on a conversation is too burdensome, too demanding. I check my phone. A message has come in from Veronica.

"Wait, we have to stop at Nordstrom's. My mother said to look at the layettes there."

"The what?"

"The layette. What you need for when the baby comes home from the hospital. It gets preordered. Baby blankets, towels, infant clothes, sheets. What the baby wears for the first few months."

Our baby, our daughter. We ought to be celebrating.

Would he care more about it if *I* were carrying our baby? Don't most husbands know by this stage of their wives' pregnancies what a layette is?

"Can we make it fast?" His face is still slack; his voice has no cadence.

"Sure, why not."

The only person working in the baby department is busy on the other side of the floor. Although we see her, James and I find a love seat near the stuffed animals and bassinets and sit together.

"Want to shop a little since we're here?" I ask.

"Not today," James says.

Up close, I realize he has a few gray hairs at his temples; his one dimple isn't as deep as it used to be. Or he isn't smiling like he used to.

"Wasn't it amazing seeing our baby?" I ask, ever hopeful that I can reel James in.

"It was. I didn't expect it to be so graphic. It made me queasy."

"Queasy, okay." I pause. "James, it's a girl. *A girl!* Now we can choose pink, today, pink!"

In the lag that follows, I recollect what we were like before we planned our baby. I wait for him to speak. There are no windows; the overhead lights make the room too ashen, the color of oyster shells.

"We should go. Both of us need to get to work," I say. "I can do the layette online. Or Aubrey will. Lately she loves baby clothes and nursery decor."

"Does she?" James crosses his legs. I don't believe he cares what my sister likes.

"James, what's going on?"

"I don't know. Are you nervous?" he asks. "You know, about having a baby, a child?"

I pivot. "Nervous? No. But something. I am observing Aubrey and it's the oddest thing. She's carrying our baby; she's my little sister. She doesn't say much about the pregnancy. I guess to protect me, in case I feel like I'm missing out."

"Do you think you are missing out?"

"No, actually," I say.

"I get that. Who could have predicted how we would feel, how much there is to plow through? From the women in town, the perceptions, Aubrey becoming more and more pregnant."

"At least both our mothers are fairly decent," I say. "At the moment."

James starts laughing, the laugh he had when we went on a trip to Berlin and we drank too much lager. I begin to laugh, too.

"I'm grateful for that." I run my hands through his hair.

"Do we have a name for our daughter?"

"We have a list," I say. "At home. Remember, we like Lila and Isabella—no, wait, we nixed Isabella. India is on the list."

"What if it's more complicated than it looks?"

James, the strong man, James the rock.

"Oh, James, please, don't say that."

If he only knew how my father stood in his own living room yesterday, crushed. If he only knew my father's lie, a double lie, one for me, one for Aubrey. I'm like my father, the one who isn't related, expected to fill the chair. Our baby daughter's precious face, my father's pain. "Your father loves you," Mom keeps saying.

"We'll be fine," I say to buoy us both.

The salesperson is coming to our love seat, carrying a tablet and a pen, ready to record our layette shopping order.

"Can we get the hell out of these shops?" James asks.

"At once," I say.

We jump off the love seat with a spring in our step. Suddenly I understand Veronica's debacle, how it must have been to bring me, and then Aubrey into the world. How it is to shore up one's husband first.

CHAPTER 26

ELODIE

When I walk into our kitchen, it is past seven o'clock. James is at home, playing Neil Young from the album *Everybody Knows This Is Nowhere*. We kiss on both cheeks, as if we're in France.

"Veronica and Mimi have been on the mother-in-law group text for hours about a baby girl," I say.

"That's indisputable," James says. "Simon weighed in once and seemed pleased."

"I saw that, too." I gulp. My father had to do that, didn't he?

Standing like he's at a weight machine at the gym, James appears much more himself than he was this morning at the ultrasound. Shoulders back, stomach in, buff. He has to know about the DNA—for my sake, for his. At once. I can't stand that he doesn't. Unless I leave the night alone—then it could belong to us, we could recover from the shock of the ultrasound, we could share the hours. I might simply practice *how* to announce the news in front of a mirror and reveal it later. After I clear it with Aubrey. Instead, I keep running it through my head, how to frame this for my husband. *Honey, sit down, here's what really happened in my family. My father was infertile, Aubrey and I are donor-inseminated daughters. Two donors, a double lie. Half sisters.*

The song "Cowgirl in the Sand" is playing. Twice we went to see Neil Young perform together. Why can't I be the person who talks about that—about how his music is part folk, part country, with that hard edge in some of the songs. I might not know what Aubrey and Tyler know, but I know about musicians we were raised on. Funny that James chose a favorite of Veronica's. My mother and husband, in sync on music, the new house, Palm Beach in season. And the baby.

"Are you thinking about the baby?" he asks me. "Since we know the sex."

"I am," I say. "It's exciting."

"Names. I looked up some on the Internet. Let's not do one in the top ten or twenty, okay?"

"I agree."

The baby should fill my head nonstop, including the roster of girls' names, Eleanor, Lila, India, Annabelle. I shouldn't be lost in our sperm-bank story, wondering how one finds her bio father.

"You know, I like Tyler, he's a good guy," James says. "He makes Aubrey happy. He's a sport—look at what's going on with the pregnancy. How he . . ."

I nod too emphatically. "He is so there, for Aubrey and the pregnancy."

"Exactly," he agrees.

"James, before we get ready, before we go tonight," I begin.

"The barbecue at Longreens?" James checks his watch. "You know, we don't have to go. But your mom called and started with that rhetoric about it being 'casual.' Corn on the cob, thin-crust pizza, shrimp cocktail, steak that's blue in the middle. Piled onto one plate."

"I don't know, it's been a long day. I'd have to change."

The thought of friends, members, finding the right clothes, bangles, earrings—it overwhelms me. Is this what depression is? What unspeakable grief feels like?

James stands, stretches. "We haven't had a night at home in weeks."

We are more teamlike than we've been for a while.

"I don't know how to do this." I start pacing. James eyes my back-and-forth steps; I am not the pacer in our relationship.

"Do what?"

He's looking in the pantry for something to eat and opens a box of macadamia nuts, then a box of Carr's water crackers.

"I want to tell you what has been uncovered." I stop myself. There's the promise that Aubrey and I made to our father, there's that. To our mother. A pact that we would not share this. Except it is *our* story, too. We are the result of their narrative. How can Aubrey not tell Tyler tonight? How can she resist?

Something about my face, the lighting, the grave loss of what I believed my entire life. Where did I read that learning your father isn't your bio father is like being hit by a Mack truck?

He waits, then asks, "Uncovered?"

That's where I am, hit by that Mack, on the open highway, splat out while suffused with the truth. I wait before I speak. Why do I pity the men—Tylor, James—and not the women? Already my heart hurts for my husband.

"Simon is not my father. I'm someone else's daughter—a sperm donor's daughter."

James spits the nuts out of his mouth, into his hands. He walks to the sink and runs water over his hands, splashing it onto his face. When he twists around, his mouth is twisted, too.

"What are you saying, Elodie? You and I, we've been together for years. Where is this coming from? I *know* your father."

"Simon is not my biological father. He isn't Aubrey's, either. Plus, Aubrey and I have different donor fathers."

I'm making peculiar sounds in my throat. Even my voice is not mine anymore; nor is it the voice that Aubrey and I pitch together. It's just foreign.

James leans against the wall next to the kitchen door and freezes up, immovable. He waits for me to explain.

The room is too glary. I'm dizzy. I breathe in, out.

"We weren't ever supposed to know, not ever. The secret, my parents' secret, was supposed to go to the grave. Some kind of covenant. Then we took the DNA tests. And what I believed, what my sister believed, our entire lives . . ."

I stop, unable to go on. Whatever I said to my parents and Aubrey this afternoon has left me depleted. I have to stay with it, telling James is my panacea, part of being let out of the cage, isn't it?

These pictures in my mind, my parents laughing together, inebriated. Christmas suppers, New Year's Eves, opening dances, dinner parties, theirs, others'. My mother's teeth always show; his are always covered. I think how Aubrey is grateful and astonished, while I am curious and astonished. Longing for more information, I am unforgiving before I am beholden.

"I'm not sure I want to believe you, Elodie," James says.

"I know, I know," I say.

Then James comes over to me and begins to cry. I have not seen James cry since he told me about his father, who died. Our arms around each other, we stand in the middle of our kitchen.

"I'm so sorry, sorry for you and for your sister. For Simon," James says. "What can I do?"

"Nothing, that's the thing. Nothing can be done," I say.

The room isn't lit enough and the sun has set. There are sharp shadows. James keeps crying in that mannish style.

"Is it because he's not my real father?"

"Everything." James holds me tighter. "That he's not your *biological* father, that Aubrey and you are only half sisters—that it makes you less related to our baby."

"I thought of that. Another blow, another shocker. I'm absorbing that, too."

"He and Veronica tricked you in some way, they tricked you and Aubrey."

"Well, I've suffered and I've thrived," I say. "I'm like him about our baby—the great steps taken. How he wanted us to be his but he couldn't do it. Kind of like me."

"That's the irony, isn't it?" James says.

The songs shift and loop around. "Cowgirl in the Sand" comes on again. Have we been talking that long? James and I lurch together toward our new de facto existence.

CHAPTER 27

AUBREY

Mom, it's fine, it's all right," I say, although my mother has parallel-parked more than eighteen inches from the curb on Worth Avenue. I would offer to re-park, except she's on edge. Lately I find it easier to agree with my mother or Elodie about almost anything. Plus, in the past two weeks I've realized that getting behind the wheel to drive is more of a trick than fitting into the passenger seat.

"Great." Mom turns off the engine, pulls down her mirror, and starts primping. Sunlight hits her chin and the right side of her nose. She bends her head in the other direction.

"I'm delighted that you can come with me this afternoon, Aubrey. Going to Vintage Tales always gives me a lift."

"Well, sure, but I have a conference call in an hour," I say.

A call about Celeste, who since her gig in Miami is being invited to perform everywhere.

"This could be our big break," I said to Tyler last night. We were on the road to the Music Scene, a live band venue for local talent in Fort Lauderdale. "We can sit at our desks and book everywhere, not only local spots."

"And not travel when they perform?" he asked. "It's your family, isn't it? It's the baby, right? Why else would you have that idea?"

The old me, the me from before I promised my sister and James this baby, would have been about going with our singers. Instead, I'm looking for excuses to be nearby. Yesterday I found myself walking through the Tot Lot playground, the one for toddlers and babies, at Lummus Park in Miami. The cutest little girl, maybe two years old, walked alongside her stroller while the mother, on her cell phone, pushed and texted. I know I wouldn't do that; I'd be too vigilant. I'd watch Baby Grace's every move. I'd take her on the swings; we'd do the baby slide together.

"Maybe for a few months, like maternity leave," I said.

"Isn't Elodie taking maternity leave?" he asked.

"Yes, of course she is. I want to be available to her, in the beginning. I thought maybe if we didn't start traveling again at once, I could help out a little."

A rain had begun, falling in pockets along the highway. Tyler put on the windshield wipers. They swiped against the glass; the swish of it was hypnotic.

"It might be a good idea to hammer it out with your sister sooner than later," he said.

"Mimi keeps asking. Doesn't the baby nurse need to be

chosen before a nanny is hired? Will I express my milk for Elodie to have in bottles?"

"Good for Mimi." Tyler kept heading south. "I mean, your sister is sort of missing in action."

"Please, she's my sister."

After a while, Tyler switched on his playlist, turning to Bob Dylan singing "Sad Eyed Lady of the Lowlands." He reached for my hand, his palm calloused like a guitar player's, though he hasn't played in months.

Mom tugs her left eyebrow up toward her forehead. She's in a Lilly Pulitzer shift, a light blue print with a panel of white lace.

"I wish that Elodie could meet us. Take a half hour from her schedule. I'd like to buy you both a little something." Veronica uses her social "maybe she means it" tone.

She lets the mirror flip back up.

"I am a firm believer in punctuating good news." She has morphed into her public voice. "A baby gift for my girls."

"I don't know, Mom, I'd rather wait until we have the baby."

"Not necessarily. We'll look around, feel it out. See what Faith is consigning at the moment. Shall we?" She turns to me, perfected.

Through the window, I see the women buying, chatting, longing for things. The Estrela sofa, the Egg chair, themed items, jewelry in cases with miniature placards that read CARTIER, IPPOLITA, DAVID WEBB, TIFFANY—they're all there. The bags arranged by color, Hermès, Chanel, Fendi, Prada. A case of costume jewelry, Oscar, Miriam Haskell, Saint Laurent. Buying and selling as a contact sport.

Chimes. Mom pushes open the door. She smiles, at ease with status items, addictive shopping as a solution. "Hello, everyone."

The age-defying, yoga-loving crowd, some wearing sapphire or ruby earrings, wide diamond bracelets, diamond solitaires, pause. *Hello, Veronica. Veronica, how have you been?* Their welcomes float up toward the coffered ceiling; their gaze is on me.

Two unnamed women nod, then the usuals: Patsy Deller, Cecelia Norric, Lara Mercer. Jesus, even Jessica's and Tiffany's mothers are in the shop, together. Eve Crane, the majordomo, approaches, her stilettos clicking on the white marble tile. She carries a velvet tray of women's watches and focuses on my mother. "After your call about an everyday watch, a woman's watch, Veronica, I gathered what we have . . . including from the safe."

"My girls don't wear watches anymore, they read their cell phones," Sylvan Harley, Jessica's mother, says. "Do you, Aubrey?" She turns to me, a chance for her to stare directly at my body.

"It depends, Mrs. Harley. I like watches; they're decorative, historical," I say.

"I suppose that is a *slant,*" Patsy Deller says. "Show us what you've got!"

"Why, some of these are charming!" Mom says. "They *are* decorative, if not *useful.*" She lifts a Cartier tank on a black alligator band. "This is classic."

Doesn't she know that she's brought along the wrong daughter for the shop, for the crowd? I have not worn a watch since I graduated from college and only costume myself in designer clothes and jewelry when I come to Palm Beach. Borrowed from my mother and sister.

"Aubrey, try this on. It can be casual or dressy."

"Sure." I half smile at the others. I'm about to offer my left wrist, when texts start coming in. I should have turned off my iPhone.

"Is that mine?" Lara Mercer puts down the Valentino rockstud bag that she's been looking at and takes her cell phone out of her pocket.

"No, no, it's mine." I back off a few steps, start texting back quickly. First from Celeste: *Nervous about the stage.* I text back, *You are fine.* How relieved I am not to be at her performance. The decibels of songs, the chords too loud for Baby Grace.

I place my hand over my womb, as I'm always doing lately. Another text, this one from Elodie. *Uber to me now.* I text back, *All ok?*

Pls come. Please. Using only my thumbs, I hit my Uber app. Mom tries the watch on, holding her wrist up and examining the effect. Sylvan comes close to inspect it.

"Look at something younger if it's for your girls. Too old-school, too traditional. Look at the bags. Jessica would want—"

"Mom? Maybe we can do this another time. I unexpectedly have to go. I'm sorry."

"Dear, where are you going? How will you get there?" Mom asks, code for *You cannot leave at this moment.*

"We want to hear about your baby," one of the unnamed

women says. I stare at her. She's about fifty, pretty, Palm Beachy.

"Well, surely you will tell everyone," Mom says. "Quickly, before you have to leave."

"I have an emergency meeting for work."

"Of course, Aubrey. I'll keep shopping," Mom says. "I'll peruse the latest evening bags."

I lift my backpack and turn to the seven shoppers and Eve. "I'd say my mother will be best at filling you in."

The oxygen is sparse where Laurie trots me down a back hall of the Literary Society. Unlike the front offices, unlike the check-in desk made of ash wood, where staff is welcoming and professional, this is hidden away and dark.

"Elodie's in her office." Laurie is about to leave me outside a half-closed door that has no name on it. Where my sister must sequester herself when she isn't presenting an author, greeting the members, feigning a faultless life.

"I'll go in?"

"Oh, sure, she's waiting for you." Laurie pushes her hair off her forehead and tugs the sides of her light blue dress. She holds her head a bit higher. Breezy and self-assured, she reminds me of my sister. Especially how she begins to walk away.

Elodie is at a wide wooden desk, staring at her desktop. "Hey," she says. "I'm glad you came."

The office is shabby, in the style of early librarian. I look at the bookcases, where my sister has set aside titles. *As I Lay Dying, So Big, Ragtime, To the Lighthouse, Case Histories,*

Celestial Railroad. Poetry is on another shelf, Edna St. Vincent Millay, Walt Whitman, Sharon Olds, D. H. Lawrence. To the right, on the floor, is a low pile of shoes, Manolo slingbacks in nude, two worn pair of Tory Burch patents circa 2016, a pair of New Balance running shoes.

I sit in a straight-backed wooden chair. My sister looks jaundiced.

"Are you okay?" I ask. For the past three or four years, she has had this affect at times. I thought it was from taking hormones, trying to be pregnant. Then it started to disappear, until today.

"I don't know. I've felt ill ever since . . ." she says.

"I feel sick, too." I start fanning myself with my hands. "Plus, I'm pregnant."

The fluorescent lighting doesn't help. Wouldn't my sister ask the Society to take it down? Why would she want noxious lights over her every day, casting a dank fake brightness over the room? I decide not to bring it up.

"Being pregnant isn't easy. I'm not someone who loves it." Yet Baby Grace is tumbling around, there is that.

"I know. I have thanked you, haven't I? I am incredibly grateful, Aubrey." Elodie jumps up and comes over to where I am and puts her head against my womb. "I can hear her! I hear swishing!"

The air-conditioning unit makes a startling sound; then the air begins to circulate. Elodie jumps up, then back into her worn office chair, which squeaks. "I wanted to see you about James and Tyler—what we say to them next. Let's not get into the half sibs yet."

"Half sibs?" I ask.

She states this; my sister fucking states this. Like

it's ordinary stuff, nothing about how it is loaded or life-changing. I can't stand much more.

"Why am I here, Elodie? Leaving Mom at Vintage Tales, where shoppers were practically pouncing on her. Gossiping over our baby."

"I told you. Because of the half-sib situation." Elodie takes a tortoiseshell hair clip and gathers her hair together.

"What are you talking about?" I take the same tortoiseshell hair clip from my backpack and clip my hair up. I feel myself becoming the same jaundiced hue. *Half sib.* I know what she means and I don't. I don't have it in me.

"According to a *New York Times* piece that ran months ago, there was one group of thirty or more half sibs. You know, people who connected through 23andMe or Ancestry. In that article, they were young; they knew from the start that they were sperm-bank babies. This family of half sibs are in their early twenties."

"That's not the same. I read it, too. Everyone was okay *because they were aware* in that story of the bio father. With Mom and Dad's case, we're older. It wasn't out in the open. There's the loony shit cover-up," I say. "It would destroy Dad if we pushed anything."

"Aubrey, I have another half sister, so far. She's my age; we look the same from pictures. We've emailed, first through the 23andMe site, then emails, then texts. We both have a widow's peak; we love the same writers. She was born in New York, too," Elodie says.

"Pictures—you've been swapping pictures like she's your pen pal? No, please, Elodie. Please let's not add anything more. Besides, I don't have one, I don't have another half sib."

"Yet, you don't have one yet," she says.

"Well, you have me." I start walking around the small space beside my chair.

"Ah, that's true. We're sisters, *half sisters*," Elodie says. "I want to meet the others. I want to know about the donor, my bio father."

"No, no! Please don't. I want nothing to do with it. You're my sister, Dad's our dad. *Please*, Elodie."

"You don't understand. Maybe it was always fine for you, but as I keep explaining, not exactly for me. I'm *beholden* to the answer. I want to meet Alice."

Alice. I feel punched. Punched while carrying my sister's child. A twinge radiates inside me, Baby Grace flipping, diving. Elodie's hands dart along her keyboard. Is she looking up more siblings, more links to a truth that divides us?

"Elodie, I am in Palm Beach for you, for our family. That's what we do for each other. The baby, for you. Can't we talk about our baby? That's the future."

She half hears me, turns to agree, and then rotates to the screen. She's squinting, captivated. I'm mystified as to what might bring her back to the ambitious pleaser, the loyal Cutler, the sister I know.

"I've almost met her once, Aubrey." Elodie's voice is high-pitched, excited. "I only put it off so that we could speak first."

"Is that loyalty?" I ask.

My sister gets up from her desk chair again, and I expect her to make a promise. A decision to let the others, the half sibs, go. Together we'll scatter them far from us, from the existence we've shared our entire lives. Except she's infatuated with the idea of them; she's glassy and feverish at once.

"Well, yes, it is loyalty. I mean, this is happening very quickly, the half sibs. I can't help but want to know."

I'd like her to come to where I stand. We'll hug. We'll agree on a shared strategy about our father. We'll protect each other, celebrate the ultrasound. *A girl.* Except she doesn't come over and embrace me. Rather, a text comes in; she frowns as she reads it.

"I'm going," I say. "You asked me to rush over and you're being rude."

Elodie starts intense texting. She waves her free hand toward me. "Just a sec, Aubrey. One sec."

I imagine the words she is choosing carefully for outsiders she calls "family."

"Hey, Elodie?" I say. "Who do any of us belong to, anyway? Who does this baby belong to?"

My sister doesn't hear me. She shifts her attention back to her desktop, where she is bewitched by a screen. A screen that leads to the DNA of others.

CHAPTER 28

ELODIE

Again we saunter to Justine's for our "family dinner," as Veronica insists on calling it. Repeat conversations, talk of tennis, boating, member guest golf outings, acknowledging every acquaintance to the left and to the right.

My mother and I are the first to arrive. We follow Smyth, the maître'd since I was fourteen, to our table, the one the Veronica and Simon Show must have and rarely do not have.

"Well, this has been the slowest/fastest season that I've ever known," Veronica says as we are seated.

"I know," I agree.

We might allude to the passage of time in terms of Aubrey's pregnancy, how keenly we've tracked her progress, but we do not. Rather we feel it and it is unmentioned. Just as we feel the air steeped in Florida humidity and few mention it. Discussing the weather would be disloyal. Whatever day one decides to leave Palm Beach to go north or west for the summer is the day it becomes intolerable. Until then there is nothing about South Florida that is unpleasant. The Cutler/Evans clan has never before been seasonless, staying in Palm Beach during the summer. This year we remain, waiting for our baby. Veronica has labeled it a year of missed "punctuations," as she calls anything important and upbeat—Thanksgiving, Christmas, New Years, Valentine's Day.

I turn to Veronica while she discreetly powders her nose.

"Don't you ever feel, Mom, as if everything seems to be beyond you?"

"How would that be, darling?"

"Like I'm not the one decorating my home, carrying my child or—" I stop myself. It hangs in the air. *Or have the real father who I thought was mine.*

"The baby, the house, they belong to you, Elodie. You might *try* to own these things—mold them as you want them to be. I promise it's best." She runs her hands through her hair for a millisecond, sneaking the gesture since we're at a dining table and it's bad manners. Then she closes her compact.

Guests are coming in; Veronica is distracted.

"I am surprised to see familiar faces. I thought the Van der Bergs and older Sinclairs had gone to Aspen. And the Morris family to Greenwich," she remarks.

"At the Literary Society we have a full calendar of events through Labor Day," I say.

Simon and James are walking in together, a father-

and-son dyad worthy of a Netflix series. They toss their shoulders and keep their chins tipped away from their collarbones. Ever since James learned about my father, he's been *too* engaged with both my parents. He is on the phone nonstop with Veronica about the new house; he and Simon have planned two golf games together. James is asking about bridge—if he sharpens his game, can he play with my father? It's deranged.

A family text comes in from Aubrey. *All, cannot make it. Turned back on the 95, accident. Band at 9 tonight.xo*

Veronica holds her iPhone as if she's angry with it.

"We are having an early dinner for Aubrey. The idea was that she and Tyler could get on the road in time," she says.

"We should have driven to South Beach and had dinner there. It makes little sense in Palm Beach if she's got something tonight in Miami," Simon says. "She is very far along."

Veronica doesn't bother with such a thread of thought. "I'm sorry, I was hoping that Aubrey would be with us tonight."

I'm disappointed, too, but I don't want it to be worse for my sister. "She's busy," I say. Meanwhile, my father must be unhappy, too. He wanted Aubrey to sit beside him. I was to move over when she arrived. He and I were both planning for it.

James dares to whisper—since my mother forbids whispering at a dinner table. "Let's manage to say nothing out of the ordinary for the entire meal."

"That's not a challenge." I speak up. What do I have to lose?

Mimi rushes to our table and sits down. "Hello, ladies."

"Mimi, perfect timing." Veronica leans in. "You know, Elodie, Mimi and I have an idea. Dad, too. We were thinking that perhaps Nadia Sherman from *Palm Beach Confidential* could come along to your office to interview you."

"Interview me? Mom, she already did that two years ago."

"About your work at the Literary Society *and* how the house and the baby are *synchronized*. About you and your sister, a story that will satisfy everyone."

"Why would I do that? What about Aubrey?" Nothing would offend my sister more; I cringe at the idea. And that Veronica and Mimi seem at the beck and call of what other people might think.

Mom sighs. "Well, it would alleviate talk and show the life that you have. The life that Aubrey has. What she's given up for you, what you and she are doing together."

"Dad, you're okay with that? James, does this make sense?"

"Elodie, this is an *idea*. A sort of proof of what's going on," Mimi says. I want to scream. *Proof? Are you kidding, after my parents' secret?*

Aubrey's right at the center of my thoughts, probably where my husband should be. Smiling and laughing with Tyler, dancing, despite how pregnant she is, to "The Rain Song," by Led Zeppelin.

"I'm not sure that I . . ." I begin.

"Something easier on James, Elodie," Mimi says. "Appearances matter."

My mother and Mimi are almost melting into each other, like composites of faces shown in magazines. One can morph from a round face to a heart-shaped face. A person with a narrow chin and arched eyebrows might end up with flat cheeks, a wide chin, and sparse eyebrows. My mother and my mother-in-law together, complicit.

"Absolutely not, not happening," I say. "I won't and Aubrey won't. We've had enough exposure, enough is known, Mom."

Simon says nothing. He and Veronica exchange an old married, gotcha look. James turns to Mimi.

"There you have it, Mom. We can't dispute how she feels."

"Aubrey's take on it, too," I say. "I know how it is."

My mother shrugs, as if she has done her best. That's when I realize what it's about. She is wisely creating a sturdy new identity. Our baby will give her purpose; the involved-grandmother role is next. And needs some publicity, marketing.

Waitstaff scurry around; diners' voices float toward us and upward toward the coffered ceiling. The clinking of glasses and tapping of their cutlery against their dishes seems screechy. No one at our table speaks for a moment.

I excuse myself and walk to the ladies' room. At Justine's it is elegant, the monogrammed hand towels, the frosted lighting, the fresh roses. Mouthwash, makeup mirrors. I look at myself and see Alice. Alice as she is in the pictures she's sent. At an amusement park with her children. At dinner with her husband. Her chin and jawline, her eyeteeth and mine.

"Elodie? Elodie?" James knocks on the door; he's never done that.

I open it three inches. "Aren't you going to Naples tomorrow?"

He pauses. "Is that worrying you? I'm flying with Darnay in his new plane. The flight is remarkably short."

I come out to where he stands. "James, I'd like to go."

"Go? Why? What's in Naples?"

"Is there room for me?"

"I'll text Darnay. What about your work? What is it you want to do?"

"An author. A woman in her fifties who is coming out with the most amazing memoir. She lives there and we've been in touch. I know I can make an arrangement on short notice. An opportunity, off-season, to meet her." I lie easily; I will do just about anything for this to happen.

I'm credible enough that James is already on his cell, asking Darnay, his client and close friend. He clicks off.

"You're in. Who knows, maybe you need a day out of town."

I quickly, semisecretly text my other half sister, Alice. *I can come tomorrow!*

"I'm happy to go." I finally smile at my husband.

James asks nothing. He puts his arms around me.

A streak of lightning comes across the South Florida sky.

CHAPTER 29

ELODIE

Egrets and grackles, birds that favor the grounds of the Literary Society, fly over the wings of the Falcon 7X, the sleekest private jet. On the tarmac, the ground crew are signaling one another, their jumpsuits flapping against their bodies in the morning breeze. I settle into my plush, creamy leather window seat.

Although I've been on private aircraft with James in the past, mostly I've been on such jets with my father. When I was in high school, Simon flew with investors and partners to Denver, Dallas, and Cleveland. If there were meetings in New York, he sometimes scheduled them on a Friday so the family could go along. When I looked at colleges, he arranged for us to fly privately, hitching rides on a friend's jet. The smooth circus act of the Veronica and Simon

Show flourished in those days—marriage, success, looks, daughters. On paper, we were winning, stellar.

"This author—it can't be accomplished with a conference call?"

My husband who never asks why and where I go, suddenly inquisitive last night. Or worse, disbelieving.

"Yes, it could," I had said. "Somehow I'd rather do it in person. It's for my Florida series next winter; I'd like her to be part of it."

Darnay comes onto his jet and claps James on the back. Friends from the "B" school days; Darnay's hedge fund is one of James's biggest investors in ANVO.

"Elodie, I don't remember the last time I saw you." Darnay kisses me on both sides of my face. With his honed Palm Beach affect, he is tan in that healthy, friendly mode.

"Darnay! Thank you for the lift, a last-minute ride," I say.

"Of course. You aren't meeting someone clandestine, are you?" He laughs at his own joke.

"An author, she's seeing an author." James's voice sounds like he's practicing scales and has no talent.

"Your Falcon X, Darnay! I love it. What a gazelle of a jet. Poetry in air," I say.

"I waited God knows how long for it. This is our first year. Cece has only been on it once."

"I see Cece at the Literary Society and we keep talking about rescheduling a dinner," I say.

"You know Cece with that calendar—the girls, after

school, weekends, holidays. At six and four years old, the girls are overextended!" He laughs at this. We, too, laugh, stop. Does James recall that I canceled the last dinner plan with them the week of my miscarriage?

The three of us remain by my seat. The area seems very air conditioned; the freshest air ever on a jet wriggles around us.

"Does your husband tell you how I admire your father?" Darnay says. "When I was a college kid in Palm Beach, long before James and I met, everyone talked about Simon Cutler. After his golf games at the Harbor Club, he'd be on the club phone, you know, the one they'd drag out with extension cords. Your father would be giving orders like no one I'd ever seen. Very collected—what a guy."

A rush of guilt and sorrow encases me. I can't really be speaking about what an unforgettably cool guy Simon is at the moment. Not with Alice waiting once we land. But on James's second pinch to my elbow, I muster up an acknowledgment.

"That's my father," I say. "You're too kind, Darnay."

Darnay looks around. "Okay, we are about to take off. May I borrow your husband for the flight? To prepare for our meeting."

"Of course." I am relieved.

"Is your phone on airplane mode?" James asks as he follows Darnay.

I nod, covering the screen with my hand, protecting my texts. I slip it into my bag, which is only half under my seat. No one seems to quite follow rules when flying on a private plane. I haven't felt like this since my high school boyfriend, Stuart, first kissed me. Or more recently, it must be how my friends Beezy and Linnie felt when they began their affairs. The tug to meet Alice is spellbinding. I might go through the sealed door and tumble from the sky to her. What if it isn't the same for her? What if she is meeting me as she'd meet a friend, an acquaintance? What if she is only willing to chat the way women do at Brick-Top's or Pizza al Fresco, light, easy conversations? Why do I conjure up days to spend with Alice? A sense I get from our phone calls, our traded pictures, our earlobes, which are scarily the same, that we both love Galway Kinnell and Patricia Highsmith.

I ought to text Aubrey and see if the baby is kickboxing in utero this morning. Instead, I peer out the window as we cut above the clouds. Being in the air, alone in my wide seat, is exhilarating. We are high enough from Earth, I am an astronaut in a spaceship of my own making, on my own puzzling voyage.

If Veronica knew my plan, my duplicity, she would beseech me not to take this step. *Do not harm your father,* she would implore me. *Protect him, please.* There would be much back-and-forth about what I owe the parents who raised me.

If Simon were the one to ask me not to go to Alice, he would be more cryptic. He would say that Veronica needed to be shielded, and he would compare Aubrey's lack of investigation with mine. He would probe for the logic while hoping that I skip it altogether.

Both my parents would say, *Come back. Don't go to her. Don't start this.* Yet it cannot be held up, it has to begin.

While the Uber driver heads to the Ritz-Carlton, Naples, I take my iPhone out and tap the camera, then hit the icon to study my face from my clavicle upward. Could my neck possibly be crepey, my eyes that puffy? I have to look good, because Alice will, because she is the touchstone, our meeting is the game changer.

The hotel works for our plan. Being public makes the idea of us easier: If we run into someone—anyone on either side—it's a neutral place, where people congregate for myriad reasons. I rush into the main lobby and search for a ladies' room. "Dark Horse," by Katy Perry, is playing throughout the hotel, a song Aubrey would appreciate. Not yet eleven, I have a few minutes to primp and fuss. Because this connection is of another order, a seduction beyond what I know, I squint in the mirror and scrutinize. I've not fussed with hair, lipstick, the angles of my face like this since the day I married James. As a product of the Veronica and Simon Show, I assumed I'd be safe from that day onward. Wasn't James a bona fide catch? Hadn't I followed the script?

At Gumbo Limbo, the Ritz's outdoor restaurant, I choose a table on the porch, half covered by the overhead, facing the Gulf of Mexico. No sun, magnificent views. I get my bearings. My head circles my body, my body circles my head as I search for Alice. Women are coming in, some in T-shirts and cropped pants, others in colorful shifts, mothers and daughters, older women in groups. I turn my ringer on silent and, with my front teeth, bite off a chip of Benadryl Allergy—maybe four milligrams' worth—and hope it won't make me sleepy. I'm itchy; it could be our get-together or the first whiff of salsa or ceviche floating from the kitchen, pollen blowing about. In my vintage DVF khaki wrap dress and wedge sandals, the effect is neutral. Stashed in my bag is a cashmere cotton-blend cardigan that Veronica bought me before my first miscarriage, before I began at the Literary Society. Isn't that how my life is, divided into a before-and-after syllabus?

Alice is silhouetted as she walks into Gumbo Limbo. We wave, then she walks to the table, shoulders back, like Veronica has taught me. The same height, gait, weight, amount of space between our upper lips and our noses. We have the kind of eyebrows that need pencil, but only a little; the kind of forehead that goes with hair swept off, hair swept sideways. Our voices are that same pitch. She has long, light blondish brown hair. What isn't physical—our worldview, our moral core—is implicit. The two of us are more than a shocking discovery; we are the same, the same, the same.

I stand up and we do a bungled hug. We are seated and take each other in.

"At last!" I say.

"I am so glad that you came." Alice smiles.

More searching each other's faces. We have that see-through skin; small veins show on our temples. Each of us has a cowlick in the middle of her hairline; we have long fingers and slim wrists. Her eyes, like mine, are wide apart and hazel—a shade starlets wanted before tinted lenses came to be. We have these skinny necks, the kind the villain strangles in horror films. It's scary; it's a homecoming.

We take off and put on our sunglasses, like we're mimes in the same act.

"I couldn't wait," I say.

We smile more; it's awkward. Beyond falling for a man, leaving a man, missing a man, and finding him again.

"I brought a list." Alice opens her bag and takes out her iPhone and a small tablet and pen.

"No way. I did, too." I take out my Smythson pink leather notebook.

I feel the hourglass starting, our time together already ransomed. Alice tips her head back and laughs.

"Right, the checklist, what we haven't communicated through email." I look at my notes.

"You already know I have two older brothers. I've always wanted a sister," she says.

"I know you're eight months older, that you're married."

"You know my girls are six, twins, Luca and Mia, and my son, Henry, is three."

"I have no children."

She nods. "I do know."

I ought to tell her about Aubrey, yet I wait. Alice looks at her list. "Mostly we've talked about our taste in books, art, film, and plays—dramas, not musicals."

I smile. "Everything from Shakespeare to Elizabeth Barrett Browning to the Brontës. Oh, and *Hamilton* and *Carousel*."

"La Bayadere, too. That seems the easiest part." Alice clicks her pen. "You wanted to know how I got to Naples. I came back kicking and screaming. I married an accountant whose father was an accountant here. We grew up together. Naples wasn't exciting, but it was the logical step. We moved back from Northern California seven years ago. I began teaching kindergarten, then after these rough spots with infertility, I took a leave and had my twins."

"Clomid?" I ask. What hasn't been disclosed and isn't searchable.

"Yes, although I never say. I kept miscarrying."

"I know the feeling. I've had miscarriages, plenty of that and on Clomid."

Alice frowns, concerned. Texts start coming in.

The first is from James: *All good?* I quickly text back: *Yes.* When a text comes in from Aubrey with a selfie—*Last round of baggy clothes*—I force myself to text back: *Yes, great.* When a text bings not a minute later from my mother—*Breakers at noon tomorrow?*—I send nothing back. I have become unfaithful to everyone, but mostly to my sister. Sitting with Alice is an addiction, isn't it? What are those phrases people use before someone is lost to them—*at a precipice, a moth to a flame?*

Images of Aubrey clutter my head. Aubrey crawling into my bed at night for years on end, until I left for college, confiding first about the mean girls and then about the bad boys. Aubrey winning the science prize for the state of Florida and not caring a fig, while I slogged away at Princeton for every A I earned. Aubrey, who is and was ethereal, objectified since she was in third grade. Aubrey, who seems content to be carrying a baby. A shocking revelation at that.

I take a deep breath.

"My sister Aubrey is carrying our baby, a girl. Her egg, James's sperm. She's due in September."

"Why, that's phenomenal, Elodie," Alice says. "You'll have a little girl! She must be a terrific sister."

"I wonder if I should have done it. I mean, at first I was

relieved and happy. My husband, James, is excited, my mother, mother-in-law. Ever since I found out about the DNA, about us, I've concentrated less on the baby, to be honest. It's intricate."

"Aren't you happy? My children are the best part of my life. It makes me realize how desperate our parents were. I can relate to that. I did the same for my girls, you did it for your daughter," Alice says. Something my mother or Mimi might have said, and I would have been offended.

"During the pregnancy, I've worried if my sister ever had a drink, smoked a cigarette." I can't believe I'm telling her this.

"Someone who would agree to carry a baby for you wouldn't put herself in harm's way, would she?"

I know she is right, that Aubrey is wary, that having children is meaningful. I won't admit how being childless too long, eyeing my friends with their babies, has made me ambivalent, a closet skeptic.

"At first it surprised me that she would do this for me. Quite a gift."

Alice smiles like I used to smile—ages ago. "And soon you'll have your baby."

The server with a name tag, Todd, comes to take our order while I sip a latte. Alice holds up her forefinger and he backs away.

"About your father, who raised you." I look at my notes. "Is that on your list?"

"Yes, yes. My social father," Alice says.

"Your 'social father,' was he good with your brothers?" I ask.

"Totally, the boys were his. After they were born, my dad caught the mumps and became infertile. My mother wanted more kids, she wanted a girl. When my father died two years ago—too young—my mother was relieved to tell me that I didn't have his DNA. What about your father?"

I shake my head. "Both my parents were indignant, angry at us for learning about the sperm donor."

"Really?" She is surprised.

"For me, the disclosure was a good thing," I say. "There was this family, yet no matter what I did, how I tried to match my father, it didn't feel like a fit. Did you have that?" I say.

"I did and I didn't. I mean, it was a divided family. The boys belonged to my dad, while I was more for my mother. I thought it was because he was sexist—I sort of accepted it. Now I know it was because I really wasn't his."

"But growing up?"

Alice looks at her list. "Right, I was going to ask you that, too." She sighs. "My father was kind to me, loving. We were close. I never put it together until . . ."

I nod. "I know, until you found out."

"It was imperceptible and mostly it was my mother who drew the distinctions. I was their child. I didn't doubt it," Alice says.

"In our family it was another story. My father has done very well and he was always busy with work. Our mother worked, too, but she had time and she fussed over my sister and me. I wanted to please them. Where I went to school, my marriage."

"I always trusted my father," Alice says. "I revered him."

"Do you feel like you've betrayed him with the DNA kits, with meeting me?" I ask.

"No, no." Alice's tone is light, confident. "Had he not died, maybe they would have kept the secret—like your parents tried to do."

The two of us look out over the Gulf of Mexico. The waves are mild compared to the Atlantic. "Vanderbilt Beach, isn't it?" I ask.

"Yes, with gumbo-limbo trees, flora and fauna you can see in the water."

"Do you bring your children here?" I ask.

"I do. We came as kids to the beach, Samuel, my husband, and I," she says. More quasi-waves hit the shore. She opens her bag and takes out a Revlon lipstick. I open my bag and take out the same one. "Rum Raisin," I say.

We tap the lipsticks together as if we're clinking glasses. I look at her profile. So like mine, maybe more like mine than Aubrey's.

"The father who raised you is your father—that's what my mother keeps repeating to me," I say.

"He must be very upset about our lunch." Alice is reading her list.

"No one knows that we are together. I said I was meeting a writer for work. Although I'm not sure they believed it. I've never had to lie about where I'm going before in my life. My sister defends our father. She doesn't want him to feel diminished. I doubt she'll track down any donor siblings on her side."

Simon. His library and gardens, the secret he has carried for forty-one years. The force of failure versus the facade of success. "Yes, he'd be disturbed about our lunch, totally."

"Still, you did it."

"Alice, I did this for me," I say. "Meeting today. For us."

"About your question. I'm very connected to my mother. I'd like to tell her about you," Alice says. "What about your mother, what would she say?"

Connected. What would Veronica say?

"My mother isn't behind me, she's defending. My sister Aubrey accepts what has happened. We don't have the same sperm donor."

"What do you mean?"

"She's only my half sister, too. Our bio fathers aren't the same. I keep asking myself why is this different from adopting a child. It's that adoption is explained. Not a secret that made us who we are."

Alice waits, computing this. "What our parents went through—we have to honor that."

"I know, except that we were lied to and it bothers me," I say. "How my mother has acted, placating my father. Their marriage, their take on their children. Not only were we deceived but it was never safe because of their secret."

Alice straightens up and looks at me calmly.

"Elodie, what will this do for you—being unforgiving, holding your parents accountable? You yourself have been through fertility hell. So there are cracks in your parents' story, in their lives." She sighs, looks out at the Gulf of Mexico. "Maybe because I have children, maybe it makes me look at it differently. We wouldn't be born, any of us, had our parents not made the decision they did."

It is almost two o'clock yet feels past midnight when we stand up at the same second in the same manner. Out into a spotless Florida day. I'm buoyant and too heavy to lift my own body. Alice takes her car keys out of her bag.

"I can drive you to the airport."

James, on guard, already at the tarmac. "I wish, but probably it isn't wise. Thank you."

Searching for my Uber app, I plug in the airport address.

Alice comes closer. "You know what isn't on our lists and should be is how our parents were coached. Shopping for a sperm bank or an egg donor is open today; our parents had to keep it quiet. The bio ethics were not in sync with the technology."

"Aren't you curious about our bio father? Why was he chosen—what were our parents' requirements?" I ask.

"That part worked out. We're smart and . . ."

". . . look good," I say.

We laugh together.

"Hey," Alice says. "We found each other. And we can find more half sibs. I figure there are twenty or more. Probably scattered across the country, coming out of Florida, New York. Both coasts."

"I know," I say. Although I want to know *and* I don't want to know; I want us to be exclusive somehow.

"Then there's our bio father and the doctor who arranged it," Alice says.

"What?" To me, the fertility doctor and sperm donor are invisible, ghosts, not accessible.

"I've found them both. I know how to track them down. Get this, they're not hard to contact!" She squeezes my hand.

The bio father. Other siblings. What Veronica fears, what Aubrey is avoidng.

"The father, our father, I would love to know who he is, to find out about him," I say. "That might be enough for me."

"And not meet him? Don't you want to meet him?" Alice asks.

James texts. *Will you be here by 2:30?* A black Hyundai Sonata snakes across my iPhone screen as it drives up to the hotel.

I reach out to her. "I have to go, Alice."

"We'll be in touch; we'll get together soon."

A polite Uber driver opens the door for me. I fold myself into the car and look back at her, standing where I've left her, waving.

CHAPTER 30

AUBREY

"Café Boulud is the best choice for a baby shower because of the terrace," Mimi says. Together we stand at the entrance to the restaurant. She is spruced up today in a St. John dress and her low-heeled Manolos, carrying an initialed Goyard bag in bright blue. A part of the Goyard frenzy. In South Beach young women carry them to the beach.

"I am sure it will be a lovely party." She looks at me and past me as she speaks, in search of my sister, who ought to be here.

"It will be." I smile at Mimi. Bizarre how I've come to appreciate my sister's mother-in-law. She's the one who wants what she wants without an agenda. Except today her words slur; I swear she's been drinking.

"You know what will be sublime, Aubrey? When I finally

have my grandchild. My son and your sister have been together for over a decade."

I nod, wondering if Mimi and Elodie will be closer once the baby is born. Didn't I just read a blog where the daughter-in-law confessed to loving her once-hateful mother-in-law ever since giving birth to a son?

We walk inside, where half the tables are set up. The other half are on the terrace, each with a bouquet of pansies. The summer light through the blinds is strong. The cake, a replica of a baby cradle in pink and white, designed by Anya, is surrounded by baby's breath and white orchids. *Baby Cutler-Evans*, it reads in a bright pink icing. Chosen by my mother and Mimi, along with Ryana Delce, party planner for every occasion. I call it "the baby shower" because I can't tell if it's mine or Elodie's, if we share it. When Mom, Elodie, Mimi, and I worded the invitation, it was more a debate than a family effort. The language was critical to the mothers. After much back-and-forth, Elodie decided. "It will read 'A Baby Shower for Elodie Cutler, Mother, and Aubrey Cutler, Carrier.'"

While not riveting or global, the "Cutler-Evans baby" is an uncommon baby to be. My mother has been the press secretary about town, labeling it "a collective baby shower," while Elodie calls it a "coming-out party for a sister who carries her sister's baby." At least she can make a joke, since she's seemed downcast for weeks. Mom keeps pretending it's fine. James is obsessed with the house, his fancy new creation. Then there is Dad, who has become icy as if he's cut himself out of our family picture ever since it was divulged for what it is. "Dad goes through the motions but isn't really there," I told Elodie yesterday. "Do you think so?" she asked, sounding distant herself.

"I want the afternoon to be successful and to vanish." Mom comes over to us, scans the dining room, hunting for Elodie. "Would you look at how many guests are down off-season? Along with year-rounders."

"Mom, you wanted a shower, you told us it was important," I say. "You said no one would come after May; you predicted a small party."

"It's irresistible, two mothers for one baby? There are guests who coordinated their schedules to be in Palm Beach this week—decorators to see, trunk shows at a few shops, *and* the baby shower!"

"Right," Mom says. "What's Tabatha's broken engagement on the Turquoise, or two husbands caught for tax evasion, or Lara Mercer's affair with her pilot, compared to this?"

The part where our mother takes it too seriously, longs to be beyond rebuke—of any sort.

"Mom, it's not like we're breaking the law," I say. "And I assume Tabatha would believe being jilted at her engagement party a little more disturbing than today's curiosity."

Mom raises her eyebrow as far as she can. "Where is your sister?"

Although it is really annoying that Elodie is late, I say, "She's en route."

Hors d'oeuvres are being served on the terrace. Guests are prompt—Mrs. A., Faith Harrison, Cecelia Norric, Betina Gilles, Margot Damon. My friends Tiffany, Heather, and Jessica; Elodie's friends from the Academy and Wellington, where they rode horses together, Beezy, Nina, Carly, and Linnie, have arrived. Women I've never seen smile at me as they should; their Aquatalia mules and Gucci slides tap against the stone floor. The false lashes, long skirts, short skirts, toe cleavage of the young, medium, old. My friends in pastel flowing dresses that sway and swing.

Then those cousins of Mimi's, two sisters—chic, thin, snooty, second cousins once removed, whose names aren't memorable. Their sons, who have tormented Elodie by existing. Kids' birthday parties—for what, eight years—that she had to attend as Mimi's dutiful daughter-in-law. Their sly looks because Elodie had *no* baby and now because of *how* Elodie is having a baby. Mimi has grown a bit short with them herself, while Elodie has always linked them to the time she miscarried at one child's third-birthday party. She called me, crying because she couldn't carry a baby to term. I didn't even know the phrase "to term" at the time. The sisters sit at Mimi's table in vintage Pucci dresses, talking only to each other.

Mostly conversations skim across the room—rainstorms, valet parking, the temperature of the restaurant versus that of the lobby of the Brazilian Court, small dogs and their biscuits, Valentino, Gucci, Escada when in doubt. Vhernier bracelets, Seaman Schepps always, the school calendar. Bellinis are polished off and voices are louder.

It would be Elodie whose stilettos hit the ground differently—more a staccato tapping—than the others when she walks into Boulud. She is a nonpregnant goddess or I'm too pregnant to judge. Every woman is thin and glamorous to me these days, while strangers on Collins Avenue in South Beach and Worth Avenue in Palm Beach glance at me and look away, fearful I'll go into labor where they stand. I'm hungry every hour; Baby Grace flips and skids across my womb. I have heartburn if I eat arugula with balsamic, angel hair pomodoro, or pizza, the only foods I want. Tyler and I haven't had sex in three weeks. The last time we did it, the baby was practically a part of it. I look around at the women—pretenders, aren't they? My sister's hair is shimmering; she wears it down, which she's done twice in the last six months. In her off-white column dress, she seems taller than she is and smiles in that rigid style our mother values, no matter what.

"Elodie, Elodie! . . . Lovely. . . . Hello, so chic. . . ."

Elodie pauses like a celebrity would. "Hello, hello." She looks around, walks to the cake in the middle of the terrace. "Oh, it's beautiful! Look at the artwork!"

She gives a radiant smile. On Hulu or Amazon Prime, she'd be a character to watch closely. There's a strange mix of tranquillity and edginess about her. She has crow's-feet that weren't there before the pregnancy. Her chin is softer, while I'm the one who has gained twenty-four pounds. We are both very pale for Palm Beach, that kind of milky pale that works better in cities.

"Where were you?" I ask my sister.

"Ran late, work, you know," she says.

"No, I don't," I reply. "This is the shower for our baby."

"Really?" Elodie tosses her head.

We look at each other, the half sibs—hers, not mine— hang between us. She's up to something, I know it.

"Hey, I'm present and accounted for." She links her arm in mine.

Ryana snaps her fingers and Jill, the photographer, who is about my age and very quick with her camera, gets a few pictures with her Nikon.

As the guests hone in, no one missing that I look like I swallowed a beach ball, Elodie comes close and places her right hand on my womb. She winks. "We love our baby."

"We do. Already she's a cause célèbre." I put my right hand on top of Elodie's. *Our baby* flips, as if I've choreographed it. Both our hands are pushed into the air. We squeal; then I burp. I've been doing that a lot lately. Elodie opens her cross-body bag and hands me a Rolaid. Each of us pops one into her mouth. Mom is beside us in a matter of milliseconds. She grasps our wrists and breathes deeply.

"Let's get more pictures, girls," Mom says.

"Did you see her camera?" I ask. "It's a twenty-four-millimeter . . ."

"That's fine, Aubrey," she says. Her grasp is tighter. Elodie wiggles her arm.

"Girls!"

We pose for consecutive shots. Our mother whisks us past the gift table, where boxes from Lori Jayne, Betty McCarter, Ralph Lauren, and Bonpoint pile up. The photographer motions for us to pause, pose more.

"We are not opening presents during the luncheon," Mom whispers as she turns to the guests. Both Elodie and I nod. Except I do want to open them. I want to see what Baby Grace will have, how adorable each outfit will be. What books will be given, puzzles, smock dresses (this is Palm Beach), a Raggedy Ann and Andy, stuffed bears and bunnies. A locket—someone will give her that, too.

"Mom, are you sure about the gifts?" I ask. "I'd so like to open them."

Elodie bites her lip. Mom steps in front of us. "Ladies, lunch is served."

Each guest reviews the menu in pink ink on parchment paper. Gaspacho, a choice of lobster roll, yellowtail snapper, or grilled chicken and kale salad. Afterward, the cake that, once cut, will destroy the cradle, figuratively. Has no one picked up on that? The only item I want at Boulud is their key lime pie. I might ask a server to slip me a piece while orders are taken. Instead, I listen to the whispering guests. *Right out of* People *magazine. . . . Who is the father? Whose egg was used? Artificial insemination . . . both the aunt* and *the biological mother . . . For years, Elodie grappled . . . talented at work . . . an unmarried sister . . . too-small a town . . . that family, always apart in their thinking . . . an idea that . . .*

Does my sister hear the talk about us? I can't tell, because she is doing an A-list acting job, standing with her childhood friends, trading iPhones for photos of children, houses, maybe husbands, too. Isn't this what is done? The sharing *and* envying of one another's glittering prizes as Elodie is, at last, about to have the final prize.

"Come," Mom says to me as I wait beside her. "I'll walk you to your friends, darling."

Together we move to the table to the left of my mother's. Elodie sits down at hers and does a zoomy wave—we're her fans.

On her way back from the ladies' room, Mrs. A. puts her mouth close to my ear. The scent of lavender soap and Caleche is dense. "Aubrey, dear, who is the shower *for*?"

"I'm sorry, Mrs. A.," I say, "I'm not sure what you mean."

"The deserving one, the woman of the hour."

At the end of it, my father, James, and Tyler work their way into Café Boulud in that exact order. Tyler lags behind, while my father, like an old actor, and James, like someone who dabbles in acting, are in step. James's part, that of the father who expects a child, is important. Tyler looks like he loves me, not like an actor. Like he's the hero in a Disney film who balances out the story.

"Here they are!" Mom seems pleased.

Forks tap gently against the china; guests polish off the baby cradle cake. My mother wants this wrapped up.

"Can we get a picture of the mother- and father-to-be?" Jill, the photographer, practically shouts. She places her hand on my back and circles around to find Elodie. James walks toward Elodie, slides his arm around her waist. She bends into him. Jill starts snapping more pictures. Everyone stops talking; the women gawk as the lens opens, then shuts faster and faster. Tyler slips his hand into mine. In an alternate universe, we are body doubles for the couple expecting a baby.

We are the next to last to leave the baby shower, while Mom, Mimi, and Dad are still inside. The heat hits our shoulders and the humidity makes the air dirty when Elodie walks me to my car.

"Did you see that Dad is settling the bill?" I ask.

"No, I didn't see that. But Tyler and James are packing up the gifts in Veronica's car."

"Yeah, well, he is, which makes me sad. I mean, it has to be déjà vu. Another level of posturing. His grandchild-to-be." I'm wistful.

Elodie pats my arm. "I know, it's surreal for him, isn't it?"

I could be overheated; the sun is too glaring. I'm always tired. The third trimester is like that, according to Dr. Noel's team and every book that I've bought.

"I waddle, don't I?" I say.

"No, you don't," she lies.

We stop, as if we need to think about it.

"Well, a little," Elodie admits. "Soon it will be over."

I hold on to her elbow, like the old ladies in the Publix parking lot who count on others for balance.

"I'm afraid, you know." Elodie speaks to me as if it's a secret; her voice is low and somber.

"Me, too. I am afraid of the delivery. I have to pee every five minutes, I sleep with four pillows—for my back, between my legs. I get heartburn, serious heartburn! Tyler and I can barely hold each other, let alone have sex."

Elodie starts laughing. "Oh my God!"

"The thing is, every time the baby, *our* baby, kicks, I want to comfort her. Tyler and I talk about the songs we can play for her. 'Golden Slumbers' from the *Abbey Road* album; 'Tura Lura Lural'—there's a recording of The Band with Van Morrison singing that lullaby." I stop; I've said too much.

Elodie pauses. She seems surprised by my zeal.

"I meant . . ." I say.

"It has to be most of the time. She must be kicking

constantly at this point." My sister stares back at Café Boulud almost with nostalgia.

"I know. She's big." I run my hands over my womb.

"What about afterward? How do women get back in shape? Some of my friends have done so well; others are more stuck." Elodie shakes her head sympathetically.

"I don't know the secret sauce. At Soul Center, near my apartment, a few months ago, a woman was talking about it. How she'd had a baby in the spring and she's gone from someone who worshipped her own body to someone who is like a martyr for her offspring. When our instructor asked her about her weight gain, she said, 'Oh, no worries, as soon as I stop breast-feeding, I'll tend to that.'"

Breast-feeding. My sister and I look at each other—our bodies so near, our faces can touch. We could whisper kisses with our eyelashes.

"Aubrey, I'm afraid to take care of the baby." Elodie's voice is flat.

"That's what you're afraid of? I wouldn't be afraid of that." I sound like a cheerleader.

"You might be the better mother, Aubrey." My sister says this in one breath, then becomes static.

"Please, don't think so." I, too, am static.

"Mother Earth. You know that." Elodie stares at my body, then at my face.

"You'll be a fantastic mother to such a sweet little girl." Again, I sound like a cheerleader. *Baby Grace.* Dare I say her name aloud?

"So could you." Elodie sounds sure of this.

"Do you believe that? I suppose I could. It's true that she's always on my mind," I say.

Baby Grace tumbles and flips. "Feel this—the baby's elbow. How she's pushing against me, how she wants to get out?"

Elodie places her hand over the baby as she kicks ferociously.

"What you're doing for me—I couldn't do it for you. I know it, Aubrey."

My big sister, the reliable one, my idol.

"We're almost there," I say.

CHAPTER 31

AUBREY

Where are the baby presents?" Tyler asks. "I thought I hadn't made room."

His files for singers, contracts, his Mac Air, and a pair of running shoes are piled in a heap on the chair that might have held the gifts.

"At my parents' or at Elodie's," I say. "I wanted to open them at the luncheon. My mother said no."

"What about Elodie?" Tyler asks.

"I'm not sure what she wanted to do," I say.

I imagine boxes. It occurs to me that some are filled with pink baby clothes. Dresses and sweaters that will fit her until she is one or two. Knit hats, booties. Someone will have chosen a snowsuit for a trip up north.

"Why don't you ask about it?" He pauses. "Hungry?"

Tyler swings open the door of the refrigerator; it's obvious he's gone food shopping. I haven't, that's for sure.

"I'm texting my mother and sister."

He squats like an acrobat, a catcher for a professional baseball team. He ought to be in a mask, thumbs up, ball whirling by. Not that I've ever watched baseball much, but once Simon pointed out the players and explained their roles. I was about eleven. It was the two of us in the den. My sister was already at Princeton. Mom was at an event for Mothers and Children. Christina had gotten married and no longer lived in, as Mom used to describe it to her friends.

Tyler stands up and shows me he has drinkable yogurt and organic blueberries. "Maybe this? It's after six, and I doubt you ate much at that gig this afternoon."

"I'm okay, thanks."

A text from Elodie. *Whenever. Time?*

I start texting back.

He winks at me. "Dulce de leche ice cream?" He's about to squat again, dig around in the freezer. I shake my head.

"Hey, what's on your mind—beyond the baby presents?"

"They don't belong to us anyway." Dozens of times I've meant to say, *Sorry, sorry, and sorrier.* I don't speak.

His bald head shines and dazzles in the kitchen light. I've forgotten how buff he is; his muscles show through his polo shirt, the one I encouraged him to wear today. I go to him and we kiss, although I smell like someone who has been out too long on a hot day. He doesn't smell.

He whistles a song I haven't heard, a new song from a new singer. A song about the despair of winter, a nonpolitical song with a tune I already love. I'd ask him to sing it or play it, except he might remark how absent I've been, avoiding clubs with loud music, asleep by ten P.M.

"We have a quiet night at least; it's ours. It's been a long while," I say.

"We should talk." His voice sounds weighted down by rocks. He's got that yogurt in his hand. I take it from him and open the cap.

I want to be covered up, never naked again. I want no one to ever say that we "should talk." Like I've been put on a pill with side effects. Flashing lights and people who might or might not be dead roll around in my head. My father's mother, Grandma Lise. She was patient with me. Did she know what they'd gone through in order for me to be born, for Elodie? Then my mother's mother, Renata, who had too many rules. No shoes in the house, nothing could be hung on a door handle. She taught me about appearances, everything just so. Manners first, true thoughts second. No wonder we're such train wrecks.

"It's been insane, the baby, the DNA, my mother doing her best at subterfuge."

"She's good, I'll give her that," Tyler says.

"She's been at it a long time." I glance out the window; the daylight is still strong. I pretend we're in Stockholm, where the summer sun shines through the night. A place we've talked about going together. I pretend that I haven't anything much ahead, nothing that might be an out-of-body experience. We could eat dinner at midnight; we could take a boat ride to the Archipelago.

We're both standing there.

"I miss you," I say.

"I miss you, too."

"You hate my family, right?" I toss the yogurt in the trash and wash my hands. "You hate Palm Beach."

I start eating the blueberries without rinsing them.

"I don't hate them." Tyler takes the berries, places them in a colander. "I don't *hate* Palm Beach."

"You hate what they've done, asking me to have Baby Grace, going up to Palm Beach too much, hardly booking the groups, leaving it for you."

"I want you, Aubrey."

He comes up, holds me gently from behind. With his arms around me at what was once my waist, his hands barely meet. I notice the music has changed; he's turned it up. "Fields of Gold," a slow-dance song, one I first heard when I was sixteen. Elodie and James were driving me to the Breakers at Christmastime to meet our "winter friends." I had no boyfriend; everyone else did. They were grown-up, savvy, my sister and James; they'd seen it all.

"Tighter, hold me tighter," I whisper.

"The baby, I don't want to crush her," he whispers back.

"You won't, can't." I know this because of how guarded I am with Baby Grace.

That's when he carries me, the floating blimp, to the bedroom; that's when he undresses me. In the mirror, he is sleek. I am clumsy. In his face I see how he loves me.

"You, I want you. What we share," I say.

He kneels down, kisses my navel, which is distorted, like there was never a belly button. Yet it's okay; we're both in awe of what it takes—how Baby Grace grows. I put my hands around his neck.

"Will she be all right?" he asks. "I mean, if we . . ."

"It should be okay. Dr. Noel told me until I'm too uncomfortable, I'll lie on my side. We can . . ."

"Shhhh." He stands up, taller than James or my father. He kisses me like I'm a babe. I open my eyes in the middle of it. Through the slatted blinds, a watery, tired light is moving in, Florida end of day. I crave him, but I must take care of the baby, our baby. She is vital, tangible. Any love-making now could be sensed, felt by her.

"Will you spoon me?" I ask.

Tyler stretches me out as if I'm nimble. In our bed, there is a foggy memory of me before I signed on for the baby.

"We can do that," he says. "Or do you want to be on top?"

"Let's try both. Or either," I say. The thought of him that close is intoxicating, although I can't conceptualize how this might work out.

"If you're on top, we face each other." He kisses my fore-head. I want the intimacy of our faces close, yet I'm afraid. Baby Grace is a gymnast inside me. Sex at the moment is unspeakable, really. I'm contemplating it only because of Tyler. There is the ongoing marvel of loving him.

"I am safe with you," I say. "Safer than I've ever been."

He props himself up on his elbow and strokes my shoulders, runs his hands over my uterus. His touch is knowing.

"A hundred percent." Tyler leans back on the pillows. "We don't have to do this, Aubrey."

"I know." I try to snuggle close. Gently, he tugs under my arms and moves me beside him.

"You know, when that photographer called for the parents, the parents-to-be today, I dunno, why wasn't it us?" he asks. "All these months, people have seen us around and assume this is our baby."

"Tyler, you know why. It's always been the deal, the two of us on the sidelines—you dragged into the drama, me a half-willing participant." At least at first, half-willing.

"Well, it's become different over time. The three of us, you, me, the baby, like we're a unit. That's how it is."

"True," I say, "completely true."

Had I never agreed to the baby, Elodie's sorrow—what she was missing—would not be my responsibility. Nor the overriding matter with Tyler.

"Baby Grace. We think she's ours, don't we?" Finally, I have the courage to ask. Tyler moves onto his side and I stay on my back, two pillows beneath my head. Our bodies are very close.

"Yeah, we do," he says.

I picture how she'll be, the baby inside me, who is soon to be born.

CHAPTER 32

ELODIE

Mom, you sounded in despair," I say to Veronica as she stands to the east. The waves do a low screech along the shoreline.

"Did I?" she asks.

"Maybe tired," I say.

She nods. "Definitely that."

She seems peaked, apprehensive, when she should be pleased. The baby shower was a hit; soon the baby will arrive. Instead, she has called for this "meeting" and we stand at her poolside, the air not only hot but clammy and damp. I wish Aubrey would appear. When Veronica asked for an "immediate lunch," my sister was fast asleep. Then she called Tyler, who arranged for Aubrey to take an Uber. According to her text, she's a few miles away.

Our last gathering at the pool was back in the winter.

I remember how dedicated Veronica was that morning. She had assumed that Aubrey's pregnancy was the reason we were together. Instead, we slammed her with the DNA tests and asked her to defend herself. Now she sucks in her breath. "Here's Aubrey."

Moving like liquid lava, Aubrey comes through the house and onto the patio. She veers to where we are sitting at the table under the umbrella. The chair scrapes against the slate when she yanks at it.

"Aubrey, please, don't be tugging on heavy things!" Veronica says. "Elodie or I will be happy to assist."

"I'm fine, Mom." Aubrey sits down. "Maybe it will induce labor."

I feel guilty at how wide my sister's thighs look—her entire silhouette. Very unlike her.

The baby contorts herself and Aubrey gasps. Through the thin fabric of her maternity dress—she's finally wearing these ugly third-trimester tents—each baby twist is distinctive. My sister's skin bunches, ripples, and relaxes.

"Isn't that an old wives' tale?" I ask. "That lifting or scrubbing floors will begin someone's labor?"

Veronica coughs, or is it a short laugh? "That's speculative," she says.

"Where's Dad?" Aubrey fans herself with her hands, then places them on her stomach. "Could we go into the house and sit in air-conditioning?"

Veronica grimaces. "Let's stay outside a few more minutes. Christina isn't in. Dad is in his office unexpectedly. His bridge game was canceled."

"Is there anything to eat?" Aubrey looks at the empty table.

"I have a Lara bar in my bag." I start fishing around, although if it's at the bottom, it's probably too close to the Purell to offer.

Aubrey watches. "That's okay."

"I wanted us alone together to tell you the rest," Mom says. "Now."

Aubrey and I look at each other and then at the Intracoastal, where the water is a faded blue. On the bulkhead are two pelicans, side by side, beaks at the same angle.

"I'm not sure what you mean, Mom," I say.

"I have a confession," Mom says. "What happened, a long time ago."

Aubrey puts her hands right beneath her breasts; the baby pushes a foot, an elbow, something at her. "We don't want or need a confession, Mom. Do we, Elodie?"

An overdue piece of the truth—how could I *not* want it? "That's up to Mom."

"No, honestly, there can't be more to learn, there *can't* be," Aubrey says. "No more, please."

I could be like my sister, searching for the part that doesn't crush you. I could choose lightness. Or I could be the next to confess, right after our mother—what more has she to tell anyway? I should speak up with a dramatic reveal: *I've met my sister Alice. She means the world to me. I see myself in her. She searching for our bio father.* Who is capable of outdoing that?

"Believe me, girls, there is more. You were born because your father and I *had* to have children."

"We know that, Mom," I say.

"Well, something happened first." She runs her fingers across her forehead. "I terminated a pregnancy."

Aubrey speaks after a full minute. "Mom, that's fine. Who hasn't? Elodie had one 'termination' and I've had two."

I need to check incoming texts. From Laurie, although the Society is calm; from James, whose obsession with our certificate of occupancy is beyond irritating. From Mimi about the baby nurse she insists is best; from our contractor about an end of day walk-through. Since our Naples meeting, Alice and I text constantly—it borders on fervid. Like now when I text Alice back that I, too, wonder what our bio father looks like.

"Elodie," Veronica says. "This might resonate for you. When you made your decision, you thought you were too young to have a baby; you thought you and James deserved time alone together, in your young marriage."

"I know, and you tried to talk me out of it," I say.

"And then later, years later, look at what it is," she says.

Is Veronica attempting to churn up my regret? I try never to revisit what I did and how the window closed, the chances lessened. I let myself go from young to too old, as if I were hypnotized and had no awareness. I used to be angry with myself over that, for years. I am still terribly sorry.

"Why does that matter today, Mom?" Aubrey asks. "Please. Can't we go inside, get something to eat? It's too hot out here, too humid. The umbrella isn't helping."

Aubrey puts a handkerchief from Maltese that Veronica bought us, the one with two embroidered butterflies, on the nape of her neck.

"We can't go inside yet," Veronica says. "I've told you, Dad is there."

"Right," I say. "But maybe we could sneak into your

bathroom, pile in and whisper. It's clearly large enough and probably only sixty-eight degrees."

"No, no. This has to do with Dad." Our mother wrings her hands.

"I don't understand. Was it another sperm donor? Is that what you want us to know?" I ask. Has our mother had three different men trying to produce a family?

"Before your father left, before Vietnam, I was pregnant. I didn't know until he was deployed. I might have written him, told him, and had the baby. I might *not* have told him and had the baby, put the baby up for adoption. Or I could have pretended we were married and I was waiting for him to come home. I asked Grandma Renata. I'm not sure why I listened to her. I couldn't ask anyone else back then; you couldn't get support, only friends judging you. It was in the early seventies—I was twenty-two years old; what sounded wisest was to abort. Grandma felt that, too. 'What if Simon never comes back,' she said to me. 'What about the neighbors? What about how you aren't married?' I paid attention. I went to Planned Parenthood." She pauses. "I aborted Dad's biological child. Then he came back and couldn't have his own."

Aubrey squares her mouth and I do the same. We are, in this moment of our mother's secret, equally astonished, a mirror for each other.

I place my hand on Veronica's forearm. "And you never told Dad what you did."

"No, never," she agrees, "because it would be crushing for him. It's enough of a blow that he was damaged in Vietnam, never mind that I took what I did away from him."

"Dad can't ever know," Aubrey says.

"Only my mother knew and now you girls," Veronica

says. "I wanted to tell you, to have you understand. I wanted to be absolved."

I look back at the bulkhead; the two pelicans have taken flight.

"We get it, Mom," Aubrey says. "Don't we, Elodie?"

I nod. "We do."

Veronica traces her upper lip with her index fingers. "I had no idea when he came home, when his service was over. I thought we'd have children, start a family. I thought we'd live in New York—the city, a suburb."

"Mom, let's not do this. It reminds me of—"

"Of you, Elodie!" Aubrey says. "That's who!"

"Aubrey!" our mother says.

"Except what about Dad?" Aubrey is about to cry. "I mean, maybe he does know—subconsciously. Or maybe what happened with the 23andMe test is too much; he's been hurt, duped."

"I used to think about it every day and then I pushed it away. I had you girls and that was enough for me. Harder for your father, except when we moved to Palm Beach. Dad got the life he wanted, and being very successful in his business helped, too. He is seen as a man who has it all, his company, his wife and girls. Yet pretending about the sperm donor, that is constant—it's been an exhausting chore, for years on end. What we did, it's there—like a specter. You always sense it."

"So that explains your Palm Beach lifestyle, " I say.

"It does," Veronica says. "Warm weather, beauty, outdoor sports, successful husbands. It sort of fed our marriage. What I had . . . why I was okay is that I had my daughters."

"We're fine, Mom," Aubrey says.

"Are we?" I ask.

"Yes," Aubrey says, "we are absolutely okay."

"I was never smart enough, was I, Mom?"

"Of course you were. Look at what you've accomplished, Elodie."

"I wasn't smart enough no matter that I went to Dad's schools and had the same accolades."

"You weren't his," Aubrey says. "I mean, in that way. But you are his, we are his." That's how deep it goes—Aubrey stating the obvious. The obvious that we've each avoided.

"That would be okay with you, wouldn't it, Aubrey?"

"I'm sorry?" my sister says.

"Yes, it would be okay; it would be enough that you aren't his biological daughter. Because you never tried to be like him," I say. "While I did."

"I am like Dad; I'm the part that's more dreamy. That's why he's patient with me."

"That's why?" I ask.

"Girls, please," Veronica chides. "Don't do this. If Dad has treated you differently, it is because you came at a different time in his life. He had become very prominent with his work by the time Aubrey was born. He was more open to the idea of a sperm donor. He wanted two children."

"It doesn't matter. We love you, Mom, we love Dad," Aubrey says.

I want to say, *Please shut the fuck up.* I don't mention how mercurial he is, how he gives and takes—how he is a cold man.

"No one talks about Vietnam, about the men," Veronica says.

The past few months, since 23andMe, our mother has made the case repeatedly that Dad was entitled to his whims—he had been harmed in the Vietnam War.

"I tried to be part of the crowd, to be a couple whom people sought out. I thought being here, living in this house . . ." Mom views the gardens and bougainvillea, the infinity pool, water views in both directions. "I thought if we had the right life, it could be our reality. Why not, in this town?"

Veronica, a young woman who loved a man. She expected him home in one piece, and he returned to the outside world as such. Her disclosure is shocking; she has carried it for decades. I'd like to be in the Aubrey phase—completely sympathetic. Except somehow I'm too close to Simon's experience. If I'm distancing myself from this family, the one I was raised in, it is how he does it. Except that I have an alternate universe with Alice. It isn't like sitting here, beleaguered yet serene. If anything, Veronica's avowal, the weight of it, makes me want to learn about my bio father rather than deal with my mother's regret. Hers is gut-wrenching, maybe contagious.

"Stop this goddamn plan," James has pleaded with me in the days since I met Alice, after he found her on my iPhone. Not that he and I check each other's iPhones or that we lack a faith in each other. Still, after the Naples trip, I was doing yoga on our screened-in porch. End-of-day texts kept coming through. Had I turned my cell on silent, James would have missed the residual dinging that made him intervene. Flat on a mat, my thoughts floated, transporting me. The briefest hour, an escape, except that James, with our baby so soon to be born, checked that there was no message from Aubrey. He read Alice's three gushy texts, a tenor we have both taken on since our hours at the Ritz. *Keep thinking of you, of us. Call soonest. Next rendezvous?*

He marched to where I was. "Who is he? How can you do this?" he demanded. "Naples, is that it? Is that why you went?"

I tried more lies, tried to defuse things. "A woman author, someone I met, a new friend. We've become close."

"I don't believe you," James insisted.

As I pulled myself off the mat, I thought of what to say to my husband. That I'm not in love with another man, that it is my half sister. That we both read Galway Kinnell and Louise Gluck, shop the sales at Neiman's, that she, too, is a runner. That our teeth, our wrists, our giraffe-like necks make it palpable. She is the sister who dared come true. The one who explains Simon's silences.

"Elodie!" He raised his voice. I had not heard him like that before.

I confessed. Afterward, James kept repeating his concerns, reminding me of Veronica's focus. "Please don't pursue the others, the halves. You have your family, our baby."

A damp wind picks up. Each of us pulls her hair into a scrunchie, which we keep on our wrists.

"Dad has done so well. But it wasn't only about money. It was his ego, his secret," Veronica says.

"He has done well," I say.

"A way to win," Aubrey adds.

"I'd trade my soul to have it like it was before you girls took the tests. Before any of this started." Our mother seems frail.

"It's okay, Mom." Aubrey puts her hands over Veronica's. "Isn't it, Elodie?" I breathe in salty air. I count. They breathe it in, too. Our lips pull into the very same line, our chins at that forty-degree angle.

"Totally okay." I put my hands over Aubrey's.

The three of us threaded together by our mother's cogent secret.

CHAPTER 33

ELODIE

An artful text comes in from Laurie at noon. *Will you be introducing?* James's text that follows Laurie's isn't as cloaked. *What is going on? Where are you?*

At the Literary Society the staff is setting up for Delfina Barkow, the novelist. In an hour, she'll be talking about her mother/daughter novel and antimotherhood dreams. Having long admired her early work, I sought out Barkow and booked her before Aubrey became pregnant, before her message would seem ironic, an odd twist. I simply wanted to hear her read and discuss the implications of her themes. What seemed a controversial speaker for the Palm Beach crowd, scheduled for the off-season, is a popular event. We are sold out, with a number of young women having signed up. Guests will file in, avid about the noon lecture, followed by a Q&A. The part of me that loves the Literary Society would have stayed to listen; the part of me that has recently disentangled has chosen to drive south instead. I ignore James's texts—three in a row, as he pushes at what can't be touched, the piece of me that belongs to no one.

That's the glitch: I won't be introducing. I'm on my way south to Sunny Isles to meet Alice at the Acqualina Resort and Spa. Her husband has a conference there and she has left her children with her mother-in-law in Naples. In order to see me—no wonder my bio family fills my head. Meaning Alice and where she'll lead me in our mutual enchantment.

When my GPS reports that I'm seven minutes away, a text from Aubrey bings. *At Society. Came to surprise you— for D. Barkow.*

That is when I panic. I was about to text her that I'd visit her in South Beach—a perfect cover for my time with Alice. Anxiety washes over me—I am an unfaithful wife of sorts; I am a cheater. One who feels fine *about* the affair, justified in her travels to and from her lover. The getting caught aspect, put to the fire, is a crafty narrative. How much easier it is to be acrobatic, justified versus duplicitous. Another Aubrey text. *Dad and James are here, too!*

I keep driving toward my destination, reckless, fearless, petrified. No one is supposed to be around today, no one in my family is coming for the Barkow event—that's why it was easy enough to make the plan with Alice. Simon, preoccupied with his three residential properties in Cleveland, has finally closed and is playing golf at a club in Boca. James is in scheduled meetings with Darnay and new investors. Last night Mimi and Veronica announced they would be driving to Bal Harbor this morning.

My phone bings one more time. Laurie. I text back: *Cover for me. Do intro.*

Alice is more distinctive this time than when we first met. She stands at the concierge desk at the Acqualina Hotel, waiting. In our constant hall of mirrors, whatever there is about me that isn't like Aubrey and my mother belongs to Alice and me. Can't anyone and everyone in the lobby tell we are sisters, practically twins? When she walks toward me and we hug, the rest of it—that I've escaped Palm Beach, that my family is about to flip—disappears. We walk together to the lawn, where the red lounge chairs are set overlooking the Atlantic. In the sunlight, the fine lines around our mouths, those deep little lines above the lips, and our crow's-feet show. Whatever she has, I have.

"I hope it was no trouble making the time today," she says. Her sunglasses, like mine, make an indentation where the pads touch her nose.

"A bit dicey, but I made it," I say. "Totally stolen hours. I didn't expect it to be complicated."

We are seated beneath an oversize beach umbrella.

"Then let's start with the news," Alice says. "In case you have to leave earlier than planned. In case your baby is—"

"News?"

"News about our bio father and our half sibs."

I want the news, although the two of us must exist in some exclusive combo. Which is illogical. According to my latest research, Alice and I have more half sibs than we can juggle.

"Isn't it the beginning for the sibs?" I ask.

"Two half sisters, three half brothers so far. They live in California, Pennsylvania, and Denver. Would you meet them?"

I nod. Alice is pleased.

"Do they want to meet us? Not everyone wants to. Aubrey isn't interested in her half sibs, in any of it."

"We'll follow how it plays out, half sib by half sib," Alice says.

My trepidation. My mother's anguish, James's suspicions. Simon, our father. Alice and our bio father. Aubrey's half sibs, her bio father. The index of surreptitious fathers. Aubrey's decision to stay away from the others on her side. I haven't her credence; I'm enthralled by the crucial facets, the unveiling.

"So what about our father? What do you know?" I ask.

"I have pictures." Alice lifts up her cell phone.

Our father. I try to imagine his face; it blurs and then becomes clear. Unknown, but mine. Hers. I'm shaky.

The ocean rolls in toward the beach, there is an undertow. No one is in the water. Alice hands her cell to me. "He must have been good-looking, dapper. Actually, he is in recent pictures, too."

Two full-blown pictures of a man who looks exactly like us. The first photograph is at least thirty years old. A black-and-white. He is a young man leaning against a building. His smile is for someone specific, not for the camera. The second is more recent, taken five or ten years ago. He's in a button-down shirt, carrying two books. His hairline is thinner, while his face is that face. I stare at the photographs; they will never be out of my head.

I hand back her cell.

"He's mesmerizing," Alice says. "I couldn't stop staring at him."

"He is unbelievable. How did you find these?"

Alice shrugs. "It took hours. After I got a lead, I figured out his name. Through his children, you know, his own family. Facebook, Instagram."

"Oh my God, Alice."

"Yes, it's incredible. That's why I wanted to show you, not text or do a phone call. I mean, we could have but . . ."

"No, no, I'm glad we're together." A bizarre grayness begins. Alice and I are linked together not only by what has happened but by what is ahead.

"Are you okay to investigate, Elodie?"

I nod. "I hope so."

"Okay, two more photos. I'd say he's in his early forties in the first and maybe around sixty in this one?" She holds up the second, spreading it out to cover the entire screen.

I touch the screen and it pushes Simon farther away.

"He went to Harvard. He's a doctor. He lives in Chicago."

"How do you know that?" I ask.

"I have been googling him since we met in Naples. I started to tell you when you were leaving that day."

She takes back her phone and makes the first picture full size. His features converge.

"I have his name, his address, his office number. We can meet him, Elodie."

Meet him? Isn't it enough that he exists?

"Do you want to?" I ask.

"Do you?"

"I'm not certain. I don't know. I wanted to meet you," I say. "I mean, I'm so happy to know who he is, that he's well, still he's our phantom father, isn't he?"

"He does have a family with his wife, children whom he raised," Alice says.

"That's his life, not us."

"Maybe that could include us, too, if he'd like it," Alice says.

My iPhone, which I've silenced, gives a quiet ping. I move it around in my bag to read the screen. *James.* I decide to wait.

"Not really. He doesn't know about us; he might not want us. It was sort of like giving blood for him. That's what he did, selling sperm. For us, he's our fantasy," I say.

"I'm not sure what to do," Alice says. "Let's mull over both sides of the situation."

My cell starts undulating in my bag. Calls, one after another. As much as I want it to be only Alice and me, I've gone missing and Aubrey is due. One more text, another call.

"I have to see what is going on. You know, Aubrey is due and . . ."

Simon's number is across the screen. "It's my father." We both smile at the confusion, the father/our father, the life/our story.

I pick up. His voice is garbled, as if he's calling from a tunnel.

"Elodie, Aubrey is in labor. Her water broke at the Literary Society. Tyler is on the way, your mother and Mimi, too. James and I are at South Palm."

My heart flaps around in my chest. *Aubrey, our baby.* My sister cannot deliver until I get there. The colors of the day bleed out and I'm left with what I've done. I've gone astray, sneaked out and been caught.

"I'll be there, Dad. I'm getting in my car." I click off. "My sister is in labor. I have to go."

"This is exciting!" Alice is sincere, as a mother, as a sister. "You have to go—hurry, but don't speed. This minute!"

"I can't believe it."

She's staring at me. "Listen, I'll drive you. We'll talk in the car."

"I have to tell them something about where I've been. About my car. I can't say it was an author again, that I came to meet a writer. I have to explain to James, who is already unhappy that we've met. I have to get to the hospital."

The sunlight over our umbrella is too intense, blinding. When I stand, it seems the hotel is sinking, pulling me with it. Water might envelop me, drag me downward.

"My car . . ." I say.

"Elodie, your sister is in labor. It'll take a few hours, at least." Alice puts her cool hand on my wrist. "Your car can be worked out. I'll help get it returned to you in Palm Beach through the concierge. You shouldn't drive back alone. Not today."

When Alice drops me at the South Palm maternity entrance, she leans across, kisses me.

"We are so lucky to have found each other. You are going to *your* family for *your* baby. Our family, the one we're learning about, it's there, we'll be there."

I close the car door too hard, unintentionally. When I turn around, Alice is heading toward the exit.

Alone, my father paces in the waiting room. His golf clothes are wrinkled and he is swinging his arms like a soldier does before a salute. On the walls are hues of inescapable hospital green. He doesn't belong in these surroundings.

"Where's Mom? Where's Mimi?" I ask.

"They are parking. They've just gotten back, too."

"James? Tyler? They're in the delivery room, right?"

"They are."

How dual it is, how we double up, cheering for our baby, for Aubrey.

"I have to get changed, wash up, and get in there," I say.

"You do." My father takes heedful steps toward me.

"Elodie, I've been wanting to speak with you. I owe you this conversation. I hope that you know how much I love you and respect you."

I am a statue.

"Elodie, did you hear me? I realize it's very late to be telling you. Saying how much you mean to me."

There is the stubble on his face, not like when James or Tyler do it deliberately, but like a father who isn't clean-shaven. That has not happened before.

"What is important, what matters is that you don't do what I did. That kind of separating oneself from one's children. Because of a history—an element that has nothing to do with the parent and child and what they can share." My father is speaking as if he's a lecturer; the topic is too painful. His voice is stilted, self-conscious.

"So," he continues, "if you need distance, distance yourself from how your child came into the world and embrace that she is here. Don't push away your daughter. She is yours. Just as you are mine."

I nod.

"Let's start again, together this time with your baby girl."

"Okay."

He reaches for my hands and lifts my right hand to his heart, then lets it go.

A nurse comes into our space. She wears navy scrubs and is carrying another set in a sealed packet. "Are you the mother?"

"Yes, she is the mother," Simon says.

"Then follow me, please. I'm Rosemary, I'll be in the delivery room with you. Your sister is in the labor room. She's been asking for you, over and over."

Together Rosemary and I rush through the maternity ward to Aubrey. Sounds swell toward us, women moaning in labor, men walking heavily down the corridors, confused, waiting for their children to be born. I hear my own sandals pad against the flooring and remember the day Aubrey came to South Palm to soothe me. The day I thought I'd never have my own child.

Rosemary asks, "Do you have a name in mind for your baby?"

"I do," I say. "We definitely do. Her name is Grace."

CHAPTER 34

AUBREY

The early morning is crisp for December in South Florida. Upstairs in Elodie's new house, she and I sit on matching love seats in her master suite. As far as the eye can see, her rooms are swathed in shades of cream and white. I face her, with Grace in my arms, while beyond us the sliding glass doors are open. Two imposing super-yachts glide by on the Intracoastal.

"This is very magical," I say. "What a view, what rooms!"

Elodie stands and paces about, looking at us and away, toward the water.

"I'm leaving," she says. "To meet my bio dad, another half sib. I'm taking a flight to Chicago."

I rearrange Grace's palest pink onesie and smooth her matching baby blanket across her small body. I hold her to my chest as if a storm is sweeping through.

"When?" I whisper.

"Soon," she says. "Very soon."

Grace gurgles. We both look at her wide eyes, her perfect forehead. Then I notice that Elodie is in navy cropped pants and black suede flats; only her shirt is white. She has a yellow cashmere sweater tied across her shoulders. Not exactly dressed for our plan to go to Benny's at the Beach for breakfast at the pier. I tug at my jean shorts; I stop myself from tightening the laces on my left sneaker. I wipe away the drool on the right shoulder of my sweatshirt.

"Does James know?" Again I whisper.

Elodie shakes her head. "He doesn't."

She sucks in the filtered air that mixes with the outdoor air. She keeps pacing.

"I never should have done this—had a child, a child with James, with you. Maybe I should never have lived in Palm Beach, basking in this . . . this story, where few mistakes are allowed. Or followed the Veronica and Simon Show. Any of it. Especially the baby."

I raise Grace up in the air with both hands. Her narrow feet do their own jig. She is almost smiling with excitement.

"But look at her, look at her. Elodie, look at her! Isn't this enough for you?"

"Is she? Well, she's presumed to be." Elodie stares into a space beyond us, like she's a member of a cult and her time here is inevitably wrapping up.

"Grace is all that matters," I say.

"There is a lot of love. There are plenty of Grace lovers. You, first and foremost, Aubrey."

She comes over and hugs me; she plants a kiss on the top of Grace's cotton cap.

"I have to get to the airport."

With purpose, Elodie leaves the center of the sitting room and closes the sliding doors. She sidesteps the stone floor, which is only exposed at the rim of the room.

"When will you be back?"

My sister doesn't answer; she doesn't glance at me. I hold on to Grace, nearer, tighter, as my sister tears herself free, leaving a searing pain beyond my reach.

"She's three months old," I say.

Then I move past Elodie to walk downstairs.

A moment later, Grace and I are on the terrace. At the dock, James is practicing a golf swing. Tyler, inquisitive, is watching the moves. I look back at the house—is that my sister by the glass doors? I can't be certain.

"Hey, Aubrey, c'mon. We're ready," James shouts.

I look up once more; no one is there.

"We're ready, too," I say.

Tyler looks at me; I know he knows. He taps James on the shoulder and together they come to where I'm waiting. The wind has shifted, kicking up from the west, blowing at our faces.

The three of us circle around Grace.

ACKNOWLEDGMENTS

I am grateful to the following people: Alice Martell for being the smartest agent ever; Jennifer Weis for bulwarking the concept of this novel; Alexandra Sehulster, my editor, for her significant input and insight. Jennifer Enderlin and Sally Richardson, publishers, for their encouragement and the entire team at St. Martin's Press, including Mara Delgado-Sanchez, Carol Edwards, DJ DeSmyter, and Meghan Harrington. Alexandra Shelley for her expertise and guidance; Meryl Moss and Deb Zipf for their campaign savvy.

Those who see me through: Patti Abramson, Anton Balbona, Helene Barre, Richard Berkowitz, Linda Berley, Meredith Bernstein, Brondi Borer, Mary D'Alton, Cole Dennis, Nancy Fisher, Jane Gordon, Justin Haworth, Kara Ivancich, Sunil Kumar, Sandra Leitner, Katinka Matson, Sarah McElwain, Helen Metzger, Thomas Moore III, Suzanne Murphy, James Parry, David Ressler, Sarah Ressler, Emily Ressler, Katie Schaffstall, Jane Shapiro,

Judy H. Shapiro, Mark L. Shapiro, Francine Silberstein, Jonathan Stone, Zachary Torkos, Kim Weiss.

My father and my late mother, who adored living in Palm Beach. My daughters/muses, Jennie and Elizabeth; my son, Michael; daughter-in-law, Elizabeth B; and son-in-law, Max. Howard Ressler, ever present, ever certain.